THE
NIGHT JANITOR

T. F. ALLEN

ISBN: 978-1-7329455-3-1
Copyediting: Cypress Editing
Cover Design: Jeroen ten Berge
Proofreading: Amanda Kruse
Book Interior: 52 Novels

Para Luzmaria

CHAPTER 1

No one had shot at Luke Johnson in three months. He had been careful this time. Few people in Port Arthur gave him a passing glance.

But tonight a man in a suit had shouted his name—his real name, not the one on his janitor uniform—chased him into an alley, and pointed a gun at his chest.

"You don't have to," Luke said.

The windows in nearby buildings had gone dark hours ago. Two overfilled dumpsters and a tower of cardboard boxes decorated the alley. A security lamp spotlighted the gunman's Astros baseball cap. Everything else was a black silhouette.

The man stepped forward. "It's my job."

"You kill for her?"

"Among other things."

Ten feet separated them. A chain-link fence blocked his only escape. Luke's pulse surged through his eardrums, creating a rush of white noise.

"Tell her I forgive her," he said.

The gunman adjusted the brim of his cap. "You what?"

"Tell her she doesn't have to worry. I'm the last person who wants to hurt her."

"She needs to make sure."

A rustling sound erupted from behind the stack of boxes. The gunman glanced toward the noise. Luke saw his opening and charged. The man's shoulders lifted, and his gun wavered. Luke closed half the distance between them before the gunman fired.

The crack of the silencer quickened his nerves. A bullet tore into his shoulder, bringing a flash of pain. He ignored the sensation and kept running.

Another shot punctured his right lung, stealing his breath. He lunged forward, grabbed the barrel, and pushed it aside as it fired again. His momentum crashed him into the gunman's chest, driving them both to the ground.

Heat from the silencer seared his palm, but he didn't let go. The gunman turned him over and tried to pin him down. Luke's adrenaline surged. He fought through the pain, forced his strength into his hands, and twisted the gun away.

Black spots dotted his vision. He couldn't catch a breath. His fingers searched for the trigger. His shoulder and chest burned. A hard punch landed on his jaw, rattling his teeth. For a moment his eyes couldn't focus.

He found the trigger and shoved the gun forward until it met resistance. He fired two quick rounds. The gunman hovered for a moment, then slumped to the pavement beside him, facedown and unmoving.

Silence flooded the alley. Luke rested his head against the warm asphalt, stared into the night sky, and wondered if these were the last stars he'd ever see.

As the adrenaline left his body, so did his strength. The gun tumbled from his fingers. He struggled to move his arm. Darkness tugged at him. He felt himself slipping away. With one last surge of effort, he swung his hand to his chest.

He covered the hole in his rib cage with his fingertips.

Closed his eyes and concentrated, letting the power flow through him.

His collapsed lung filled with warmth, but not the same kind that came from the bullets. Its tissues flared and vibrated.

Capillaries repaired themselves. New flesh grew from the fissures the slug had torn open. He coughed. Fluid from his lung shot through his windpipe and sprayed across the asphalt.

The bullet retraced its path through his chest, inch by inch, as if pulled by a magnet. The flesh around it closed and healed. He inhaled a deep breath. The bullet broke through his skin. He pinched the tip and pulled it free. The hole behind it disappeared.

His fingers crawled toward his opposite shoulder. The bullet worked its way out of his muscle and into his hand, leaving no scar and no internal trauma, only healthy and rejuvenated flesh.

He climbed to his feet, then turned and faced his attacker. He rolled the gunman onto his back. The man's injuries looked fatal, and definitely well deserved.

God, this one was just a kid, no older than twenty-five. He'd probably taken this job to prove his bravery. Luke wondered if the attacker's boss had warned about his special ability. Probably not. That was just like her, sending others to do what she couldn't do herself.

Others, he reminded himself. Sometimes she sent more than one.

He grabbed the man's wrist and found a pulse—faint but still there. He covered the man's wounds with each hand. Closed his eyes and concentrated.

"How'd you do that?"

He turned. A wrinkled old man with huge eyes stared at him from beside the stack of cardboard boxes. "You an angel or something?"

Luke touched a finger to his lips. He turned toward the unconscious gunman and closed his eyes again.

After he finished, he snatched the Astros cap and fit it on his own head. He walked toward the man by the boxes. "Don't talk about this."

The old man, clearly a frequent visitor to this dark alley, backed away.

Luke held out his fist and opened his hand, showing a collection of four bloodstained slugs. "I'd find another place to sleep tonight." He dropped the bullets and pointed with his thumb over his shoulder. "When that guy wakes up, he won't be happy."

He left the alley before the man could answer.

Time to get out of Port Arthur.

CHAPTER 2

Annamaria grabbed her Fendi purse, adjusted her D&G sunglasses, and climbed out from the rear passenger seat of a black Audi SUV. She told the driver to wait, then shut the door. After a pause, she opened the door and grabbed the tiny yellow stuffed bear she'd left on the seat. She tucked it into her purse and shut the door again. Then she paced down the sidewalk of the strip center, toward the most unlikely place she thought she'd ever visit.

A nail salon and a dry cleaner sandwiched the business on either side, but no one could miss the neon signs blazing from the windows of Psychic Readings by Nick. The largest panel featured a Capricorn goat, a horned Taurus, and a long-fingered hand with an eye in the center. Other signs boasted the services Psychic Nick offered: Spiritual Advisor, Tarot Cards, Healings, Readings, Connecting with Lost Loved Ones.

Jackpot. She hurried inside.

When she crossed the threshold, her anxiety level spiked, but she forced it down with a deep breath. She dug a fingernail into the top of her blond wig and scratched. She could pull this off, no problem.

"You must be Diana." A twentysomething woman looked up from a magazine resting in her lap. She closed the pages and stood.

Annamaria removed her sunglasses. "Where's Nick?"

"He's finishing a call with a client." The woman motioned toward a couch along the opposite wall of the lobby. Every surface looked covered with a blanket of grime. "I'll let him know you're here." The woman disappeared behind the only door in the office.

Annamaria picked out the cleanest-looking section of the couch, sat, crossed her legs, and tried to look calm. She opened her purse and slid her hand inside. She found the tiny bear and stroked its well-worn fur. This was it—the moment she'd dreamt about since she was thirteen. Answers that had eluded her would soon come within her grasp, but only if she kept it together.

The door opened. A large man strode into the lobby. Despite his size, he looked smaller than she'd imagined, even wrapped in a Tibetan robe. His gray-streaked hair ran from the center of his scalp to the edge of his shoulders, nearly masking the crow's feet etched into the corners of his eyes. But what a set of eyes—so deep, so green, so electrifying, they explained how he could draw a steady stream of customers to such a hellhole of an office.

"Diana, please come with me."

Another deep breath.

He led her to a room with dark violet curtains lining each wall. A shelf to her right held a collection of crystals. They sat at opposite ends of a small, round table situated beneath a globe-shaped glass chandelier. A set of tarot cards lay spread in an arc in front of Nick. She had to hand it to him. Even though he was surely a fake, this room held the pulse of a genuine psychic energy.

As if there were such a thing.

Nick struck a match and lit a votive candle, then placed it on the table between them. "What kind of reading are we doing?"

"What do most customers ask for?"

"I'm a tarot specialist." He scooped the deck into his left hand and flipped the bottom card to the top like a skilled poker dealer.

"When you say 'specialist,' does that mean you're good?"

"Best in Greater Memphis, honey."

Annamaria's stomach clenched. No one called her honey and got away with it, especially not this guy. She swallowed and forced a smile. The prosthetic latex covering her nose tickled against her skin. It felt unnatural and smelled like toxic chemicals, but she worked to suppress her reaction. Instead of cringing, she focused on the bright side—the wig and fake nose must be working. Psychic Nick definitely didn't recognize her.

"It works best if you have a specific question," he said.

She leaned forward. "I'm trying to find my parents."

"I see." He pushed the stack of cards toward her. "Did they pass away recently?"

"You tell me."

Those charming green eyes twinkled as he laughed. "I'm happy to do that. But we need to cover something first. I have a policy of receiving payment up front. I'm sure you understand."

"I have a policy of seeing what I pay for."

"I'll show you plenty. But not for free."

Dammit. Just like she'd expected, Nick was a disciplined con artist. He'd probably danced these same steps a thousand times. No use fighting it. The money didn't matter. She opened her purse. Her toy bear stared up at her. She gave it a gentle squeeze, then pulled a hundred-dollar bill from her wallet and passed it across the table.

"Okay." Nick swept up the money and tucked it inside his robe. A tuft of white chest hair poked through the opening he created. "To get started, mix the cards any way you like."

Annamaria stared at the chandelier and shuffled, trying not to think about the hundreds of desperate people who'd touched these cards before her.

"Let the cards absorb your energy, your questions, your future, your past."

Psychic Nick wasn't helping, not one bit.

"Think about your parents. Concentrate on what you remember about them."

She twisted the deck so violently a few cards snapped loose and flew from her hands. Two landed facedown to her side. A third flipped over and leaned against the votive candle.

"Ah, the Magus," Nick said. "The Magician. You must be thinking about your father."

Dumb luck, of course. She decided to go with it. "What do you see?"

Nick touched the card with his index finger. "A man who is powerful, adept. A master of many skills. Incredibly charismatic."

She blinked. Her father was all those things and more.

Nick reached for the pile of cards she'd abandoned. "The next two will tell us about your past."

"I already know my past."

"Maybe they can show you something you missed, something you didn't realize at the time."

Heat rushed to her cheeks. No wonder this man's tacky office doors stayed open. Nick spoke in such a way that she found herself wanting to believe his words were true. Of course, she knew better. But the draw of his voice was unmistakable.

He flipped the top card. The picture showed a man in a long cape, his head down, his shoulders turned away from the artist who drew him. Three overturned goblets lay scattered near his feet. Two more stood upright nearby.

"The Five of Cups," he said. "Also known as the Lord of Disappointment. Your father must have let you down in some way. Or maybe it was you who disappointed him?"

Annamaria looked away. This was such bullshit. Millions of people probably believed their father had screwed them at some point during their childhood. Her past wasn't that unique. She folded her arms. If she was going to play this game, she'd make him earn his money.

"Does any of this resonate with you, Diana?"

"Not really."

The next card revealed a profile of a woman sitting up in bed with her head buried in her hands. Mounted on the wall behind her were nine swords, each with gleaming sharp points.

"Oh dear." Nick ran his fingers through his hair.

"What is it?"

"Now I see why you want to talk to him. He hurt you. He hurt you so deeply you're still feeling it."

"Is that what the card says?"

He held it up for her. "The Nine of Swords is never easy to discuss. It's a catalyst, an intensifier to the cards around it. When paired with the Five of Cups, it suggests you suffered a disappointment that was particularly intense." He reached across the table and grabbed her hand. His touch sent a chill through her. "This wrong was inflicted on you by someone who lacks compassion."

She leaned back, pulling herself from his reach. "My father left when I was a kid."

"I'm sorry."

"Yeah."

"The important thing is you survived." Nick glanced at her purse. "You persevered and overcame, made yourself into a successful woman."

This man had no idea.

"But you didn't come here to understand your past." He covered the tarot deck with his massive hand. "Your question is about the future."

He was right, in a sense. But she'd never leave something this important to the draw of a card. Psychic Nick might try to find meaning in the random selection of miniature painted pictures, but she stayed more focused on his every movement, on each inflection of his voice. The key to her future couldn't be read from any card. It lived inside the man sitting opposite her.

"Here we go." He pointed to the image on the next card. A large and powerful hand surged from a puffy cloud. Its fingers gripped a long, straight branch of wood still green with sprigs and leaves.

"The Ace of Wands represents the beginning of a new life. It signals a rush of energy—a raw and powerful energy." He grinned. "Soon you'll become a force to be reckoned with."

She allowed herself a smile. Again, he had no idea.

Nick moved faster, as if he could sense her patience waning. "This one's called the Tower, one of the Major Arcana. A sudden change is coming. Something big—something connected to the energy revealed by the Ace of Wands. Does that make any sense?"

She leaned forward. "New energy? A sudden change? That's so specific. You really are the best in Greater Memphis."

Nick pursed his lips. "You're free to believe them or not. But I promise these cards never lie." He pushed the deck in front of her. "I want you to pick the last one."

"Why?"

"To prove I'm not manipulating this. I'm a proud man, Diana. My reputation means everything to me. I can't let you leave thinking I'm a fraud."

His stare pierced her so deeply she felt it in her chest. "Any card I want?"

"As long as you don't look at it first."

She spread the deck in a line across the table. Nick probably had a lecture prepared for each card. She ran her fingers along the edges, then plucked one out of line and turned it over.

This card easily held the busiest image yet. Several figures suspended in unnatural poses formed a scene too complicated for her to decipher.

"You picked Aeon, the symbol for judgment. In Christian circles, this card represents the Final Judgment, like in the book of Revelation. But pagans see it differently."

"What about you?"

"See this figure?" He pointed to a small child in the center. "That's Horus, the Egyptian god of redemption. He also suffered a tragic loss of his father at a young age. Like you, he managed to persevere and overcome. He became a wise ruler, and eventually a god."

"So I'm like an Egyptian god?"

"You're going to make a decision that will affect the rest of your life. You'll make a judgment—a final judgment—that can't be taken back. This card is warning you to weigh that decision carefully. If you choose the right path, your potential is unlimited."

The skin on her forearms tingled. Again, he'd nailed it. But his warning came too late. She'd made her decision long ago. No way she'd turn back now. In his own way, Psychic Nick helped confirm what she already knew to be true.

"I don't know how you saw it, but that's exactly why I came here."

"Not sure I believe you, Diana."

"I know how I sound, but I really mean it this time. With that last card, you clarified things. You were right about every-thing—my father, the betrayal, the new energy I've found, and the final judgment that's coming."

"Really?"

She didn't need to fake her excitement now. The words spilled out like an avalanche: "My father was a preacher, of sorts. We moved a lot when I was young. I had to keep my things in one small bag in case we needed to leave in a hurry."

Nick narrowed his eyes. "I see."

"Then one night my parents disappeared. They grabbed our bags and left the hotel without me. They didn't even pay the bill. I was thirteen. I didn't have any money. The hotel manager called the police, but it was too late. They never came back."

His keen emerald-green eyes darted left and right across the room, looking everywhere at once. She didn't let it stop her.

"I promised myself I'd make them pay when I found them. I survived, earned an Ivy League education, and developed a power my father could only dream of possessing."

Psychic Nick wouldn't look away. The color drained from his face, and his cheeks trembled. He grabbed the arms of his chair.

"My father was a faith healer—the kind that blows into small towns, performs a few healings, takes a collection, then disappears before everyone realizes it's just an act."

"Annamaria, wait—"

She kicked the table across the room, sending the tarot cards and the votive candle flying. "My father was a fake, but I'm the real thing. Here, let me show you."

Nick bolted for the door. She lunged after him, jumped on his back, and tackled him. Turned him over and sat on his chest. She grabbed his left wrist and pulled his hand close to her face.

"Where are you going, Daddy? This reading isn't over yet." She pressed her thumb into his palm. "It's my turn to read your fortune."

CHAPTER 3

Another city, another uniform. Another building that needed a night janitor. Luke had started over again.

The elevator doors opened. He pushed his cart into the hallway of the seventh floor. He checked the map posted on the wall and headed toward the critical care unit.

The term *hospital* didn't begin to describe the University of Texas MD Anderson Cancer Center in Houston. The main campus included a dozen buildings and spanned two zip codes. Cancer patients from around the world seemed to flock here in search of miracle cures, and the staff spared no efforts trying to provide them. The evidence was everywhere—nurses filling out patient applications for cutting-edge clinical trials, pharmacists cross-checking drug interactions while ordering the thirty different prescriptions each patient was taking, doctors staying late to explain to family members the risks of an experimental procedure. In a place permeated by constant death, it encouraged him to see so many people stay committed to the mission painted on the hospital walls: Making Cancer History.

He pushed a large stainless steel button on the wall. Two automatic doors swung open. A woman in scrubs rushed past him, chasing an alarm that sounded like a landline busy signal.

No surprise. Even in a place as massive as this, the night shift covered more patients than the day shift. Management figured with fewer doctors and visitors there'd be less to do. But cancer never slept. This new job required him to spend more time cleaning the rooms of patients who'd died than in any other place he'd worked.

This was also the most invisible job he'd ever held. Nurses and family members regularly walked through his mop strokes, sometimes even stepping on the mop while he tried to pull it out of their way. Doctors engaged in detailed conversations in front of him, discussing patient treatments or personal finances as if he wasn't there. Nobody ever noticed the cleaning guy, which made it the perfect job for Luke.

He pushed his cart into room 751A. All the lights were off, except for a backlight above an empty bed. It spotlighted a set of rumpled sheets and covers—mostly white with faint yellow stains near the middle. He checked the whiteboard near the door. Apparently a patient named Luis Rodriguez had fought his final battle in this room hours ago.

Luke walked to the side of the bed, placed his hand on the pillow, and bowed his head.

"What are you doing?"

He looked up. A woman with mocha skin, curly hair, and puffy reddened eyes stood in the doorway. She flipped on the lights and walked in.

He rushed to his cart and pretended to arrange his cleaning supplies.

"Were you praying?" she said.

"Cleaning. I was cleaning."

"It's okay. I won't tell anyone." Her tone softened as she moved closer. "Last time I checked, prayer was still legal in Texas."

He pulled off the sheets, bundled them into a pile, and stuffed them into a laundry bag that hung from his cart. All the while he could feel the woman staring at him, watching him work.

"Thank God. There it is." She strode past him and retrieved a leather purse resting on a recliner in the corner. Instead of leaving, she walked to his side and stared at the empty bed. She placed her hand in the center of the mattress, touching it with her delicate fingers.

After a moment, she turned to him. "You know what they say about this place? Angels roam the hallways. Some patients actually see them. Papa saw one earlier tonight." Her eyes grew watery, but she didn't blink them clear. "He was reaching for one when he died."

Every part of Luke believed her. He thought about her watching her father slip away. If only he'd arrived a few hours earlier.

"I'm sorry about your dad."

She patted his shoulder, then walked toward the door. "Remember what I said about this place."

"I will."

Ten minutes later he'd turned the room, making it ready for another critically ill patient. He pushed his cart into the next room.

This room's layout was a mirror image of the previous one, but the bed wasn't empty. An older black woman, her body emaciated by whatever version of the beast she was fighting, reclined at a forty-five-degree angle. Her right arm hung limp, taking in a yellowed mixture of the contents from four IV bags hanging next to her. The television screen on the opposite wall showed a rainbow-colored test screen. Her eyes seemed to focus on it like it was an Impressionist painting.

He checked the two recliners set against the far wall. No purses, no rumpled blankets, no mobile phone chargers plugged into the outlets.

The whiteboard listed her name only as Ms. Holmes. He'd read enough of these boards to know what information typically appeared: patient name, allergies, food and medication restrictions, attending doctors' names and their disciplines, and always an emergency contact with a telephone number.

Ms. Holmes's whiteboard didn't list an emergency contact.

He pushed his cart deeper into the room and pulled the door halfway closed—the most he could conceal himself without getting into trouble. He moved to the side of her bed and leaned into her field of vision.

Though her mouth hung slightly open, her cheeks looked like she was sucking them in. Her teeth were missing, and her eyes had drawn into their sockets deeper than he thought possible. He assumed she was asleep or in a trance, but then her eyes locked onto his. Her entire body stiffened, and her fingers dug into the sheets.

He placed his hand on hers. "It's okay. I won't hurt you."

"Take me quickly," she said.

"You don't understand." He lifted her hand and curled three of her fingers into her palm, forming a pointing gesture. "Show me where the cancer is."

Her finger moved in a wide circle, then paused over her forehead, sank to her neckline, stretched toward her abdomen, to her hips, down one leg, as far as her arm would reach.

"You're too late, son. It's everywhere."

"I can take it away."

She shook her head. "You mean well, I can see that. But I don't want your help."

"What about your family?"

"They're waiting for me. On the other side."

He pulled off his sanitary gloves and cradled her hand in his arms. Her skin felt so cold, so stiff. He tried to rub some warmth into it. "At least let me take the pain away."

"That's what these bags are for." She glanced at the IV stand. "I'm comfortable now. That's the most anyone can do for me."

He stood there a minute longer, gently massaging her fingers, her palm. Sometimes the most difficult aspect of his ability was not being able to use it.

She forced her head deeper into the pillow before speaking again. "I thought of something you can do."

He leaned in close but didn't speak.

"Make sure my room is clean for the next person."

He placed her hand over her heart and covered it with the blanket. "I can do that."

"You are the janitor, right?"

"Yes, ma'am."

"But you're not just a janitor."

"No, I'm not."

She graced him with a wide, toothless grin—an image he knew he'd never forget. He kissed her forehead, then grabbed his cart and pushed it into her bathroom. He needed to get busy. His shift ended in three hours, and the seventh-floor CCU held dozens of rooms to clean, floors to polish, and people to see.

CHAPTER 4

Clyde Merritt shut his laptop and kicked the underside of his particleboard desk. His latest video had earned only a thousand views—barely enough to pay for the half-eaten lunch in his refrigerator. The number of Facebook shares and Twitter retweets looked pathetic. He couldn't deny it any longer. This episode of *ShowMeClyde* was a failure.

He grabbed two fistfuls of his curly hair. Somehow things always worked out. Never mind that his rent was due. He'd been this low before and knew how to spin out of a funk. His next viral video hid only a few keyboard clicks away. All he needed was patience and perseverance. He closed his eyes and concentrated on his breathing.

Rich, cool, oxygenated air rushed in.

Hot, negatively charged carbon dioxide flushed out.

There, he felt better already.

He opened his laptop and checked his email. Over a hundred new messages waited. Most would turn out to be hoaxes, which wasn't necessarily a bad thing. Viewers seemed to like those as much as the crazy-but-true stories he discovered. But each day it grew more difficult to provide original and compelling content. Content YouTube deemed worthy to decorate with ads. Content that might help pay this month's rent. He clicked on the first message.

The doorbell to his basement apartment rang—three quick notes that startled him out of his chair. He rushed to the door and opened it. An overweight man dressed in a Tibetan robe leaned against the doorframe. Sweat coated the man's forehead, and red sores covered the skin on his hands and neck.

"Don't worry. It's not contagious," the man said.

Clyde tried to shut the door, but the man stepped into the threshold and stopped its momentum. "I need to talk to you."

"Not interested."

The man leaned against the doorframe. His emerald eyes glimmered when he spoke. "You're ShowMeClyde, right? From the YouTube channel?"

"Do I owe you money?"

The man chuckled, but his laugh quickly degenerated into a deep, rumbling cough. "We can talk about that later, after you've heard my story. And boy, do I have one."

Clyde kept pressure against the door, making sure the robed man hadn't lost his resolve. "Give me the short version."

"I've been murdered."

"You don't look dead to me."

"I will be soon. My daughter killed me three days ago."

He let the door swing open but didn't step aside. "What do you mean? With poison?"

"It's more complicated than that." The man pointed toward a camera stand in the living room. "We need to film this."

"You should call the police," Clyde said.

"Already have. They don't believe me."

"What about reporters?"

"They called the paramedics, who gave me a ride to the hospital."

Clyde looked the man up and down. Jesus, even his ankles were covered with sores. "Maybe that's where you belong."

"I'll be there again soon enough." The man coughed into his fist so violently it seemed like he'd bring up a lung. "You're my best chance. You have to help me tell people what she did."

Everything about the man set off alarm bells in Clyde's head. Logic demanded he shut the door and return to his emails, but the electricity behind the man's eyes suggested he carried an explosive story, one powerful enough to compel him to leave the hospital and force his way through Clyde's door.

"I'll give you five minutes."

Clyde kept his distance as he showed the man inside. He grabbed an old bedsheet from a closet and spread it over his couch. The man sat across from the tripod stand while Clyde readied the camera and adjusted the lighting.

"This better be good."

"Don't worry," the man said. "I know what your viewers want."

"Just tell your story." Clyde tossed a wireless mic to the man and motioned for him to clip it on the lapel of his robe. He pushed a button on his remote. A red light on the camera flashed on.

His voice shifted into performer mode: "Welcome to a special episode of *ShowMeClyde*. Today we have a visitor with a story that sounds too amazing to be true. Tell us your name and why you're here."

No amount of makeup or lighting tricks could hide how sick the man looked. The reddened and raised sores, the yellow pallor of his skin, the layers of sweat that stained parts of his robe a deeper shade of crimson. Clyde couldn't believe a hospital would let someone walk out their doors in this condition.

But once the camera came on, the man's demeanor transformed. His posture straightened and his eyes widened, exposing a set of green irises that looked backlit by tiny flames. He also seemed to shift into performer mode when he spoke. "My name is Nicholas Gabor, and I'm a dead man."

Clyde worked to suppress a grin. Whether or not the man was telling the truth, Nicholas clearly possessed a natural talent in front of the camera. Clyde would edit in his own reactions later, once he had time to collect his thoughts. For now, he'd simply bark questions from off-screen. "How's that possible?"

"My daughter murdered me three days ago. I'm only alive because she wants me to suffer. But I'll be dead by Sunday. She told me so when she cursed me."

"She cursed you?"

"There isn't a word for what she did to me, but *cursed* comes the closest." Nicholas held out one arm and pulled up his sleeve, exposing a never-ending pattern of red and bumpy sores. "Shingles," he said. "It's the most uncomfortable sensation I've ever felt."

"But it's not fatal," Clyde said.

"I'm just getting started." Nicholas erupted in a coughing fit again. This one lasted over a minute. No worries, Clyde could edit that out later. The important thing was to keep Nicholas talking.

"You're saying she gave you the shingles."

"Not just that." Nicholas pointed to his chest. "Pneumonia." His finger moved to his temple. "Brain cancer." To his abdomen. "IBS." Back to his chest. "Angina. Congestive heart failure." His hand reached lower, toward his groin. "Prostatitis. Bladder cancer." Now his knee. "Blood clots. Bone spurs. She even gave me restless legs syndrome."

Oh boy. Clyde had a live one here. "Last I checked, most of those aren't contagious."

"She gave them to me, all at once. She came to my office, tackled me, held me down. Grabbed my hand and spoke the words, sent these illnesses deep into my bones. The woman is a killer—the most prolific killer the world has ever known."

"Did anyone else see this?"

"Even if they did, would it matter? No one will ever believe me. Not the police, not the media, not even my own doctors. By any legal standard, she's as blameless as the Virgin Mary. But I'm telling you, she did this to me." Nicholas thrust his bare forearm in front of the camera. Any hint of showmanship had drained from his voice. "And she'll do it to others."

Clyde motioned for Nicholas to back away from the camera. "Are you saying your daughter can make people sick by saying a curse?"

"I don't know exactly how it works. But she can do it at her whim, to anyone, as many times as she wants."

"Who is she?"

"I named her Annamaria, but she's probably changed it by now. I've been hiding from her for twenty-nine years, hoping she'd forget and move on. I thought she'd given up. But she never stopped looking. She finally found me. And then she murdered me."

"Where can I find this woman?"

Nicholas leaned into the couch as far as the cushions would allow. "You don't want to do that. Believe me. And you definitely don't want to confront her."

Clyde's heart went out to this guy. Nicholas seemed truly scared for himself and anyone who might cross his daughter's path. Of course the man was delusional. Even if he suffered from half the diseases he listed, Nicholas would be dead within a month. And that cough might do him in sooner if he didn't get antibiotics fast.

Clyde hit pause on the remote. "I'll make you a deal. You agree to let me take you to a hospital, and I'll promise to upload this video."

Another coughing fit erupted. This one sounded like it hurt. Nicholas's face turned purple. Clyde wondered if he'd made his offer too late, if this man might die on his couch in the middle of his interview.

Just when he thought Nicholas might pass out, the man stopped coughing and stared at him. "I need more than that. This is a huge favor. I'd do it myself, but obviously … "

"What is it?"

"Turn the camera back on."

Clyde hit the remote. The red light flashed on again. Nicholas settled into the couch and raked his fingers through his long gray hair. "There's only one way to stop my daughter. Her ability defies every principle of science except one: Newton's third law. Forces always occur in pairs, equal and opposite. That's how the universe remains stable." He drew a deep breath. "Annamaria commands a force unknown to this world. But she's not the only one."

Clyde forced the lens to zoom in on Nicholas's face. "What are you saying?"

"I also have a son."

CHAPTER 5

Luke kept to himself as he walked along the massive glass-enclosed skywalk that connected MD Anderson's Mays Clinic to the main building, over a quarter mile away. Open-topped golf carts zoomed by on his right, their electric engines humming as drivers carted passengers toward their destinations.

The shuttle drivers were making their final runs of the evening. Fewer people crowded the hallway, allowing him to glance out the windows. He noticed buildings belonging to Texas Children's, St. Luke's, and Methodist. Farther north but out of view were Ben Taub and Memorial Hermann—a massive group of hospitals that employed more people than an average city. He'd never find a better place to operate under the radar.

A clean-cut man in a European suit clipped his shoulder as they passed each other. Luke turned. The man reached out and tried to grab him. Luke evaded the man's grasp.

"You okay, sir?" the man said.

Luke relaxed when he noticed the name tag on the man's lapel: Fazer Pharmaceuticals. This wasn't an assassin, just a pharmaceutical salesman trying to promote his drug.

"I'm fine."

The man walked away. Luke stood there for a moment. This was what his life had become. He needed to treat each encounter as a potential assault. The ability he once hoped might bring people together now kept him isolated, paranoid, and hunted.

Another electric cart rolled past, slowing near the stop that served the Faculty Center. He noticed a preteen girl wearing a T-shirt that read Cancer Sucks. Next to her sat a Hispanic female nurse dressed in pink scrubs. The nurse smiled at the girl, then looked in his direction. A spark of recognition danced in her eyes. She glared at him as if he were a child molester.

He turned away, then glanced back. The nurse's stare intensified. She hugged the preteen girl sitting next to her, grabbed her purse, and hopped off the cart. Luke walked back the way he'd come, doubling his pace to make sure she wouldn't catch up.

Fifteen feet later, he felt a tap on his shoulder.

"Hey, you."

He kept walking.

A hand clenched his forearm, tugged, and spun him around. It was her. "Don't pretend you can't hear me."

Easily a foot shorter than him, the curly-haired nurse pointed a finger at his chest. "I saw what you did last night."

"What are you talking about?"

"Room 751B—Ms. Holmes. Sound familiar?"

"I clean a lot of rooms." He turned to leave, but she darted in front of him.

"Do you know what *CCU* means? The patients on that floor need critical care around the clock. Many are taking experimental drugs. Their immune systems are severely compromised." She blew a strand of hair out of her face. "Then the *cleaning* guy decides to hold hands with one of the patients."

"I was only trying to help."

"You could have killed her."

"That's impossible."

"Oh yeah?" She licked her lips and paused. People around them stared curiously as they passed, but no one looked willing to interrupt. "Are you a doctor? Do you know what kind of pathogens hide in toilets and trash cans? No offense, but you're a walking death trap when you're working here. The last thing you should ever do is touch a patient."

Dark bands of eyeliner came together in sharp points near the corners of her eyes. Her Spanish accent made her words bite harder than normal. He understood her perception of what he'd done. Ignoring infection control procedures could earn anyone in a hospital a reprimand, even doctors and nurses. More importantly, it put patients at risk.

"What were you trying to do?" she said.

He could never explain his ability to anyone else. He'd tried before. It always ended badly. Even if they wanted to believe him, no one could ever fully understand. "I felt bad for her. She looked like she needed to feel a human's touch. I didn't think it through."

The woman's expression softened, but not her tongue. "Don't touch another patient in my CCU."

"I won't."

She reached for his ID badge and held it close. "I'll be watching you, Luke Johnson. Once someone gets on my radar, they never go off."

He leaned forward and read her badge. "Message received, Marisa Cruz."

The left side of her mouth pulled upward. It looked like she was trying to force it back down. She spun around and paced down the skywalk toward the main building.

He waited until she'd walked a hundred yards, then followed behind.

She never looked back, not even once.

CHAPTER 6

Annamaria stared at the ceiling of the San Francisco Fairmont's penthouse suite while a makeup artist painted a second coat of mascara on her lower lashes. She hated having to be still while a pair of unwashed hands hovered around her face like mosquitoes. But at least she didn't need to wear that disgusting blond wig or fake nose anymore. Her naturally dark hair shimmered in almost any light. She smiled. Soon dozens of lights would shine on her, each as bright as the sun.

Her aides stood far away but within earshot, silently awaiting instructions. Gilbert and Noordhoek—she'd never cared to learn their first names—seemed to take their jobs as seriously as she demanded. No coincidence they'd also worked for her longer than any other employees. They never spoke out of turn and never took vacation days. They also never called in sick. Funny how those things went together.

The makeup artist backed away, then searched through a case that held enough makeup to paint the Sistine Chapel. Annamaria called for her aides. They swept into the room and to her side with a silent urgency that couldn't be taught.

"Any update on Psychic Nick?"

"He checked into Baptist Memorial at three p.m.," Gilbert said.

"They admitted him directly to the ICU." Noordhoek shook his head. "It doesn't look good."

"Sure it does." She stood and grabbed Noordhoek's tie, straightening it with more force than necessary. "Remember, people earn their fate."

"Of course."

She could feel the tension building in his shoulders, the fear that coursed through his bloodstream when she touched him. Noordhoek outweighed her by a hundred pounds, but he'd never raise a hand against her, not even in self-defense.

The rush lasted only a moment before it left her. She returned to her padded chair and looked away. "What about our fugitive?"

"No sign of him in Port Arthur." Gilbert glanced at the makeup artist. "Our man lost him after their meeting. We're checking facilities nearby. He'll turn up again soon."

The makeup artist approached with a powder brush in her hand. Annamaria closed her eyes and lifted her chin. "What's the nearest big city?"

"Houston is less than two hours west," Noordhoek said.

"That's where he's going."

She heard Gilbert and Noordhoek shift positions in their suits, but neither spoke.

"Yeah, I know it's big. But you need to find him. You need to make sure."

Light brushstrokes swept across her face. A puff of powder flew up her nose and made her sneeze. She flashed open her eyes and grabbed the makeup artist's hand. "That's enough. You're done."

"Sorry," the artist said. "It was an accident." She turned and packed up her case.

A bald man Annamaria hadn't seen before poked his head into the room. "Ms. Varner, they're ready for you in the ballroom."

Time to turn it on. Annamaria drew her lips into a smile. "Be right there."

Gilbert and Noordhoek traded glances. She placed a hand on each man's shoulder. "Find him quickly. I'm counting on you both."

Both men nodded.

She dug into her clutch purse. Under her toy bear was a rolled-up slip of paper. She pulled it out. "Here's the last one." She tucked it into Gilbert's palm. "Find him, but don't engage. I'll handle this one myself."

Gilbert shoved the paper into his pocket without reading it. Noordhoek acted like nothing had happened.

The makeup artist finished packing her zebra-print case and turned to leave. Annamaria stood in her way. "You did a phenomenal job." She offered her hand. "I hope we can work together again."

The artist raised a painted brow. "Are you sure?"

"This is a big night. I let it get to me for a moment. It won't happen again."

The artist's expression brightened. "I'm available anytime—even if it's an emergency, like earlier this week." She glanced at the tip of Annamaria's nose, then winked.

Annamaria clasped both hands around the artist's fingers. She bowed her head and blinked so quickly she doubted the woman noticed.

"Parkinson's," she said.

"What?" The artist pulled her arm back, but Annamaria wouldn't let go.

"I said parking's probably expensive here. Make sure you get validated."

"Thanks, but I use Uber."

Already she could feel the tremors in the artist's hand. "I guess you're all set, then." She released her grip and watched the artist walk away.

"Ms. Varner," the bald man said. "I'm sorry to ask again—"

"Gilbert, Noordhoek. Let's go." She strode across the room, flanked by her best men.

The bald man led them to a secure holding area connected to the Fairmont's Grand Ballroom. During their trek he filled the silence by providing directions he claimed would help her performance: the senator will stand to your left, the party chairman on your right; teleprompters are mounted on each side of the podium; the words roll up on cue; the speed automatically adjusts to your pace.

She ignored them all. Best to let her instincts take over and live in the moment. That was why the public loved her. They adored the grieving widow who'd somehow found the strength to step into the national spotlight at a time when people needed her most.

The stage waited twenty feet ahead. Senator Blair, his golden hair a study in Aryan perfection, spoke into the microphones. "She began her career as a legal clerk for Justice Franklin on the Supreme Court. Then she served as a federal prosecutor, earning the highest conviction rate in the history of her department. She's a champion for justice, not afraid to take on the biggest corporate CEO or the most hardened criminal."

Annamaria focused on the senator but whispered a message she wanted only her aides to hear: "After tonight, things will be different. But I'll still need you."

"When she met Governor Varner, they formed the ultimate power couple," the senator said. "She worked behind the scenes to implement his policies, helping transform the state of California into a model of innovation for the country."

The senator spoke the truth. No need for embellishment. She'd known from the moment she met Bobby Varner he was the man she should marry, the one she'd use to climb near the top of every social and political ladder. And now she'd climb even higher, into an atmosphere where few dared to tread.

The senator glanced in her direction. "Robert Varner was a true patriot who dedicated his life to public service. We were all shocked and saddened by the governor's sudden passing. But I'm proud to announce I've found someone worthy to step forward and take his place by my side. I can think of no one more qualified, no one more dedicated to the causes the governor held so dear."

"Here it comes," the bald man said. "Get ready."

Senator Blair waved her to the podium. "Ladies and gentlemen, it's an honor to introduce my new running mate in the upcoming election, the next vice president of the United States, Anna Varner."

CHAPTER 7

Clyde had spent the last twenty-four hours doing things he never thought he'd do. He drove a man who claimed to have already been murdered to the hospital. He edited himself into the most bizarre interview he'd ever conducted. After uploading the video, he sat openmouthed and watched the number of views grow exponentially, saw the social networks go wild with shares and retweets, and read hundreds of comments along the lines of "I once knew a bitch who thought she could do that." The online chatter sounded like gold coins spilling out of a slot machine.

His inbox overflowed with emails from amateur cyber-sleuths. They sent him links to articles about hospital patients claiming to have been miraculously healed by a stranger. They repeated Nicholas's challenge and begged him to find the dying man's lost son—the son with a supernatural power that could save Nicholas and stop his homicidal daughter.

At first Clyde thought it was all bullshit, but the article links kept pouring in, dozens of accounts detailing similar yet ludicrous claims from patients at hospitals and nursing homes in different cities: an angel touched me, the janitor healed me, I dreamt of a wizard who waved a staff over my body and took away the pneumonia.

After reading a hundred emails, he knew it was all bullshit. But people believed this stuff. They *wanted* to believe in a man who could heal by a simple touch. Millions of people went to church each Sunday and prayed to a god they believed could do such a thing. Off camera, Nicholas admitted to having made a living for twenty years by pretending to do it. Half of Clyde's subscribers seemed convinced it was his duty to track down and interview this miracle worker. Just as many begged him to do it so he could prove the believers wrong.

So he'd filled his Mitsubishi with gas and driven to Port Arthur.

According to the most recent article links his subscribers had sent him, an unidentified male had roamed the halls of St. Mary's Regional Medical Center less than a week ago, entering at least three patient rooms and healing two different patients. Eyewitness descriptions of the mystery man varied wildly, forcing Clyde to take a different approach as he strode past the welcome booth and angled toward the elevators.

He looked for the floor that held the CCU and pushed the button. Experience had taught him that people who walked confidently into restricted areas rarely got caught. It was all about acting like you belonged. The shirt, tie, slacks, and dress shoes didn't hurt, either. For all anyone knew, he might be a hospital administrator checking in with the head nurse of the CCU. The only thing missing was the badge.

The elevator doors opened. He marched into the CCU. Three steps later, a nurse stopped him cold with a stiff arm to the center of his chest.

"What are you doing here, sir?"

"I need to speak to the head nurse."

"You found her. Now answer my question."

Clyde said the first thing that popped into his head. "I represent Paramount Insurance Company. I'm here to investigate a claim by one of our insureds regarding the care they received in this CCU."

The nurse crinkled her freckled nose. "What kind of claim?"

"That an unauthorized person entered their room and administered medical treatment without their consent."

She folded her arms. "When you say 'unauthorized person,' do you mean a person pretending to be someone they're not?"

Heat rushed to his cheeks. He looked around. Other nurses were staring. "Look, we have to investigate these claims, no matter how silly they sound. Do you remember the last time someone gained access to this CCU without proper authorization?"

"About twenty seconds ago."

A large man with a red goatee and a gold security badge appeared behind the nurse's shoulder. Without looking, she seemed to know he was there. "Do you have a business card, sir?"

Clyde pretended to dig through his suit pockets, but he knew it was a losing effort. After a moment he threw up his hands. "Must be in my other suit."

The nurse nodded to the security guard. "Rusty, show this man to the exit."

Clyde couldn't believe they made uniforms large enough to fit a man Rusty's size. Rusty quietly escorted him out of the CCU, down the elevator, through a network of hallways, and out the back entrance to the hospital, his fingers clenched firmly around Clyde's triceps. Clyde peppered Rusty with questions, but the man never responded. Rusty didn't need to. The strength in his grip spoke for him.

"This isn't the way I came in," Clyde said. "How do you expect me to find my car?"

Rusty raised one of his massive arms and pointed toward two loading ramps that fed into an alley along the back side of the hospital. The alley seemed to lead around the corner, in the general direction of where Clyde had parked. He adjusted his tie. "Thanks for the hospitality."

Rusty turned and marched back into the hospital.

Clyde scratched his chin. Plan A was now officially dead, but he still had options. He looked around. In a way, Rusty might have done him a favor. This entrance didn't look nearly as fancy as the one he'd used. It faced the back side of a cinder block building with all its windows boarded up. Nurses, cleaning staff, and surgeons filed through the hospital doors in both directions. To his right, six men with scrub pants and no shirts launched basketballs at a goal mounted on the hospital wall. He walked in their direction.

As he approached, an errant shot bounced hard off the backboard and rim, launching the ball over the players' heads and toward the alley. He angled to the left and snatched the ball just before it would have landed in a puddle.

"Nice save," one of the players said.

He spun the basketball in his hands, threw it in the air, then started dribbling. "You guys have a three-point line?"

"It's the blue mark," another player said.

Clyde dribbled forward, his eyes focused on the rim. He bounced the ball on the mark, set his feet, and released a jump shot that splashed through the bottom of the net.

The bare-chested players looked at each other. "Do you play?" one of them said.

"Wish I could, but I have to work."

The tallest of the group, a black man with tiny beads of sweat dotting his bald head, passed the basketball back to him. "You new here?"

Clyde dribbled to the side and crossed the ball between his legs. "I'm a journalist based in Memphis. I came here to investigate reports of a stranger roaming the hospital healing patients."

"What, like some modern-day Jesus?"

He pulled the ball close and swished it through the rim. "I'm not saying it really happened. But at least one patient thinks it did."

"Maybe they're talking about me." The man flashed the whitest teeth Clyde had ever seen. "After all, I *am* the best surgeon at St. Mary's."

A few players groaned. Clyde played along, acting impressed. "You guys haven't heard any stories like that, have you?"

Several players shook their heads. The tall surgeon called for the basketball. "We deal in miracles every day. One patient dies, another lives. Usually there's no rhyme or reason."

Another player stepped forward. "Especially with elderly patients. Many are in such bad shape they expect to die. When they survive, they call it a miracle."

"What about a stranger? Have you guys seen anyone hanging around who doesn't belong?"

The surgeon attempted a shot from the same distance as Clyde's swish. It clanged off the rim. "This is a small town. Everyone knows each other. The only people roaming these halls are employees or family of patients." He pretended to straighten an imaginary tie around his neck while a few other players snickered. "Strangers are easy to recognize. You're the first one I've seen this week."

Clyde figured he wouldn't get a chance to launch another shot, or even another question. The players turned away and resumed their game. He turned and walked toward the alley.

Over five hundred interstate miles separated Memphis from Port Arthur. By the time he returned, that meant three tanks of gas. Plus a hotel room, food, and the piña coladas he'd order later tonight. But he hadn't run out of options. Thanks to his subscribers, the notepad in his pocket held the address of one of the patients who claimed to have been healed. He took a cleansing breath—drew the positive energy in, pushed the bad energy out. That seemed to work. He picked up his pace.

When he approached the corner, an old man jumped out from a hedge and blocked his way. The man looked dirty and smelled even dirtier, with dark lines marking the creases of his face. The man's eyes seemed so large Clyde wondered how they fit into their sockets. "You searching for the miracle healer?"

Clyde took a step back and watched the man's hands. No weapons in sight. He put his own hands out. "I don't want any trouble. Just trying to find the parking lot."

"I heard you talking to those men, asking about the guy who healed those people." The man's eyes grew even larger as he spoke. "The one you came all the way from Memphis to find."

"What do you know about him?"

"I saw him do it," the man said.

Clyde sniffed but couldn't detect any alcohol. Maybe it was buried under a week's supply of body odor. "What do you mean you saw him do it? Were you in the hospital last week?"

"Not in the hospital." The man hunched his shoulders and grinned like he was holding a secret in his pockets. "I saw him get shot in an alley close to here. He healed himself, then he healed the guy who shot him."

Clyde smelled something else now. This man was either crazy or on drugs. "You have a good day, sir." He turned and walked away.

"Wait." The man raised his voice. "I have proof. Let me show you."

Clyde spun around. The man dug into several different pockets, his fingers working faster than a thief's. "Here they are." He stuck out his palm and produced four shiny lumps of metal.

"What are those supposed to be?" Clyde said.

"The bullets he pulled out of himself and the other guy."

He snatched one piece out of the man's hand and inspected it. The tip looked badly misshapen, and the sides were stained with dark blotches. He closed his fingers around it. "Interesting, but it isn't proof."

The old man swung at his hand. "Give it back. He gave 'em to me. They're mine!"

"Calm down." Clyde held the slug between his fingers and offered it to the man, who swiped at it like a child reclaiming a toy from his little brother. "Did you talk to the guy?"

"I asked if he was an angel, but then I didn't see any wings, so he couldn't have been. But he sure healed that guy."

"Did you get a good look at him?"

The old man stared at the sky for a moment. "Tall guy. Dark hair. A half-circle scar on his right cheek. He wore a dark blue uniform, like he was a mechanic or something. Had his name stitched on it, but I couldn't see what it said."

Clyde remembered the name Nicholas had mentioned. "Did it say 'Lucian'?"

"What kind of name is Lucian?"

"Never mind," Clyde said. "He's probably using an alias."

The old man scratched at the side of his face. "If you ever find him, tell him I said thanks. That guy saved my life. Told me to get out of there before a second gunman showed up."

"*Second* gunman?"

"Yeah, another guy came running five minutes after the healer left. I'd already crawled back into my hiding spot. Neither of them saw me."

"Where did this happen?" Clyde said.

"Two blocks from here."

"Can you take me there?" He dug into his own pocket and pulled out his phone. "And would you be willing to make a short video detailing everything you told me?"

The man's large brown irises darted left and right. "Don't know. I'm really hungry."

"We'll stop by an IHOP."

"Really thirsty, too."

"One bottle. That's it."

The old man tugged on a knot he'd made by tying the sleeves of his jacket around his waist. "Now you're talking. Let's go."

Clyde strode toward the parking lot with a renewed sense of purpose. Maybe Lucian was a real person. Maybe he even held a special ability. At this point it still didn't matter. After his viewers watched his next video, they'd scream for more.

He glanced over his shoulder. The old man was doing his best to keep up. Taking a homeless person to a restaurant and a liquor store seemed like a small price for another viral video. Plus, it was warm enough for him to roll down the windows of his car.

He tapped a few keys on his phone, then held it to his ear. "I'm calling for Nicholas Gabor, room 335."

The woman on the other end sounded anything but friendly. "That patient is no longer in that room."

"Could you connect me to his new room?"

"Sir, are you a friend or family member?"

"I want to sell him insurance." Clyde took a deep breath and blew it out. "I'm a friend."

"I need to transfer you to Patient Services."

Clyde froze. "What are you saying? Did he leave the hospital again?"

"No, sir. He didn't."

CHAPTER 8

Luke waited while dozens of commuters dressed in either scrubs or long white coats squeezed out from the METRORail train onto the platform of Dryden Station. This aboveground stop marked the population epicenter of the Texas Medical Center, especially in these early morning hours when the night shift passed their torches to the day shift.

Once the doorway cleared, he stepped inside, took a seat near the back, and stared at the floor.

An electronic bell sounded. The doors closed. As the train lurched toward the next stop, Marisa Cruz flung herself into the seat next to him.

"We need to talk."

"I didn't touch anyone last night."

"I know," she said. "I asked one of the nurses on your floor to watch and make sure." She settled her bag in her lap. "I'm talking about the three patients in my CCU who claim an angel held their hand and took away their cancer."

He clenched his fist—the one she couldn't see—as tightly as he could. "I don't know what you're talking about."

"At first we thought they were delusional, or that someone might've screwed with their medication. But their vitals and labs improved so quickly, the doctors decided to run scans."

Luke checked the schedule posted near the roof of the train car. The next stop was one minute away.

"You know what they found?" She planted a hand on his knee and pushed her face in front of his.

"No, I don't."

She leaned in closer and didn't blink. "All three came back one hundred percent clear."

"Their families must be elated."

Marisa's nostrils flared and her pupils dilated. "What did you do to my patients?"

"Nothing."

"I checked the security tapes. You were the only person who entered their rooms during the time they claim they were healed."

Luke's blood ran cold. He'd been busted again, this time quicker than ever. Marisa couldn't prove anything or else she'd have brought security. But she showed no signs of backing off.

She squeezed his arm. Her fingernails bit into the fabric of his work suit. "You're the one they were talking about. You did something to them."

"I cleaned their rooms. That's all."

"*Mentiras.*"

"What?"

"Lies." She let go of his arm, stared down the length of the train car, then back at him. "Tell me what you did."

The train slowed. An automated voice announced the next stop. Luke hopped over the seat in front of him and ran down the aisle. A group of medical students stood near the doors with their backs facing him. He elbowed his way through. When the doors opened, he darted out of the train and into the morning sun.

The platform straddled the median of a busy street. He bypassed the walkway ramp and sprinted across the southbound lanes without checking for traffic. When he reached the curb, he risked a look back. Marisa had already cleared the platform. She charged in his direction.

He needed to outrun her—lose her, grab his things, and escape to the next city. This time it was his fault. Every time was his fault, but he couldn't help himself. He'd never stop trying to make up for the damage his family had done.

He ran south, across another intersection.

First came a screech of tires, then the impact, a sweeping blow that knocked his legs from under him. His head slammed against something hard. He glimpsed the sky, then everything went black.

Dude, are you okay? I didn't even see you.

Get back. Call 911.

Whoa, look at his leg. That's messed up.

Come on, Luke. Wake up.

He opened his eyes. Marisa stared down at him, a halo of sunshine behind her shoulder.

"There you go. Stay with me. An ambulance is on its way."

He tried to sit up. Dizziness forced him back down. He raised his hand and touched his forehead. He held it there when Marisa tried to pull it away.

"What are you doing?" she said. "Just stay still."

A sharp, intense pain throbbed in his right knee. It felt like someone had taken an axe to it. He blocked it out. The dizziness faded. Once his head cleared, the pain sliced back into his knee. He raised himself onto his elbows and looked. His pant leg was damp with blood, his knee bent at an impossible angle.

"I told you to stay still." Marisa pushed against his chest. "It's better if you don't look."

The driver of the car crept closer and stared. Luke ignored him and reached for his knee. Marisa slapped his hand away.

"Don't make it worse," she said.

"Just let me do this."

He reached again. This time she left his hand alone. He closed his eyes, felt the warmth rush into his ligaments and tendons. They grew and repaired themselves, pulling against his other tissues.

The pain crested. His lower leg started to move. The driver gasped when Luke's leg snapped into place.

Marisa shuffled backward, along with the driver. She stretched out her arms as if warding off evil spirits.

Luke climbed to his feet and sprinted as fast as his repaired knee allowed. He didn't look back. He could never look back again.

CHAPTER 9

"Welcome to the race."

Annamaria raised her glass of Krug Clos du Mesnil and clinked it against Senator Blair's. She drew it close to her lips. "Don't you mean welcome back?"

"Of course." The senator took a long sip. "You've always been part of the team, even when you were standing behind Bobby. It's a no-brainer for you to take his place."

She set her drink on the table and looked out the window of the senator's chartered jet. Even after living as a governor's wife for seven years, the way people treated her since she accepted the senator's offer surprised her. Here she sat, sipping champagne at thirty-two thousand feet, heading toward the first of five different states they'd visit before the sun dipped below the horizon. When they landed, every door would open for her, and every camera would turn in her direction. According to the talking heads on television, the entire country wanted a piece of Anna Varner. She could get used to that.

Senator Blair flipped through the pages of a report his aide had placed in front of him. His toothy smile made Annamaria want to retch. Instead she batted her lashes, just like he expected her to.

"This is amazing," he said. "The overnight numbers are through the roof. We're up in nearly every state. You've pushed us ahead in

Ohio, Pennsylvania, and Florida." He flipped a page. "We're up in Nevada and Arizona. Damn—we're even competitive in Texas."

She knew Blair wanted to see her campaign-winning smile. Instead she stared out the window and tried to peer through the clouds. Lucian was down there somewhere, probably trying to save the world one pathetic sick person at a time. If a reporter found him and learned his story, everything she'd built would fall apart.

"Anna, did you hear me? I said we're killing it."

She folded her hands in her lap. "That's great news."

The senator refilled his own glass then spiked the bottle into the ice bucket. He didn't even glance at hers. "This was a stroke of genius. After Bobby's heart attack, I thought I was finished. Our supporters were demoralized, and the media got offended when I held a rally the night of the funeral." He threw the champagne down his throat like it was a shot of whiskey. "I mean, what's wrong with trying to win?"

Annamaria took comfort in knowing Blair cared for her dead husband even less than she had. It proved they saw Bobby the same way: as emotional currency that needed to be spent before it expired.

"But then I remembered you, Anna. You were the one they really loved, not Bobby. You're young—politically speaking—smart, charming, and beautiful. Plus you're comfortable standing behind great men."

She leaned forward and touched his hand, then closed her eyes. It took every ounce of restraint in her body not to say what she was thinking.

"I'm sure he would have wanted it this way," she said.

"Look at you." He covered her hand with his. "You always say the right thing. You're a natural at this. I'm counting on you to push me across the finish line."

She pulled her hand away and wrapped her fingers around her glass to try to cool them. "We'll cross that line together."

"Absolutely." The senator lifted the bottle from the ice bucket, shook off the condensation, and poured the last of the champagne into his glass. "We need to talk about your stump speech. My people have prepared a few notes." He pulled a document from the stack of papers in front of him. "We want to keep it short and sweet. That way there's less chance of a screwup." He slid the paper across the table.

"Screwup?"

"With the schedule you'll be keeping the next few weeks, it's bound to happen. It happens to every candidate at least once in a campaign."

"I never screw up," she said.

"Read it. It'll help." He motioned for an aide to roll away the ice bucket stand. "You'll get ten minutes to my thirty. Shake some hands, pose for a few selfies, say your lines, then stand back and look pretty. That's how we win this thing."

Annamaria squeezed her glass so hard she thought it might shatter. Before today, she figured the smartest approach might be to allow Blair his moment in the sun, let him move into the West Wing and do all the heavy lifting of setting up his administration before giving him a debilitating disease that would force him to cede the presidency. The scenario offered a certain amount of grace and dignity to the man who would help her take that final step into the most powerful position in the world.

Now she knew she couldn't allow this prick the pleasure of enjoying even one day in office. He deserved a painful, embarrassing demise. And she'd be sure to deliver it.

Justice, swift and mighty, would soon swing its hammer through the senator's house of cards.

Soon, but not now.

The dull roar of the airplane's engines lowered an octave in pitch, marking the beginning of their descent. She looked out the window again. Clouds no longer blocked her view. A gleaming city waited in the distance, its buildings filled with people eager to catch a view of the newest candidate for vice president of the United States.

The senator flashed his porcelain smile. "What do you say, Anna? Are you ready to make history?"

"More than you know."

CHAPTER 10

Luke dashed around his hotel room, grabbing his belongings and stuffing them in his canvas duffel bag. He ran to the bathroom vanity and raked in his toiletries with one swipe. He opened dresser drawers, scooped out his underwear and socks, and tucked them into what little free space remained in his bag. He closed the zipper and charged toward the exit.

Time to get out of Houston.

When he opened the door, Marisa was waiting outside. She still had that look on her face, the one she'd shown when he healed himself in the middle of a busy street. He dropped his bag. The *thunk* it made when it hit the carpet was the only sound between them.

He waited. She looked like she wanted to say something, but her lips didn't move. They hung there, slightly open but seemingly unwilling to form any words.

"How did you find me?"

"I have friends who work in HR."

She'd never sounded like this before. For the first time, he didn't immediately think she wanted to bite his head off.

He reached for his duffel bag. She stopped him with her words: "I need to apologize."

"No, you don't."

"I shouldn't have attacked you like that. I practically forced you into that accident."

"I'll live."

"So I see." She leaned forward. "Can I come in?"

"I was just leaving."

"This will only take a minute." She stepped closer. "Please."

He looked both ways along the balcony walkway. No one else was in sight. He moved aside and let her in.

They sat in the same two uncomfortable chairs that seemed to come with every hotel room he'd ever rented. She planted her elbows on the skinny, round table between them. "Where are you going?"

"I don't know yet. Maybe Austin. Maybe San Antonio."

"And what will you do there? Find another job near sick people?"

"Something like that."

She narrowed her eyes. "How long have you been doing this?"

"Janitorial work?"

"You know what I mean. How long?"

He leaned back in his chair. No one had ever asked him that before. He tried to remember the number of years, the number of jobs, the number of times he'd needed to cut and run. They all ran together in his mind. "This is the only thing I've ever done. It's the only thing I know."

She shook her head. "I never would have believed it. Back at the METRO, I thought maybe you were working for someone, carrying out some sort of experiment. Or maybe you practiced Santeria."

"Practiced what?" he said.

"Never mind." She pinched the pinky ring on her left hand and twisted it back and forth. "Then I saw what you did in the street. That was no trick or experiment. It was real, just like my patients' scans. I thought about it all the way here. I've turned it over in my mind a thousand times. There's no logical explanation." She reached across the table, grabbed his wrists, and held them up to the overhead light between them. "It's like you have the hands of Jesus."

"You're wrong." He pulled away, grabbed the duffel bag, and stepped toward the door.

"Wait." She stood and blocked his way. "You didn't let me finish. I didn't mean it like that."

Luke considered pushing her aside. He didn't own the hands of Jesus, or those of any other prophet or god. His hands could also punch, push, and squeeze the trigger of a pistol. Comparing him to someone like that proved she didn't understand him at all.

"Let me explain," she said. "I think I can help."

"I don't need help. I just need to keep moving." He stepped on the bed to get around her. He reached for the door handle.

"What if you didn't?" she said.

He turned the handle but didn't pull.

"I won't pretend I understand what you can do. Whatever it is, I know it comes from a good place. You're saving lives. That's why I want to help." She moved between him and the door, then leaned against it. "I'm willing to do whatever it takes to keep you at my hospital."

"It's no use. People will talk. They always do."

"I'll make sure they don't." The corner of her mouth turned upward like it did the first time he saw her. "I know people—people who can help us stay unnoticed. I could protect you, give you access to patients you could never reach on your own."

She pulled his hand away from the door and pressed his palm between hers. "I know you want to do this. Part of me thinks you need to do this. Let me help."

Her heartbeat pulsed through her fingers so forcefully he could feel it. Marisa looked sincere, but she didn't know him. No one had ever offered him a deal like this. It implied a level of trust neither of them had earned yet.

"You don't know what you're asking," he said. "It's dangerous to be near me."

"What's so dangerous about a healer?"

"People are looking for me. People with guns." He turned away and paced in front of the dresser. He glanced at the mirror. The scar on his cheek caught his eye. "They always find me, no matter how careful I am."

She picked up his bag and set it on the bed. "Why would someone want to shoot you?"

"Long story," he said. "That's the reason I need to keep moving. Once word gets out that a stranger is healing random people, they show up and try to kill me."

"Sounds like a spy movie."

"It's my reality."

She walked to the window and peeked out the curtain. "When was the last time they caught up to you?"

"A week ago, in Port Arthur."

"How did you get away?"

"I almost didn't. They shot me in the chest."

"*Dios mío.*" Her hands moved to her own torso, like she was checking herself for wounds. "Can they kill you?"

He winced, remembering the sting of the bullets. "I'm pretty sure they can."

"Of course, you're just like anyone else—unless you're an alien or some type of superhero?"

"Sorry to disappoint."

She walked toward him and touched his shoulder. "You need to give this a chance. I can make it so you're put at less risk. I'll watch your back, make sure no one with a gun gets close enough to use it."

"You can't guarantee anything you're saying."

"It's better than taking chances on your own," she said.

He didn't know if she was right or not. But it looked like she wouldn't take no for an answer. "If I stay, how are we going to keep things quiet?"

"I have a few ideas." She opened his duffel bag and started pulling out his socks. "Let's get you unpacked first, then we'll talk."

CHAPTER 11

Clyde had spent nearly two hours with the star of his latest video before he asked the man's name. Billy—the homeless guy with large brown eyes and an appetite for pancakes and bourbon—had proudly reenacted every aspect of the shoot-out in the alley. Watching Billy gesture with his fingers acting like a gun, hearing him try to mimic the sound of a silencer popping off rounds, listening to his colorful description of how a mystery man had pulled bullets out of his own body, Clyde knew every bit of it was pure internet gold. He was so sure of its appeal that he'd spent the rest of the day editing the footage on his laptop in his hotel room, working straight through dinner.

Apparently his subscribers shared his enthusiasm for Port Arthur Billy, as one fan had dubbed him. The overnight views confirmed his instincts. Making this month's rent wouldn't be a problem after all. It wouldn't be a problem for the rest of the year.

His only regret was Nicholas would never see the story Billy had acted out in front of a smartphone camera. They'd never shoot a follow-up video set in Nicholas's hospital room like he'd planned. No tearful reunion between father and son. But Clyde wouldn't drop this story just because his original source had died.

He parked on Ninth Street in front of a one-story brick home surrounded by oak trees and thick St. Augustine grass. He pulled out his notepad and checked the address again. The black numbers on the side of the house matched those on his paper, so he shut off the engine and climbed out of the car. A towering refinery dominated the horizon to his left. He inhaled but smelled nothing. The wind was probably blowing in the opposite direction. He smoothed the lapels on his suit coat and strode up the sidewalk toward the home of Riley Sankey.

According to an online article, Riley had recently been discharged from St. Mary's with a clean bill of health only two days after a priest performed a last rites ceremony. He also claimed to have seen a mysterious visitor not listed on the ICU logs during that same time, though he refused to identify the person. Several religious bloggers highlighted his story as proof a miracle had occurred. One of them was Riley's own grandson, who also happened to be one of Clyde's subscribers. Most news organizations had ignored the reports, but Clyde owed it to his followers to attempt a visit.

Two minutes after ringing the doorbell, Clyde found himself sitting on the old man's couch and holding a glass of sweet iced tea. Riley Sankey struck a grandfatherly profile, with a barrel-sized chest, skinny legs, and thick steel-colored hair. He balanced his torso on the edge of a padded chair and stared at a large television on the opposite wall tuned to FOX News with the volume muted. The house smelled like aged tobacco, and the ceiling sported several faded yellow patches. Riley appeared to be chewing on something, though Clyde hadn't seen him put anything in his mouth.

Two large dogs barked from the backyard, but Riley didn't seem to notice. "I'd rather not say how it happened. I just know I can breathe without any trouble now. I can walk up a flight of stairs without stopping for oxygen. I can be intimate with my wife without passing out." He winked. "Haven't been able to do that since I was forty."

Clyde took out his phone and set it on his thigh. He set the iced tea on a coaster and leaned forward. "I'm interested in what you remember about the man who helped you. Had you ever seen him before? Did he look familiar?"

Riley shook his head. "Things were a blur the whole time I was there. You can't tell it now, but I was in pretty bad shape." He tapped the toe of his boot against an oxygen tank standing next to him. Its metallic resonance filtered into Clyde's ears. "COPD kicked my ass for thirty years. Docs said it would put me in an early grave, but that man proved them wrong. He set me right faster than you can snap your fingers."

"Can you describe what he looked like?"

Riley squinted toward the ceiling. "Tall guy with a curly fry–shaped scar on his cheek. His skin was darker than yours or mine—probably Mexican or Native American. I thought he worked there. Not as a doctor or a nurse, though. Might have been a contractor. His uniform looked like the FRCs I used to wear in the refinery."

Clyde unlocked his phone and started recording video. He angled the camera lens toward Riley as discreetly as he could. "Did he say anything to you?"

"We talked about the Astros. I'm a baseball junkie. He seemed interested enough to ask questions. So I told him how they'd rebuilt themselves into winners faster than anyone thought possible. I must have gone on for ten minutes. It took a while because I needed to stop and catch my breath."

Clyde shifted his weight while he worked to keep the camera steady. Nicholas's son must be a better man than Clyde was. Riley's baseball stories might've put him to sleep in less than a minute. "What happened after that? Did he place his hands on you? Did he pray?"

Riley's expression changed before Clyde could finish his question. His eyebrows crashed over his eyelids. "What happened in that room stays between him and me. I promised I wouldn't tell. That's the only payment he required."

"But he healed you, right? You suffered from late-stage COPD before he walked into that room. And when he left you were cured."

Riley folded his arms. "I don't remember."

"COPD is a degenerative disease. Patients never regain their lung function. Yet here you sit, breathing as easily as a newborn. How do you explain that?"

"I don't need to explain anything." Riley stood, and for the first time, Clyde realized how massive the old man's frame was. "I'll tell you what I told the others. You let that man be. If he doesn't want to be found, I'm not going to help anyone find him."

The room lighting seemed to dim several shades darker. Clyde angled his phone upward, trying to keep the old man in the frame. "Even if his father is dying?"

Riley brought a hand to his chin. The backyard dogs went quiet for a moment. He paced in a tight circle, then eased himself back onto the edge of the chair. "What's wrong with his daddy?"

"You name it. He's in a Memphis hospital connected to a breathing machine."

"They don't talk to each other?"

"He hasn't seen his son in twenty-nine years. That's why I need to find him."

"Should have told me that earlier." Riley rested his elbows on his knees. "His name is Luke. Never mentioned a last name. I don't know where to find him, but I know he's not in Port Arthur anymore. Poor guy gets ambushed every time people start talking. He has to keep moving. Such a shame a man like that never gets any peace."

"Did you ask why he heals people?"

"Something about repaying an old debt. I got the sense he felt guilty about something."

Clyde dug a business card out of his back pocket and walked it over to Riley. "I'll keep trying to find him. If you think of anything else, please call."

The man reached for the card, then tightened his hand into a fist. The skin on his neck reddened. "What are you doing with that phone?"

"Nothing." Clyde tucked it into his pocket.

"Are you recording this?"

"Of course not. Here, take—"

Riley grabbed him by the collar and nearly lifted him off the floor. "I knew it. You're just like the others. You don't even know his daddy. Do you, peckerhead?"

"I can explain."

Clyde's feet struggled to keep up with his body as Riley dragged him through the living room toward the foyer. The dogs in the backyard barked louder than before. A jolt of terror passed through him. Everything was happening so fast. He hoped the old man didn't own a cellar.

Riley threw open the front door, then tossed him across the porch. Somewhere along the way Clyde must have dropped his business card. He patted the outside of his front pocket. It felt like his phone was still intact. And hopefully still recording.

He climbed to his feet and dusted himself off. Riley stood in the doorway with his arms crossed, like a bouncer guarding the entrance to a nightclub.

"I'm not a reporter. I swear."

Riley reached into his shirt pocket and pulled out a pack of Camels. He shook it until a single cigarette popped up. "Leave that man alone. And don't come back, or I'll show you my gun collection."

CHAPTER 12

Annamaria worked her way past a line of starstruck voters and toward a black limousine parked on the corner of Forty-Ninth and Rockefeller Center. She shook every hand, posed for every selfie, even flashed an enthusiastic thumbs-up whenever anyone shouted Senator Blair's campaign slogan: "An America Worth Saving."

A Secret Service agent pushed the limo door closed. She stuck her hands out, spread her fingers wide, and squeezed her eyelids closed while Noordhoek wiped away the grime with a disposable wipe. The thought of what she might have just touched, all the snot and sweat from the Great Unwashed, made her work to suppress her gag reflex. Noordhoek cleaned her fingers and palms methodically, scrubbing every inch of skin at least twice. She didn't open her eyes until he'd finished.

Her mobile phone sounded. Noordhoek answered it, then handed it to her.

"This is Anna."

"That was the best damn interview I've ever seen." Senator Blair's deep voice echoed into her ear. Apparently she wasn't important enough to be taken off speakerphone. "I've never seen a candidate discuss foreign policy and cook beef bourguignon at the same time. Where did you learn that?"

"I took culinary classes during law school."

"This opens up a whole new world of possibilities. Do you realize how many potential voters watch cooking shows?"

"I'm running for vice president, not first lady."

Someone else in the room—not the senator—chuckled under his breath. She wondered how many members of Blair's staff realized what an ass he could be.

"Of course you are. I just wanted to say you're doing a great job. You're everything I thought you could be, and more."

"Thanks."

"Good luck at your next stop. Those blonde reporters from the morning show will try to trip you up. Be careful."

"I'm not worried."

"Me neither." The senator ended the call.

She tossed the phone to Noordhoek. "Give me a warning next time."

"Your package arrived at the hotel during your interview," he said.

"What package?"

"The one from Memphis."

She searched for the privacy window control on her armrest and pushed it down hard. "We need to stop by the hotel."

The Secret Service agent in the front passenger seat barked something unintelligible into his sleeve, then said, "Ms. Varner, that would put us behind schedule."

"I'll only need five minutes."

The agent whispered into his wrist again. The driver changed lanes and hooked a sharp right. Annamaria reversed the controls on the privacy window. Noordhoek stared at the floor of the limo. She knew he wouldn't look at her again until she got what she needed.

The Secret Service agent sitting across from her obviously possessed no such instincts. He leered at her from behind his sunglasses. She just knew it. He probably wondered why a woman as self-assured as the former first lady of California needed to make a pit stop at her hotel between interviews. At least the senator didn't try to mask his misogyny behind a pair of dark shades.

She forced the thought out of her mind. The day was still young. She'd have plenty of time to deal with a judgmental agent later.

The limo stopped at the Waldorf Astoria. Noordhoek and the agents ushered her into the hotel and up to her suite.

"Everyone out," she said. They complied.

The package waited on a table near the bedroom door. Per her instructions, a private courier had flown this box, one foot square by sixteen inches high, from Memphis to LaGuardia earlier this morning. She rushed toward the table and attacked the package with her fingernails, pulling off tape, prying open staples, tearing through the extra-thick cardboard until the top ripped open.

She pulled a cocoon of bubble wrap from the box and set it on the table. The final protective layer came off easily. She picked up the exposed vessel—a short, ceramic pot the size of a teakettle with a shiny silver band near the top—carried it into her bedroom, and shut the door.

Anticipation consumed her. She fell to her knees and lifted the vessel near her face. She stared at it so intently she swore she could see the brush marks of the artist who'd painted it. She checked to make sure the door was still closed, then whispered, "Hello, Daddy."

She placed the urn on the fireplace mantel and sat on the edge of the bed. Her father still possessed an unmistakable magnetism. She couldn't stop staring at him. He'd spent twenty-nine years hiding from her, running from all the pain he'd caused, all the damage he'd wrought upon a scared little girl. She fought back tears. Even now, she wouldn't give him the satisfaction of seeing them. He didn't deserve to witness how deeply he'd hurt her.

She grabbed her elbows and rocked back and forth. The decorated urn taunted her with silence.

"Why did you leave me?" she said.

Of course he wouldn't answer. He never answered her, not even after she'd pinned him on the floor in his office. Now she'd turned him into a pile of ashes. Her father would never talk again. And she hated him for that.

She reached into her purse and drew out her yellow bear. Its tiny dark eyes stared back at her. "This was all you left me—a stupid fucking bear." She clenched her hand around it and threw it at the mantel. It bounced against the urn and fell to the floor.

Immediately she regretted her decision. She lunged after the bear and gathered it into her hands. She gave it a soft squeeze, then tucked it back into her purse.

Her father's urn rested mere inches from her face. She'd grown so used to his absence that his presence, even in this state, pressed into mind her like an overwhelming psychic force. Her father had claimed to be able to heal people and affect their thoughts. But she knew that was a lie. If he held any powers, he wouldn't have tried to crawl away when she cursed him.

"You tried to hurt me, but you only made me stronger."

She pulled the lid off the urn, dug two fingers into the ashes, and scooped out a small pile. She stared at the charred remains of Psychic Nick, then shoveled them into her mouth.

He tasted like rotten eggs, sand, and parchment paper. She chewed through the grit and swallowed. There, she'd won. Her father could never run from her again.

She carried the urn into the bathroom, lifted the toilet lid, and dumped the rest of the ashes into the bowl. Tiny chunks of bone clinked against the porcelain. Now the empty urn felt weightless in her hands. She threw it against the marble floor. It shattered into tiny pieces.

Noordhoek and the Secret Service agents shouted her name from the main living area.

"Everything's fine. I'll be out in a minute."

She opened her mouth in front of the mirror. Her father's chalky stain still coated her tongue. She grabbed a cup from the vanity and filled it with water, then washed the rest of him down with deep, angry gulps.

She pushed the handle on the toilet, washed her hands, and marched out of the bathroom. Noordhoek met her when she opened the bedroom door. "Everything okay?"

"I want this place cleaned by the time I get back. It's a total mess."

CHAPTER 13

"Are you for real?"

Luke gazed upon the cutest six-year-old he'd ever seen. She wore a flannel set of Teenage Mutant Ninja Turtles pajamas with hot-pink socks, and a skull-and-crossbones scarf covered her head. The sticker on her chest suggested she'd scribbled her own name without any help. Sarah had raced to his booth as soon as the nurses at the Children's Cancer Hospital at MD Anderson finished the opening announcements and released the children into the Centrum.

"Of course I'm for real." He pointed at the canopy that covered them—a pop-up shade volunteers had decorated with sheets and curtains to make it look like an Arabian tent. "You are in the presence of Rajah the Mystic. I'm the best fortune-teller in the world."

Sarah's face lit up like she'd seen a magic trick. The line of children waiting behind her oohed and aahed when he said the words. Marisa silenced them with a wave of her hand, turned to him, and winked.

Every detail of this setup had been Marisa's idea. His costume—complete with a fake beard, a gold turban, and a flashy sherwani jacket—looked like she'd borrowed it from a movie set. Marisa, dressed in an outfit that reminded him of Princess Jasmine from the *Aladdin* cartoon, waved her arms wildly as the children charged through the Centrum. Their booth was one of several created for Carnival Day. The Centrum boasted dozens of stations, from balloon darts to ring tosses to picture booths. The children could choose from any number of games and activities that provided a brief escape from the life-and-death challenges they faced.

Luke motioned for Sarah to sit in the chair opposite him. A fake crystal ball anchored the center of a plastic table between them. She placed her hands on it before he could ask her. "What will I be when I grow up?"

Luke reached under the table and switched on a flashlight mounted directly beneath the crystal ball. The sphere lit up with a flash of blue light. Sarah's grin stretched even wider.

"You ask about the future. That is my specialty. Rajah sees all. Rajah knows all." He placed his hands on top of hers.

Per the guidelines set by the hospital, he wore sanitary gloves. But Marisa had cut away a tiny section near the thickest part of his palms. Marisa looked at him now, her eyes large and glossy, but didn't say anything.

The skin on his palms touched Sarah's hands. He closed his eyes. Felt the sickness flowing through her veins in the form of damaged white blood cells. He searched through her body, sensing deep into her bones. The warmth passed through him and into her arms. She tried to pull away, but he held her hands firm. "Wait, little one. Rajah is nearly done."

"But it's so warm."

"That's the magic gathering. Don't let go."

She relaxed, and he went back to work. The marrow inside Sarah's tiny bones hummed with an energy he knew might make her feel uncomfortable. But it lasted only a few seconds. He searched her bloodstream again, sensed the damaged cells repairing themselves as they floated by. Her marrow had also become like new. Each blood cell her body created would now work exactly as designed.

He released her hands. "I see a pirate ship with a huge sail. Do you like the ocean?"

Sarah blinked. "How did you know?"

"You have saltwater in your veins. Rajah can feel it."

"That's just the medicine."

He glanced at Marisa. She dabbed at the corners of her eyes with a turquoise handkerchief.

"I see great things in your future, Sarah. You will command the seven seas. You will become a fearsome pirate, more famous and wealthy than Jack Sparrow. Rajah is sure this is your destiny."

"Wow, really?"

"Rajah never lies." He folded his arms and lifted his chin.

Sarah jumped from her chair and threw her slender arms around him. He froze. The sensation she caused made him want to laugh and cry at the same time. She planted a kiss on his fake beard. "Thank you, Rajah. When I become a pirate, I'll give you a ride on my ship for free. And I won't stab you with my sword."

Marisa peeled Sarah's arms from his neck. "That's enough. We need to let others have their turn."

Sarah dashed out of the tent and into the chaos of the carnival. Marisa whispered into his ear. "How did it go?"

He couldn't answer. Instead he just nodded.

"Ready for another?"

"Let's get all of them."

In the next three hours, Luke told the fortunes of thirty-seven different children. Each would go on to live bold and exciting lives. A few would discover new planets and solar systems. Others would help save animals that had been mistreated. And all would proudly claim the title of Childhood Cancer Survivor.

After the last child ran out of the tent, Marisa collapsed into the chair across from him. Her handkerchief was damp and marked with mascara. "Did we really just do that?"

He wrapped his fingers around the crystal ball and closed his eyes. "Rajah says it is so."

She slapped at his hand. "You can stop now."

"That's my problem. I can't."

"I'm counting on it." She leaned forward and lowered her voice. "If you stay, there's no limit to how many we can help."

He opened his mouth to answer but stopped. Two men dressed in expensive suits strolled through the Carnival Day area. Each man scanned the Centrum with eyes that looked as dark as they were small. He recognized the shorter one as the man he'd healed in the alley. The taller blond one didn't look familiar, but Luke couldn't be sure. He'd never hung around long enough to get a good look.

Marisa saw them, too. She marked them with her suspicious stare, even when they passed so close to the tent Luke had to turn away.

The men marched to the other side of the Centrum and turned a corner that led toward the main hospital. Luke drew a large breath. With all his attention focused on the two men, he must have forgotten to breathe.

She turned to him. "You know those guys?"

"I told you. They always find me."

"Are you sure?"

"The shorter one with dark hair—he shot me twice last week."

She wrapped the handkerchief around her knuckles. "I'll be right back."

He grabbed her wrist. "You don't understand. These guys don't play by the rules. They're always armed—always. And they're not afraid of nurses, security guards, or even the cops."

"You're right. I don't get it. Why are they trying to kill you? Who are they working for? The government? The mafia?"

"It's complicated." He climbed out of his chair and checked the corner where the men had disappeared. "You'll never believe me."

"That's not fair." She stepped into his line of sight. "You don't get to tell me what I'll believe. I took a big chance for you today." She snatched his hand and turned it over, exposing the cutout section of the sanitary glove. "You're not a one-man show anymore. I deserve the truth."

"I'll tell you later. We need to get out of here."

He waited while she gathered her bag and put on a light jacket. They checked the corner again, then headed toward the opposite end of the Centrum. The gold turban weighed heavily on his head. Each person who passed seemed to hold their stare a second longer than normal, but the looks didn't spook him as much as they would have otherwise. They took turns checking behind themselves all the way into the parking garage. Luke didn't take off his beard and turban until Marisa had driven half the distance to his motel.

She accelerated through a yellow light, then spoke. "Okay, spill it. Who are they?"

"Hired guns who work for my sister."

"Your sister? *Dios mío.*" She made a clicking sound with her mouth. "Who is she?"

"I don't know exactly. We lost touch several years ago. She must have changed her name and made a few powerful friends."

The knuckles on her fingers whitened as she took a turn too fast. "They're in my hospital right now."

"Don't worry. They're only after me, no one else."

"Why does your sister want you dead?"

He looked out the window and thought about Annamaria. They'd shared the same childhood frustrations. Both hated how their father had dragged them from one small town to another when they should have been making friends in school. Being forced to perform in elaborate healing ceremonies, pretending to be cured of scoliosis, whooping cough, and scarlet fever, knowing their father was a liar in every sense of the word, that every dollar their family earned came from people who couldn't afford to lose it—that kind of history would carry an effect into anyone's adulthood. But each of them had handled it differently. Once he discovered his ability, he used it to try to bring everyone together, starting with his own family. But his father had only seen bigger dollar signs. And Annamaria had only seen red.

"Hello?" Marisa punched his arm. "Don't you know it's not smart to ignore a Latina?"

He grabbed the overhead handle and scooted closer to the passenger door. "She must see me as a threat. That's all I know. I've tried talking to her men before. I tried to tell them I meant her no harm. But they wouldn't believe me. They said she needs to make sure."

"Is she like you?"

"Yes and no. She's different, and much more dangerous."

"She must be a powerful woman if she can afford hit men."

"*Powerful* is a great word to describe her."

Marisa took one hand off the wheel, reached across the seat, and popped open the glove box. She pulled out a handgun with a huge black barrel and dropped it into his lap. "You might need this."

He froze, thinking back to the last time he held a gun. It sat there on his lap, all shiny and heavy, the antithesis to everything he wanted to do. "No, I won't."

"Keep it close—at least until things blow over."

"Nothing's going to blow over, Marisa. Once these guys show up, it's time to run."

A traffic light turned yellow. She slammed on the brakes. "You're going to bail on me? After what we did today?"

"They almost killed me last time."

She grabbed his hand. "Last time you were alone."

"Doesn't matter to these guys."

Waves of heat radiated through her skin. She stared at him while the traffic light burned red. She released his hand, snatched the gun from his lap, and tucked it into the center console. When the light turned green, she pushed the accelerator to the floorboard. "Some hero you turned out to be."

Things always ended this way. Anytime someone took an interest or tried to help, the men with guns would show up and throw everything into chaos. Sometimes Luke got to say good-bye;

often he just grabbed his bag and disappeared. But he never failed to disappoint the people in this world who'd actually given him a chance.

They rode in silence another mile or two, until he saw his motel in the distance.

"I'm sorry," he said.

"For what?" She jerked the wheel as she changed lanes. "Running at the first sign of trouble? We saved thirty-seven children today. And we could save others, day after day, as long as there are sick people in this city. But you're too scared to try."

The motel parking lot was nearly full. She stopped near the balcony stairs and shifted into park. The engine kept running. She didn't reach for her seat belt. Instead she stared at the windshield like she was trying to shatter it with her thoughts.

"You don't think I feel guilty?" he said.

"I don't know what you feel."

He unbuckled his seat belt. "Maybe I'd rather disappoint you than watch you get killed."

"You're not responsible for me. I'm here because I accepted the risk. It's worth—"

A car slammed into the rear door so hard Marisa's car fishtailed ninety degrees. The impact knocked Luke into Marisa. They bumped heads. For a moment he forgot where he was. Then he looked out her window.

Two men in dark suits climbed out of their damaged car. Both reached inside their coats and rushed toward the driver's side.

Marisa reached for the gearshift. Luke reached for the gun.

Bullets struck the car like a roofer's automatic nailer. Marisa ducked. The side window shattered. Luke aimed through the opening and fired six times.

She screamed. The car surged forward. The men blurred out of view. Marisa peeked up long enough to guide her car through the motel lot and onto the street. She slammed the gas pedal and tore across three lanes of traffic toward the freeway on-ramp. The engine roared as the speedometer climbed past seventy.

"Are you hurt?" he said.

"*¡Pinche méndigo!*" She pushed against the steering wheel so hard he thought it might snap in two. Her breaths came in heavy thrusts. Her shoulders dipped each time she exhaled. He leaned over and reached toward the left side of her jacket. Sticky, wet blood coated every surface he touched.

She winced. "*Dios mío.* Be careful!"

"Stay still and keep driving."

"Don't know how long I can."

He searched with his fingers and found three bullet holes. Each was smaller than he expected. Maybe the bullet had splintered as it pierced through the door. He covered her wounds with his hand. Closed his eyes and concentrated.

The bullet was broken into three fragments. Each had torn a slightly different path through her insides. None of the wounds were deep; the bullet hadn't done serious damage. Marisa growled. The fragments vibrated and moved. Hot tears fell on Luke's sleeve as he pulled the pieces through her skin and into his palm. Her tissues healed as quickly as the fragments moved. By the time the pieces fell into his hand, she was like new.

"How do you feel?"

She shook her head like she didn't believe him. "Let me see."

He opened his hand in front of her. The fragments rattled against one another in his bloodstained palm.

She mirrored the same look little Sarah had given him in the hospital. "Thank you."

"You sure you feel okay?"

She glanced at him. "Shouldn't you know?"

"Just checking."

The speedometer held steady at eighty. Everything else shook like they were traveling on an unpaved road.

"Slow down," he said.

Her triceps flexed. She wouldn't look anywhere but straight ahead. It looked like she'd overdosed on adrenaline.

"Slow down. They aren't chasing us."

"How do you know?"

"I shot one of them."

"Good. I hope he's dead." She let up on the accelerator and settled into the normal flow of traffic. "How'd they find us so quickly?"

"They must know someone in HR."

"Or they tracked us from the hospital. Either way, you were right. Someone definitely wants you dead."

She wouldn't take her eyes off the road, and he couldn't stop staring at her. Sitting in her bloodstained Princess Jasmine costume, driving her smashed-up car through late-morning Houston traffic, Marisa looked nothing like the overaggressive nurse he'd met in the skywalk. In three short days, he'd changed her life forever. Surely Annamaria's men had noted her license plate. Soon they'd know more about Marisa than he did, more than she'd want anyone to know. Getting out of Houston wasn't just an option now; it was their only choice. Neither of them had to say it.

"We need a change of clothes," she said.

"And money." He patted his thin costume pants. Everything he owned was back in his motel room. He hadn't even brought his money clip when she picked him up earlier. "We can't stay in this car, either."

"I know." She rubbed the side of her torso, like she was checking his work. "We'll stop by the bank. I'll take out as much as I can from the drive-through ATM. Then I'll ditch my card."

"Marisa, I'm sorry."

"Don't say that. I'm the one who showed up at your door, remember?"

"Things are different now."

"Why? Because they wrecked my car and shot me?" She twisted her lips like she'd taken a shot of vinegar. "Those *pendejos* aren't going to stop us. Not if we stick together."

"What about your family?"

"My parents are dead. My sisters still live in Monterrey." She dabbed the corner of her eye with her jacket sleeve. "So stop trying to talk me out of it and come up with a plan."

"I know a place," he said. "It's where I go when I get tired of running—a kind of safe house. Somewhere we can hide and figure out what to do next."

"Sounds perfect. How far?"

He buckled his seat belt. "Ever been to El Paso?"

"That's a twelve-hour drive into the middle of the desert."

"You'll like it. I promise."

"Whatever." She blew a curly strand of hair out of her face. "But there better be skin moisturizer."

CHAPTER 14

Clyde covered his ears while the METRORail train screeched to a stop nearby. He pulled out his phone and recorded video as the cars unloaded passengers—mostly people dressed like hospital workers. Everything about this place told him Nicholas's son might have come here after he fled Port Arthur. The Texas Medical Center in Houston looked larger than most cities' downtowns, with dozens of tall buildings and busy traffic—the perfect place to blend in and disappear.

"Dude, it didn't happen over there." A blond-haired medical student tapped Clyde's camera hand. "The guy ran across the street from this corner. I never saw him coming."

Clyde didn't need much time to find another lead on Nicholas's son. All it took was an internet search with the right keywords. *Allintext: unidentified man healed* had done the trick this time, delivering a link to an online article about an auto-pedestrian accident in Houston where the driver swore he'd seen the victim heal himself. The driver, a twenty-six-year-old UT medical school student named Justice Taylor, wasn't difficult to find. And he seemed willing to tell his story to anyone who'd listen. If this guy was telling the truth, Clyde was only one day behind Lucian. Maybe less.

"He must have been in a full sprint," Justice said. "Or maybe he suddenly appeared, like in those *Star Trek* movies. You know?"

"That might explain it." Clyde turned the camera toward the student. Already he knew his followers would love this guy. Just like they couldn't get enough of Riley Sankey or Port Arthur Billy. "Tell me what happened after you hit him."

The medical student pushed up his sleeves like he was about to perform surgery. Instead he used his hands to punctuate his words. "I hit my brakes, I swear. See those tire marks? Anyway, I clipped him at the knees—my car sits kinda low, you know—and his head slammed the hood of my Nissan. It made a huge dent." He pulled out his smartphone. "I have a pic somewhere."

"That's okay. I trust you." Clyde rubbed both temples with his free hand. "I assume at some point you got out and checked on him?"

"Yeah, of course." The student smiled like he'd done something heroic. "I was the first one there. But then I saw his knee. It was jacked—I mean, bleeding pretty badly and bent at a weird angle, like this." The student contorted his arms into something resembling a modern sculpture. How did this student's peers keep from laughing when he presented medical cases?

"Then a nurse rushed to his side—this is the Med Center, you know—and told me to stand back. She struggled to keep him calm. He was fighting her, arguing with her, trying to touch his head and then his knee. Finally she gave up and let him do what he wanted. That's when things got crazy."

"Describe crazy." Clyde held up the camera and zoomed into a close-up.

The medical student stared into the street and blinked like he was watching the scene unfold again. "Dude closed his eyes. I held my breath. He looked like he was in a lot of pain, like the reality had finally settled in. Then his leg snapped back into place. It literally popped. I heard it."

Clyde rolled his eyes.

"What—you don't believe me?"

He wanted to believe this guy, just like he wanted to believe Nicholas and the witnesses in Port Arthur. Clearly this medical student believed. But it was impossible. The scene the student described sounded like a *Wolverine and the X-Men* comic. This had to be a trick. Real people didn't stalk hospitals late at night healing patients with their hands. And they certainly didn't heal themselves during the day in the middle of the street.

"Of course I believe you." He felt a twinge of guilt for lying so brazenly. But it didn't matter. He'd edit that part out later.

"I thought you wanted to find this guy."

"I do."

The student nodded. "Anyway, he got up and ran. And I mean, he sprinted. Straight down that sidewalk like he'd never been hit."

"What about the nurse?" Clyde said. "You mentioned they were arguing. Did she know him?"

"I doubt it." The student's eyes grew large. "She looked like the type that likes to argue. She yelled at me after he left. Like *I* was the weirdo."

"Do you know which hospital she worked for?"

"Could be one of a dozen. Take your pick."

"Did she stay around to talk to the cops? Did any reporters interview her?"

"Naw, dude." The student shook his head. Clyde swore he saw a few grains of beach sand fly out of his hair. "She bolted in the other direction, running as fast as he did. She didn't even care about my car. Hey, that reminds me." He swiped the screen on his phone. "I started a GoFundMe account to help pay for the dent. You think any of your subscribers might want to help?"

"Sure thing." He patted the student on the back and stopped the recording. His phone vibrated before he could tuck it into his pocket. "I need to take this."

"Whatever." The student jogged toward the platform like he was late for another interview.

Another train squealed to a stop. Clyde covered his opposite ear. "ShowMeClyde speaking."

"Someone picked up the remains of Nicholas Gabor early yesterday morning."

He nearly dropped the phone. "Who signed for it?"

"Couldn't find out. A local funeral home performed the cremation. The director's a real ice queen."

Clyde clenched his teeth. He knew he should have sprung for a more experienced private investigator to explore the Nicholas/Annamaria angle while he was gone. He walked along Pressler Street and away from the train stop, in the same direction Lucian had apparently run. "What about your document search?"

"All I can find are birth records for Annamaria and her brother, Lucian. I came up empty on everything else under their names. No school records, no marriage licenses, no tax records, no death certificates. It looks like they both simply disappeared."

"Someone ordered the cremation. And someone picked up those remains," Clyde said.

"I might be able to find out who it was once they file the paperwork with the county, but until then, we're in the dark. We don't know what name the sister is using, where she lives, what she looks like, or if she's even alive. Same for the brother. Mr. Gabor's apartment didn't turn up even one photograph of his children. And your primary witness is dead."

"What about the mom?"

"We're ten years too late," the investigator said. "According to her death certificate, Marian Gabor died at age fifty-three from severe osteoporosis."

Clyde stopped walking. "Osteoporosis? Are you serious?"

"That's what her medical records indicate. She died in a hospital in Columbia, South Carolina. Apparently she'd checked herself in. Nicholas Gabor's name doesn't appear on any of her paperwork. Not even as next of kin."

He shook his head. Nicholas must have figured his daughter had found her mother. He was probably either too embarrassed or too scared to stay near the woman anymore. What a loving and compassionate family the Gabors had turned out to be.

"So she's another dead end," Clyde said.

"Not entirely. Are you sitting down?"

Clyde broke from his cellular haze and looked around. Somehow he'd wandered into a parking lot stuffed with cars. He leaned against the bumper of the nearest one. "Go ahead."

"I found another birth certificate."

CHAPTER 15

Luke wrapped his fingers around the stick shift and slammed it into what he hoped was fifth gear. The markings on the gearbox of their new ride—an '85 Pontiac Fiero with more body putty than original paint—had worn off long ago. Marisa didn't get picky when the owner of a salvage lot offered this car as an even trade for her smashed-up Toyota. The owner only wanted hers for parts, and he seemed satisfied with a handshake instead of a signature to seal the transaction. They only needed the car to take them the eight hundred miles between Houston and El Paso.

Judging by its performance over the last forty minutes, they'd be lucky to make it half that distance.

The clutch screamed, and the engine choked and sputtered. The unbalanced wheels jumped and wiggled so violently he couldn't push the speedometer over sixty.

"Can't you do something?" Marisa said.

"I can barely keep it on the road." He gripped the wheel even tighter, trying to quiet the vibration. Getting stranded anywhere on Interstate 10 between San Antonio and El Paso wouldn't be fun.

The farther they traveled, the greater the distance had grown between signs of civilization. The city of Junction receded into his rearview mirror. A hazy brown sun dipped toward a rise in the highway a mile ahead. He looked for the headlight switch and turned it on. Nothing happened. He tried the parking lights. Again, nothing.

"We might have a problem."

Marisa ripped a price tag off the bottom of her T-shirt. "What do you mean?"

"No headlights."

"They're not working?"

"They don't even flip up."

"What are our options?"

"Find a motel or stop and try to fix it," he said.

She held up one hand and tapped into her palm with a finger. "Let me check my phone—oh wait. Someone made me throw it out the window."

"You know we had to." He checked a passing sign. Only 430 miles to El Paso. "We'll find a place the old-fashioned way."

She stared out her window. "I'm on it."

He'd never seen her in regular clothes. Each of them had assembled their own getaway outfit while roaming the aisles of a discount superstore. The total bill was less than fifty bucks. Marisa had washed off all her makeup in the bathroom while he waited. It turned out she didn't need any. The only difference was the missing dark eyeliner.

The clutch screamed again. The stick shift broke loose and wiggled. He pushed in the clutch and shoved it into fifth. The gearbox growled and popped. Smoke rose through the holes in the housing cover.

"It's done." He stood on the clutch and pulled onto the highway shoulder. The Fiero coasted another two hundred yards, then creaked to a stop. He punched the hazard light switch. Of course those worked. The lights blinked on and off in a steady rhythm.

Marisa slapped the dash. "I knew we shouldn't have trusted that guy."

"We had no choice." He unbuckled his seat belt. "Don't worry. We'll get there some other way."

"Don't worry? We've gone from Guatemala to *Guatepeor*. We're stranded with a dead transmission. I've been shot, wrecked, and forced to leave my job without saying good-bye." She reached into the back of her jeans and pulled out a thin stack of twenties. "This is all I have left. Do you even know—"

She stopped herself, but he wanted her to keep going, to let it all out. Of course he knew. He'd been living this exact pattern longer than he could remember. But it was all new to her. Leaving everything she'd worked for, especially her job at MD Anderson, just because Annamaria's men had spotted them together was a huge price to pay. He didn't blame her for lashing out. He wouldn't blame her for walking the opposite direction once they got out of the car.

Her eyes shimmered, but she didn't cry. Instead she grabbed his knee and squeezed. "Momentary lapse. You're right. We'll find another way."

"Marisa, I know this is hard."

"It is. But you warned me." She pried open the glove box, grabbed the pistol, and pushed her door open.

He hesitated. "We don't need—"

"It's not a discussion. Let's go."

They walked east, away from El Paso but toward the nearest town. Luke remembered passing an exit with a gas station sign a few miles back. With luck they'd get there in under an hour. Marisa waved whenever a car zoomed past, but he doubted anyone would help. This wasn't the seventies. Even if someone cared enough to slow down or stop, it wouldn't take long to notice the huge pistol tucked into the back of Marisa's jeans.

She pumped her arms like she was on a treadmill. "I've been wondering."

"About what?"

"Why the scar? It doesn't make any sense."

"Happened when I was a kid, before I knew what I could do. My sister and I were playing in an alley when I found a broken soda bottle. We fought over it. Things got messy. We ended up cutting each other's faces with the glass."

"You guys fought dirtier than me and my sisters."

He shook his head. "Annamaria always won, even though she was younger and weaker. She knew I'd feel sorry for her and let up. I knew she wouldn't stop until she drew blood. So I decided to strike first." He tilted his face toward the fading sunlight. "As you can see, the plan backfired."

"*Dios mío.* How did your parents react?"

"They were more scared of her than I was. I always caught the brunt of the punishment no matter who was at fault. They took away my baseball cards. My dad threw them out the window as we drove down the highway."

Marisa tucked a strand of curly hair behind her ear. "At least you taught her a lesson with that scar."

"Maybe, but it didn't last. One night when I was thirteen, I noticed her sleeping peacefully in the bed we shared. The moonlight through the motel window highlighted the scar on her cheek. I felt guilty for ruining her smile—she could appear like an angel when she wanted to. I wished I could take it back. I reached out and tried to wipe it away. And then it happened. Her scar disappeared."

Marisa's pace slowed. She gave him that look again, the same one she made when she first saw what he could do. "Being thirteen is hard enough. But finding out you can heal with your touch? I bet you were freaking out. And your parents—I can't even imagine."

"They freaked, but not how you might think. Annamaria wanted me to prove it wasn't a trick by scratching her cheek again and again. I healed her a dozen times before she finally believed me. My mother wanted to take me to a doctor. But my father had other plans."

He told her about his nomadic childhood, about the never-ending carousel of healing ceremonies he was forced to participate in. How he'd mastered the art of mimicking the effects of polio by age seven just so his dad could pretend to heal him every other night. How, after he healed his sister, his father said they didn't need to fake it anymore. How his father had bought a bigger tent and more folding chairs, hoping for larger crowds and more money. How he'd become even less of a person in his father's eyes that night—reduced to nothing but a magic wand his father could wave to create the fortune he so desperately wanted.

Luke told Marisa as much as he thought she could handle, stopping before the night his parents had left. He didn't want to think about that chapter of his life. Better to look forward to El Paso, assuming they'd ever get there.

"Sorry you had to live that way." Marisa wiped her forehead with the handkerchief from her costume. "But you didn't answer my question."

He traced the half-circle scar on his cheek with his finger. "Why do people get tattoos?"

"I don't know. Maybe to remember something." She shrugged. "Or someone."

"Sounds about right."

A bright red tow truck with a chrome grill pulled to the shoulder and stopped thirty feet in front of them. Luke thrust his arm in front of Marisa. "Wait. Let him come to us."

The distinctive hum of an idling diesel engine masked the silence between them. He guessed the driver was sizing them up, deciding whether he'd made a mistake by pulling over. Finally the engine cut off and the driver's door swung open.

A man who looked thirty years older than Luke climbed out of the truck. The man rubbed his hip like it was bruised. He wore a tan cowboy hat and a faded pair of overalls, but his rattlesnake-skin boots looked like they'd been polished within the hour. "You folks need help?"

Marisa stepped forward. "Our car broke down about a mile ahead. We need a mechanic, and a lift."

"What's wrong with it?"

"Transmission," Luke said.

The man scratched his chin. "Not an easy fix. I got a garage in town if you want me to take a look."

"We'd appreciate it," Marisa said.

"Where you heading?"

"El Paso," Luke said.

"You're not getting there tonight." The man waved them forward. "Hop in my truck and we'll get your car."

They walked toward the truck while the man watched. "The lady in front, you in back on her side, please."

Luke understood the reasoning. The man was just being careful, keeping two strangers within sight while he drove. Maybe he'd already spotted Marisa's gun.

Bright yellow letters spelled out a company logo on the passenger door. Theo's Garage and Towing operated in the city of Junction. Luke grabbed the rear door handle and jumped inside. "Are you Theo?"

"That's my son." The man winced as he wrapped his fingers around the steering wheel. "Name's Peter. Not Pete. Peter."

"Really glad you stopped for us, Peter. I'm Marisa. He's Luke."

The man smiled with every part of his face except his mouth. "I see people in trouble, it's my duty to help them out."

"We feel the same." She glanced toward the backseat.

"You work evenings, Peter?" Luke said.

"Five nights a week. My son has a young family, so I offered to help out. I don't turn a wrench anymore, but I'm good at finding problems."

"This one will be easy to spot," Marisa said.

"We'll see." Peter slowed and pulled in front of the Fiero. He shifted into reverse and backed so close to its bumper Luke swore they must have caused another dent. "Stay here. I'll be right back." Peter tucked the keys into his pocket and climbed out of the cab.

Luke tracked Peter with his stare until the man disappeared behind the truck.

"He seems nice," Marisa said.

"But he's no dummy."

"What do we do if he gets suspicious?"

"Anything but lie."

An electric motor whirred into action somewhere behind them. The Fiero's hood rose into view. Peter grunted as he climbed back into the cab. He reached for the starter button, then paused. "You two ain't running from the law, are you?"

"No, sir," Luke said.

Peter's stare jumped back and forth between them. "Then why the gun?"

Marisa's cheeks turned pink. "It's hard to explain. We're not running from the cops, but we are running."

"I made an enemy years ago," Luke said. "And my enemy made powerful friends."

Peter narrowed his eyes. "What's in El Paso?"

"A safe place."

Peter slipped a thumb under one of his overalls straps. "Let's see if we can get you there." He started the engine and shifted into drive. "Do me a favor and toss that gun in the glove box. I'll keep it safe until we fix your car."

After Marisa did what Peter asked, no one talked for a while. Instead Luke watched the remaining sunlight drain from the sky as they cruised into Junction. Theo's Garage sat proudly under its own billboard sign on Main Street. Marisa waited in the tiny office while Luke helped Peter roll the Fiero onto the hydraulic car lift. Peter didn't look much older than sixty-five, but the grunts and hisses he emitted while pushing against the Fiero's bumper told a different story. After they were finished, the man sat on a nearby stool and shook his fingers like they were on fire.

Luke stared at the man's hands. A gold wedding band looked hopelessly trapped behind one knuckle. Many fingers looked unnaturally curled, bent in weird directions, and slightly misshapen.

"Arthritis." Peter rubbed his wrist like that somehow helped. "It came and went for a few years. Now it just comes and stays."

"How painful is it?"

Peter pushed a button on the controller. The hydraulic lift sent Marisa's Fiero above their heads, exposing its dilapidated underbelly. "I don't like to complain. We all have our burdens." He indicated a flashlight hanging on a nearby pegboard. "But if you want to hold that thing for me, I won't stop you."

Luke grabbed the flashlight and pointed its beam toward several parts of the Fiero's engine while Peter directed. Peter never said what he was looking for. Instead he took turns grimacing and shaking his head.

"How long has she owned this?"

"About six hours."

Peter turned away from the Fiero's underside and peered through the window into the small office. Marisa sat in front of a desk, picking at her fingers. "You two must be having a bad day."

"Good and bad, actually." Luke thought about little Sarah from this morning's Carnival Day. He couldn't believe how long ago that seemed. "It's hard to explain."

"This enemy you made. Why do you need to run from him?"

"My sister wants me dead, along with anyone who helps me."

Peter walked in a circle under the Fiero. He stared at the garage floor like he was looking for a pattern in the oil-stained concrete. "Why does she hate you?"

"I disappointed her a long time ago."

"Brothers tend to do that," Peter said. "I'm sure there are two sides to the story."

"She doesn't want to listen."

"I can understand being upset, but wanting to kill your own kin—that takes serious motivation." Peter scratched the back of his hand. "Must be something special about you to inspire that much anger."

"We're both special in different ways," Luke said.

Peter ignored the Fiero and stared into Luke's eyes. "Are you a religious man?"

"Not really."

"Well, I am." Peter walked toward a workbench and retrieved a worn leather-bound Bible from the top drawer. "The Good Book says we each possess a special talent, a spiritual gift from our Creator. Mine is reading people. I can tell a person's nature and intentions from the moment I meet them."

Luke didn't speak.

"I knew you two were on a mission before I climbed out of my truck. Whatever it is, I want to help."

"We really appreciate it. But we just need to get to El Paso."

Peter returned his Bible to the drawer, then glanced toward his office window. "Your friend has great faith in you. She believes in what you're doing, enough to tuck a gun into the back of her jeans. She must hold the same gift as me. But yours is different, isn't it?"

"Yes."

"I'll do what I can to help. But before I do, I have to know."

"It's not something I can explain." Luke set the flashlight on a nearby shelf. He stepped in front of Peter, held out his arms, and exposed his palms. "Let me show you."

He worried he'd made another mistake, that Peter would react like so many others and chase them both out of his garage. But he knew from the moment Peter had flexed his fingers in pain that he needed to relieve this man's suffering.

Peter stared at him, eyes unblinking. His nostrils flared and relaxed, then flared and relaxed again. He stepped back and looked through the window at Marisa. Then he turned away and wrung his hands together like they were covered with ants. Finally he came forward again. He released a nervous sigh and placed his hands on top of Luke's.

Luke closed his eyes.

The office door creaked open. Marisa's footsteps signaled her approach. He blocked it out of his mind and focused on Peter.

Inflammatory cells dominated the man's body. Arthritis raged through his entire system, attaching to cartilage and bone, invading his joints and aggravating his nerves. Peter's bones already felt like they were burning. He didn't try to pull away when the warmth passed from Luke's body into his.

"Oh," Peter said. And then Luke went to work.

The inflammatory cells relaxed and let go. They floated away from his joints through his bloodstream toward his liver. His bones and ligaments repaired themselves, regaining their previous form. The tension in his muscles fell away, their internal enemy no longer present. Peter's entire body relaxed. For a moment, Luke thought he might need to catch the man before he fell.

Peter regained his balance and grasped Luke's hands with a firm, steady grip.

"*Dios mío.*" Marisa rushed to Peter's side. "How do you feel?"

Peter let go of Luke's hands, then stared at his own, flexing each finger, each joint. His jaw fell slack, and his eyes grew large. "How'd you learn to do that?"

"I don't know. I just can."

Peter marched to his workbench, grabbed a heavy crescent wrench, and squeezed the handle as he turned an imaginary bolt. "It's gone—all of it. Like it never even happened. I can't believe it."

Marisa giggled. She covered her mouth, but after a moment she gave up and let out a hearty laugh. Peter joined her. So did Luke. He couldn't remember the last time he'd laughed. He'd forgotten what a freeing experience it could be.

But no amount of laughter could fix their car. Peter motioned toward the Fiero with his crescent wrench. "Sorry I can't do the same for you. This transmission is toast."

"We figured," Luke said.

"What now?" Marisa said. "We only have two hundred dollars."

Peter walked into the office and rummaged through his desk. It seemed every movement he made was lighter now, quicker, with more purpose than before. When he returned, he strode through the open garage door and into the parking lot. He disappeared around a corner.

"What's that all about?" Marisa said. "You think we freaked him out?"

"No, he's okay."

Marisa started after Peter. Luke grabbed her arm. "If he wanted us to follow, he would've asked."

Lights flashed on somewhere outside. They grew brighter with each second. Then came the sound of an engine, low and smooth, approaching from somewhere to their right. A blur of maroon shot into view, stopping as quickly as it appeared. Tires skidded across the gravel a couple of feet, kicking up a cloud of dust in front of the headlights. The driver's door swung open. Peter climbed out and folded his arms. "This is the best I can spare right now. Two working headlights, a full tank of gas, and a transmission that won't fall apart. I bet she has another hundred thousand miles in her—more than enough to get you to El Paso."

Luke eyed the car's profile. This Toyota Camry was no junkyard throwaway. It looked less than five years old and in great condition. "Peter, we can't—"

"Shut up and take it," Peter said. "I'm not giving you a choice. This is what *I* can do."

Marisa gave Peter a tight hug. She grabbed his face and kissed his reddened cheeks.

"Please, I'm a married man." Peter smiled and pulled away.

Luke offered his hand. "We can't thank you enough."

"Ditto."

After Peter lowered the Fiero and Marisa grabbed their possessions, they loaded the Camry and said their good-byes. Peter leaned into the driver's side window and scratched at his neck. "You know how to get back to the highway?"

"Yes, sir," Luke said.

"Sure you two don't need a good night's sleep before you head out?"

Marisa leaned forward. "The sooner we get there, the better."

"I understand. Wait here." Peter disappeared around the rear of the Toyota.

Marisa tapped Luke's shoulder. "Is it me, or is he moving faster now?"

"Like a deer."

A knock on Marisa's window turned both their heads. Peter stood on her side now, hands behind his back, a snarky grin on his face.

She pushed the button to roll down the window.

"You forgot something." Peter offered her the gun, handle first. "Sure hope you don't need it."

CHAPTER 16

Annamaria fought the urge to throw her chair through the window of her private suite in the Cleveland Metropolitan Hotel. Even though her insides were ready to explode, her body language coach didn't seem to notice. The woman fashioned her hand into a fist with her thumb resting on top, then raised and lowered it as she calmly made her point: "See this? No sharp angles, no pointing fingers, no implied threat. Your goal is to convey sincerity and conviction with every gesture. But you don't want to appear too aggressive."

Annamaria dug her fingernails into her palm until it hurt. To be fair, she couldn't blame her anxiety on this woman. If anything, it was Senator Blair's advisors' fault for making her sit through a never-ending series of debate prep sessions. Or maybe it was the last text message Noordhoek had shown her. Or that she hadn't been able to think about anything but Lucian since.

Something had gone wrong in Houston. Lucian had made the news the day before. The online article didn't mention his name, but it didn't need to. He should have skipped town immediately, should have known she was getting better at tracking him. Her men were already on the ground by the time the story was posted. But apparently her brother wasn't done in Houston. Apparently he hadn't found enough people to heal.

Gilbert and a new hire had spotted Lucian in a cancer hospital earlier this morning. They acted on standing orders, tailing him to a nearby motel. They waited until no one else was around, then attacked. That was when all hell broke loose. She didn't know any details, just the words relayed in the text message: *Gilbert hurt. Subject out of range.*

She opened her hand and inspected her palm. No blood, just four deep indentations from her manicured nails. She rubbed her hands together and watched the markings disappear.

"Ms. Varner, are you getting this?"

"That was a big help, thanks." She stood and offered a smile. "I assume we're finished?"

The coach clearly didn't look finished. But the woman gathered her notebook into her arms anyway. "Good luck tomorrow. I want you to know that, as a woman, I'm behind you one hundred percent."

"Thanks."

The coach retreated from the room, never taking her eyes off Annamaria until she crossed the threshold, like she'd been in the presence of royalty. Noordhoek replaced her, his stoic demeanor as comforting as a cashmere blanket. "He's here."

"Send him in."

Noordhoek signaled through the open doorway, then Gilbert stepped into the room. Noordhoek pushed the door closed, insulating them from the Secret Service agents in the next room.

"What happened?" she said.

"We had them cornered, but they—"

She slapped her hand on the table. "*They?*"

"Turns out he had a driver with him. She's a nurse at the hospital—Marisa Cruz."

"Your orders were to wait until he was alone."

Beads of sweat formed across Gilbert's forehead. "He hadn't been alone all morning. She was with him in the hospital, and she stayed by his side all the way to their car. They drove to a motel together. We had to assume they were working as a team."

She clenched her teeth. Lucian had never worked with an accomplice before. His ability was too unfathomable, too polarizing. Most people either ran away or shut down after they saw what he could do. "What happened next? How did you screw up?"

"We immobilized their car—at least we thought we did. We approached on foot, guns drawn. No hesitation this time. But somehow, they were ready for us."

Annamaria didn't speak. She knew Gilbert wanted her to talk, to save him, but she needed him to suffer through the process of having to share each excruciating detail. It was the only punishment she'd allow herself to dish out—for now.

After a moment, Gilbert broke. He grimaced like he was reliving the incident. "The nurse got the car working again, and your brother returned fire with a large-caliber pistol."

A chill ran across her shoulders. Part of her thought Gilbert must have been chasing the wrong guy. Lucian never carried a gun. Everything about this ran counter to his nature. "Where did he hit you?"

Gilbert slid off his jacket using only his right arm. The left sleeve of his dress shirt was missing. A bandage wrapped around his upper arm showed a dark red blotch in the center. "It's a clean shot. No arteries, no nerve damage."

"But he didn't stop to help you," she said. "You must've made him mad."

"We'll get him soon." Gilbert stepped forward. "We've collected a load of information on the woman. She can't stay underground for long. Once she surfaces, we'll find her. And then we'll find your brother."

Annamaria lunged forward and snatched Gilbert's left hand before he could pull away. She pressed her thumb into his palm. "I have a nationally televised debate tomorrow night. Millions of people will be watching. Hundreds of reporters are digging into my past as we speak. If one person with a microphone gets to him before we do, I'm toast."

She blinked, then pursed her lips, watching the terror spread across Gilbert's face. One word and she could take his life. Gilbert knew it. So did Noordhoek. But neither tried to stop her.

"I can't wait for anyone to surface. I need you to dive in and find them. And I need it done yesterday." She tugged his arm, then shoved it away.

Gilbert let out a loud hiss, grabbed his arm, and backed toward the door. Noordhoek stepped forward like nothing had happened. He produced a tablet from behind his back. "There's something you need to see."

"What now?"

"You might want to sit."

She waited to see if Noordhoek was serious. His chiseled expression held firm, even though his eyes shifted focus toward the floor. She sat and crossed her legs. He placed the tablet in front of her. The screen showed an image of her father when he was still alive—Psychic Nick in his Tibetan robe, his face puffy and red, his skin broken out with terrible sores. His neck shimmered with sweat. Disgusting. But she couldn't look away.

A play symbol lay superimposed over his image. She inhaled a deep breath, then tapped the screen.

The video started. Psychic Nick's body came to life. She reached blindly into her purse and rummaged until she found her bear. She held it in her lap between her hands, both thumbs rubbing the back of its furry head.

The camera stayed on her father, but he wasn't talking. Someone off-screen with a voice as whiny as a little girl's announced an introduction to an internet show. Finally, the voice tossed the proceedings to her father. He cleared his throat, the way he always did at the beginning of his fake sermons.

My name is Nicholas Gabor, and I'm a dead man.

Annamaria's bear tumbled to the floor.

CHAPTER 17

Luke guided the Camry into the driveway of a one-story house on Aurora Avenue, one of several homes resting near the foothills of the Franklin Mountains in central El Paso. The gravel lawn sparkled as the headlights washed over it. Marisa stirred when he set the parking brake. She'd slept during most of their six-hour journey, leaving him free to focus on the road, listen to two different late-night music programs, and think about how much he should share when she woke up.

"We're here," he said.

"What time is it?"

"Two thirty."

"In the morning?" She rubbed her eyes and yawned. She looked at the yellow house at the end of the short driveway, then all around her. "Are you sure we're at the right place?"

"Yes."

"Your safe house is in the middle of a neighborhood?"

"A safe neighborhood."

She shook her head. "How do we get in?"

A floodlight on the porch flashed on. The front door swung open. A Hispanic woman with thick white hair and a long hot-pink bathrobe stepped onto the porch. The woman squinted in their direction, then smiled and waved.

"Come inside," Luke said. "I'll introduce you." He opened his door and hurried up the sidewalk.

"*¡Corazón!*" The woman opened her arms and embraced him. Luke picked her up and swung her in a circle. He breathed in her flowery scent. "It's good to be back."

"I'm surprised you remembered the way." She smacked his arm like only a woman her age could. "It's been nearly three years." She looked past him. "Oh, and you brought a friend. *Preséntanos.*"

He turned. Marisa stood on the sidewalk, arms at her sides. The huge pistol hung limp in her right hand.

"Paloma, this is Marisa," he said. "We met in Houston a few days ago. She risked everything to get me here. You can trust her."

"Marisa, welcome. You two must be exhausted." She made a waving gesture toward the front door. "Get your bags and come inside."

"We don't have any," he said.

Paloma smiled. "Then you must have a good story. *Cuéntame.*" She led the way into the yellow house. He waited for Marisa, who strode past him with a blank look on her face.

"Your mother?" she said.

"A friend."

"What haven't you told me?"

"Not much."

The interior of Paloma's house hadn't changed since his last visit. The same gold lampshades, gold fabric couches, and gold-painted crucifixes decorated the living room. Of course, the place was spotless. Paloma swiped at an imaginary speck of dust on the couch next to her and patted a cushion, indicating where he should sit. He did as she asked. "Sorry about the hour."

"It's okay, *mi'jo.* I'm always here. Tell me, is she still chasing you?"

He nodded. "Most of the time I stay under her radar. But sometimes I screw up." He glanced at Marisa. She still looked like she thought this was a dream. "I screwed up a lot the last few days."

"I don't know about that," Paloma said. "You were trying to help people, no? That always comes with a cost."

"How long have you known each other?" Marisa said.

Paloma squeezed Luke's knee. "You didn't tell her?"

"It's been a long day," he said.

"Fine, I will." Paloma shifted her attention toward Marisa. "I met Luke fifteen years ago on a Greyhound bus headed for Albuquerque. There was an accident. I thought I would die, but he saved me, and so many others." Her pupils widened as she motioned in his direction. "I'm sure I don't need to say how."

"No, you don't."

"The other passengers reacted in shock and fear. It was a crazy scene. You'd think they would have been grateful. But no, they turned on him. Even the ones he saved. They called him a *brujo*, a witch doctor, and other words I can't say in front of Jesús." She pointed toward the crucifixes.

"Paloma was the heroine that day, not me," he said. "She waved down a passing car and dragged me inside with her before the cops arrived. She brought me here and insisted I stay until she knew I was safe."

"That's an amazing story," Marisa said.

Paloma smiled. "I'm sure you have a similar one."

Marisa's eyes shimmered in the golden light. "He helped thirty-seven children at a cancer hospital earlier this morning. And later, he helped me." She touched her chest with her fingertips. She closed her eyes like she was searching for words. "Luke has a power I can't understand. And I want to help him use it."

"I'm glad he found you," Paloma said. "He needs someone to look after him. He only lets me do it a few hours at a time."

"I'm sitting right here," he said.

Paloma patted his leg but didn't turn away from Marisa. "He's going to get himself killed one day."

"Tell me about it."

"His sister, Annamaria. She's a horrible *mujer*. Do you know what she can do?"

Luke waved away her question. "No, Paloma."

"She deserves to know. You said we can trust her."

Marisa leaned forward. "Why won't you tell me?"

"I don't want to scare you."

"Too late."

He looked away. An image of his sister flashed into his head. Not the angry, vindictive adult Annamaria, but the innocent young girl who used to gaze at him like he was a hero. To admit what she'd become meant admitting his biggest sin. And it never got any easier.

"She doesn't just hire hit men to find me. She's a killer herself—the most dangerous killer the world has ever seen. She murders by touch. Her victims never realize she's given them a deadly disease. Police never suspect her. No jury will convict her. And no one can ever stop her."

Marisa leaned into the back of her chair. *"Dios mío."*

A door creaked open somewhere in the darkened hallway connected to the living room. Footsteps sounded on the porcelain tile. Marisa reached for the gun. Luke stepped in front of her. "It's okay."

"Uncle Luke?" A boy dressed in oversized footie pajamas charged through the living room and jumped into his arms. "You're back. I knew it. Uncle Luke, you're back."

He kissed the boy's chubby cheeks. "Yes, Harry. I came to check on you, to make sure you're doing your school work."

"Yes, sir. I promise. Mama, tell Uncle Luke how smart I am now."

Paloma tousled Harry's thin, dark hair. "He's a very smart boy." She turned his shoulders toward Marisa. "Harry, this is your uncle's friend Marisa."

Harry shuffled in front of Marisa and stuck his fingers in her hair. "Wow, you're beautiful. Look at your curls."

"Harry, that's not polite," Paloma said.

"It's okay." Marisa cupped his hands in hers. "I think you're adorable, too."

Luke didn't need to explain to Marisa why Harry didn't act his age. She was a nurse. Surely she recognized the physical characteristics of a child with Down syndrome. Seeing her reaction to Harry's excitement only cemented his feeling that she belonged on this journey with him.

"Go back to bed now, Harry," Paloma said. "You can visit with Uncle Luke and Marisa in the morning."

Harry scrunched up his nose. "You promise they won't leave?"

"We promise," Luke said.

Harry strode in front of Paloma, stood at attention, and clasped his hands in front of his stomach. Paloma crossed her index finger behind her thumb, then blessed Harry in Spanish. She marked the sign of the cross over his forehead, lips, and chest, then kissed his cheek. "Go now."

Harry flapped his arm wildly. "Goodnight, everybody." He galloped down the hallway and back into his room.

"I know what you're thinking," Paloma said to Marisa.

"How many people live in this house?"

Paloma laughed. "Just Harry and me. He's my son, but I didn't give birth to him. I'm much too old for that."

"I didn't assume anything."

"In case you wondered."

"I think it's beautiful."

Paloma winked at Luke. "You found a good one, *mi'jo*."

His face flushed. So did Marisa's.

She looked away. He decided to change the subject. "What was Harry talking about when he hugged me? Why did he think I was coming?"

"He was probably just excited," Marisa said.

Paloma twisted her lips. "I wanted to wait until morning." She reached across the coffee table and grabbed an iPad decorated with comic book superhero stickers. "He saw something on the YouTube two days ago. When he showed it to me, I knew it wouldn't be long before you knocked on my door. Honestly, I was praying for it."

"What's on YouTube?" Marisa said.

Paloma grabbed a pair of reading glasses, set them on the bridge of her nose, then tapped the screen. "Sit down. This will be difficult."

Luke's mind raced in a thousand directions. Had there been cameras at the intersection in Houston? What about the alley in Port Arthur? Or in the motel parking lot? His head fell toward his chest. Cameras hid everywhere these days. It was a miracle no one had posted a video capturing him in action before. No wonder Annamaria seemed to have little trouble staying on his heels. "What did they catch me doing?"

Paloma slid a finger behind her glasses and rubbed the corner of her eye. "Not you, *mi'jo*. It's your father."

Marisa peered over Paloma's shoulder at the screen. "His father?"

A chill blasted through Luke's chest and spread to his extremities. His fingers and toes tingled. Nicholas Gabor, the father he loved and idolized as a boy. The father who'd disappeared, along with Luke's mother and all their possessions, while he and his sister slept in a dark motel room. The father he hadn't seen in twenty-nine years had somehow decided to make a video and share it with the world. Luke couldn't believe it. His mind wouldn't allow it to be true.

"Luke, sit." Paloma patted the couch again.

"I can't."

"Here." Marisa grabbed his hand and laced her fingers between his. "Whatever it is, you can handle it. *We* can handle it—all of us, together."

Warmth radiated from her fingers and seeped into his skin. A wave of calm overtook him. He was in El Paso, his safe place. If ever there was a time or location to see his father again, it was here, now. And with these people.

He sat next to Paloma. She raised the iPad and tapped the screen.

CHAPTER 18

Clyde strode across the parking lot of Graham's Funeral Home and Crematory in Memphis with his chin held high, the bounce in his step announcing to the world that he'd finally reached his potential.

Soon after he'd returned to his hotel in Houston and opened his computer, he'd marveled at how popular his videos had become. *ShowMeClyde* now trended on Twitter. His YouTube views jumped exponentially with each episode he'd posted. Fans had created Reddit posts and Facebook pages dedicated to finding Lucian Gabor. Same with Annamaria. Online theories abounded, most of them focused on a possible murderer roaming the city of Memphis—a remorseless killer the police could never arrest.

Nothing fueled an internet topic better than fear and a fascination for the unexplained. Even better, the brother held the exact opposite ability of the sister. Lucian fit perfectly into the role of reluctant hero—a man dedicated to keeping a low profile, pretending to be one of us while seeking out the injured and the sick. Apparently Clyde had uncovered more than enough evidence to convince a large segment of his followers—a number so astronomically large he still couldn't fathom it—that Lucian was the real thing. And that meant Annamaria must be the real thing, too.

Of course, he still didn't believe the Gabor siblings possessed paranormal abilities. But the money would spend well either way.

He'd checked out of his hotel, exercised his credit cards at Houston's Galleria mall, traded in his Mitsubishi for a Mercedes, and cruised back to Memphis in style.

He hopped up the steps to the front door of the funeral home, stared into the reflective glass, and ran his fingers through his hair. The bird's nest of messiness on top of his head had transformed into a sleek, close-cropped style he'd seen in magazines. It matched his new Brioni suit perfectly. He sniffed and stuck out his chest. His new cologne smelled better on his skin than the sales attendant had promised.

Only two problems threatened to spoil his mood—no one had recognized him yet, and the trails of both brother and sister were growing colder with each minute.

No worries. He knew how to set things right. He breathed in the positive energy, blew out the bad, then pulled open the heavy glass door and walked into the lobby.

A cold blast penetrated the folds of his new suit. He shivered. The air-conditioning must have been set on subarctic. An open doorway at the other end of the lobby led to a large chapel with dark wooden pews. The thick red carpeting felt like a plush mattress under his Givenchy shoes. Everything looked clean, classy, and quiet. This was the perfect place to inter a loved one. Or maybe to freeze them.

A blond woman in a gray business suit greeted him in the center of the lobby. "What brings you here today?"

"I'm following up on a cremation you performed earlier this week."

"What is your relation to the deceased?"

"Close personal friend. I'm Clyde Merritt."

He waited. The woman's expression didn't change. He offered his warmest smile. "I'm ShowMeClyde. From the YouTube channel."

Nothing.

"You must've seen his video before he passed. It earned over ten million views. I'm the guy who produced it."

Apparently the chilly air had numbed this woman's senses. Only her jaw moved when she spoke. "We can only release information about the deceased to family members."

"I don't need information about the deceased. I'm here about the person who arranged the cremation."

"That falls under the same umbrella."

"What umbrella?" Clyde sensed the negative energy building inside. He flared his nostrils and inhaled, then forced out his breath like it was toxic. "I need to see the person who actually performs the cremations."

"He won't be able to tell you anything."

Jesus, this woman wasn't just cold in temperature. Did working in a place like this rob you of your personality? "I'm curious about the process."

The woman's facial muscles twitched, proving she might still be human. "I'll see if he's in." She turned and marched toward a phone mounted on a wall nearby.

Clyde peered into the chapel. The architecture suggested this was some kind of church, but it didn't have the typical religious markers. No crosses, no Star of David, not even a crescent moon. The space near where the altar should have been lay empty. That seemed fitting. Most people only came here to worship the spirit of a person who'd passed away.

The woman hung up the phone—he couldn't remember the last time he'd seen an actual wall phone with a cord—and motioned down a side hallway. "Garry said he'll see you, but he's very busy."

Clyde thanked her but didn't wait for a reply. If he stayed in her presence another minute, his fingers might go numb. He negotiated the path toward the crematory by himself, following the signs posted at every intersection. With each step the air temperature climbed a degree. One hallway seemed to go on forever. He peered through a window and discovered a larger building just ahead. Three metal exhaust stacks towered through its roof.

He turned a corner and opened the door to a room the size of a train car. Four long pews ran from one wall to the other, all aimed at a large interior window. Beyond the glass sat a rectangular furnace with three metal doors. A man wearing a reflective apron, a face shield, and heavy gloves stood at the control panel.

Clyde tapped the glass. The man turned, then shook his head. He waved his glove in a semicircle and pointed to a door on his side of the window.

Moments later Clyde found his way to the correct door. When he stepped into the room, a wall of heat slammed him in the face. "Are you Garry?"

The man walked toward a nearby table and pulled off his face shield and gloves. His long, greasy hair had been pulled back into a ponytail. Three teardrop tattoos decorated his left cheek. "You the guy curious about cremations?"

"In general, yes. But one in particular."

"Ever see one before?"

Clyde pulled out his phone. "Can you show me?"

Garry blinked. "Oh my God. You're ShowMeClyde." He pointed at the phone. "You're blowing up. Me and my friends, we love your videos."

Adrenaline sparked through Clyde's body. Sure, this guy was only a tattooed crematory tech, but it was a start. He flashed a winning smile. "Thanks for watching."

"Are you making a video about cremations?" Garry stepped forward, invading Clyde's personal space. "Hey, can I be in it?"

The man smelled like rotten eggs and formaldehyde. Clyde backed away but kept his smile intact. "As long as you answer all my questions."

"I was about to smoke one before you came in." Garry marched to the far side of the room and rolled a gurney in front of one of the furnace doors. A coffin-shaped cardboard box labeled Human Remains rested on top. "Go ahead and start filming. I'll explain as I go. Any questions, fire away."

Clyde couldn't decide if Garry was trying to be funny. The thought of watching a body burn into ashes made his stomach turn, but he'd tough it out. His instincts told him his fans would love watching Garry at work. He pressed the record button on his phone.

Garry smiled for the camera, donned his protective equipment, and strolled to the furnace control panel. He punched a few buttons. "Need to set the oven first. Fourteen hundred to sixteen hundred degrees is what you want. This furnace runs hot, so I set it at thirteen fifty."

"How many bodies do you cremate a week?" Clyde said.

"Around twenty." Garry punched another button. A metal door covering the furnace slowly lifted, exposing a refractory-lined oven with several burners shooting blue and orange flames toward the center. The sound reminded Clyde of a jet engine. Garry seemed used to the noise. He shouted over it. "Now we slide the sucker in."

"Do you remember cremating a man named Nicholas Gabor?"

Garry pushed the cardboard coffin into the flames, then returned to the control panel. "You mean the guy from that video? The man with the daughter who's a killer and the son who can heal?"

Clyde reached inside his suit coat and pretended to dig for a notepad. He didn't need one, of course. Not as long as his camera was recording. "My sources tell me this facility handled the cremation earlier this week."

"Wow, I cremated an internet star. And I don't even remember." Garry scratched his head with a gloved finger as the furnace door dropped back into place. He shrugged. "I never look at the names. It's easier that way."

"Big guy, midsixties, with sores all over his body."

Garry looked up, as if the answer was pinned to the ceiling. "Two days ago. Yeah, I remember now. You always remember the big ones."

"Why's that?"

"Took forever to squeeze him into the oven, for one." Garry snatched a long metal pole with a scraper attachment on one end. He punched another button, and a different furnace door slid open. "He burned hot, and he didn't go quietly." He shook his head. "All that popping and sizzling."

Acid bubbled into the back of Clyde's throat. He swallowed and tried to stay focused. "So you handled the entire process—the cremation, preparation, and delivery to the family?"

Garry held up one finger. He shoved the scraper pole into the open furnace and raked through the contents like he was stoking a campfire. "You need to break up the bones to speed the process." He banged the scraper against the side of the furnace. White ashes swirled into the air. He lifted his mask and gazed at the camera. "Your guy needed over six hours to cook. After I ground him into powder, I poured him into one of those." He pointed toward a set of shelves on the back wall, where dozens of decorative urns waited to be filled.

"Got it," Clyde said, though he wished he hadn't. Sweat poured down the back of his neck and from his armpits, soaking his dress shirt. He wiped his forehead with his coat sleeve. "Who picked up the urn?"

Garry pulled off his gloves and slapped them on the table. "Someone dressed like you."

"A man?" Clyde's pulse quickened. "Are you sure?"

"I didn't feel the need to confirm it. But yeah, it was a guy."

"Was he a family member?"

Garry shook his head. "Maybe. He had a stack of papers, all notarized and legal. Everything looked legit, so I gave him the remains."

"You just *gave* them to him?"

"There isn't a black market for fat old guys' ashes," Garry said. "People show up. I check their paperwork, make sure they're paid up, and deliver the goods."

"Where's the paperwork now?" Clyde said.

"We're supposed to file it. But I'm a little behind."

He leaned forward and zoomed in on Garry's face. "Need any help?"

"Turn that thing off," Garry said. He glanced at the door. "Want to get me fired?"

"Sorry." Clyde slid the phone into his pocket. But he didn't stop recording. Old habits.

Beads of sweat formed near the edges of Garry's temples—the first sign he wasn't immune to the heat. "What are you looking for in that file?"

Clyde waited, then blinked. "Do I need to spell this out?"

Garry threw back his head. "Oh yeah. You're still searching for his son."

"And his daughter." And a third sibling, he reminded himself. The baby with no name or birth date his investigator had discovered on a heavily blacked-out birth certificate.

"I can't let you see the file. Employees and family only." Garry leaned forward, straightened his arms, and planted his palms on the table. "Lucky for you, I like to read out loud."

CHAPTER 19

The smell of cooked eggs, chilies, and onions woke Luke from a deep sleep. He lifted his head off the couch. Pain radiated through his neck and shot down his spine. He sat up, brushed the sleep out of his eyes, and looked around.

Harry sat cross-legged on the floor, elbows on his knees, eyes wide and staring back at him. The boy jumped up and ran into the kitchen. "Mama, he's up. Uncle Luke just woke up."

"*Mocoso*, I told you not to bother him," Paloma said. "He needs his sleep."

"I was quiet. I promise." The sound of heavy footsteps announced Harry's return to the den. "Uncle Luke, Mama's making breakfast. She's cooking *migas*—your favorite."

"You're right. It is my favorite." Luke grabbed Harry's arm and pulled him into a mock-wrestling hold. "Tell me, do you still give hugs for free?"

"Only to you." Harry giggled as he fought free. He wrapped his arms around Luke and squeezed. "And Mama, of course."

A hallway door opened. Marisa strode into the den wearing the same clothes as the day before. Her hair was wet. Dark shimmering spirals hung past her shoulders and framed her narrow face. She wore no makeup. She still didn't need any.

Harry abandoned Luke and ran to her. "Marisa, guess what Mama is cooking."

"Smells like a Mexican breakfast." She lowered herself to his height. "Am I right?"

"Yes, it's from Mexico. That's where *migas* comes from." Harry hopped in his footie pajamas.

Paloma's voice sounded again from the kitchen. "*Mi'jo*, come set the table. Our guests are hungry."

Harry padded toward the kitchen. Marisa joined Luke on the couch. She wedged her hands between her knees. "How are you holding up?"

"My mind's still spinning. It's a lot to take in."

"Seeing your dad like that, learning what your sister did to him—I can only imagine how it must feel."

There weren't enough words—or maybe there were too many. He couldn't decide. Seeing his father again unearthed memories he thought he'd buried forever. They came back as skeletons in his mind, bony and sharp and as scary as ever.

"He left when we were kids. He and my mother, they abandoned us."

"I'm sorry." She touched his shoulder. "Why'd they do that?"

"Annamaria had just discovered her ability. She was still young and didn't know better. And she'd developed a temper. She caused a measles outbreak. My parents got scared. They figured they were in danger, so they left."

"Were they in danger?"

"I didn't think so," he said. "Let's face it—we weren't normal kids, either of us. We lived on the road. Our father forced us to take part in his fake healing ceremonies. And we had these gifts." He lifted his hand to his face and turned it over and back, staring at each finger, each crease in his skin. "My sister needed help understanding what she could do. She loved my parents. It was their job to teach her. But they let her down."

"They let you both down." She leaned forward and looked into his eyes. "You were just a kid, too. Right?"

"My dad was a con man, my mother a quiet enabler. By the time they left, Annamaria and I were used to being let down."

Harry rumbled into the den with a folded paper towel in each hand. He extended his arms toward them. "Here's your napkins. Time to eat."

Paloma's voice echoed from the kitchen. "Ask them, *mi'jo*. Remember, we don't tell others what to do."

"I didn't force them."

"You didn't ask, either. I warned you about that."

"Yes, Mama."

Silence reigned at the tiny breakfast table as everyone ate. Even Harry seemed to sense something was bothering Luke. He dragged his fork through the mixture of eggs, tortilla strips, and salsa with his stubby fingers as quietly as could be expected. And he didn't say a word.

Paloma's mouth twisted again. Luke knew she'd be the first to speak. She seemed unable to hold back any longer once she finished her glass of tomato juice. "None of this is your fault. I hope you know that."

But he didn't know that. It wasn't like he hadn't tried finding his father before. But when someone like Nicholas Gabor wanted to disappear, no one typically found them. Certainly not a fourteen-year-old boy who also needed to watch over his little sister as they both grew into adulthood. He'd given up searching long ago. But apparently Annamaria hadn't.

"I have to see him," he said.

"No." Paloma slammed her glass on the table. "He doesn't deserve it, *mi'jo*."

"I have to try. It's what I do."

"We don't even know if he's still alive," Marisa said.

Luke wiped his mouth with the paper towel. "I'm not asking you to agree. No one else has to go."

"They'll be waiting for you this time." Marisa spoke low and fast, as if she thought Harry wouldn't hear. "She might be waiting there, too."

"I'm not scared of her."

"You should be." Paloma's cheeks turned bright red, matching her ruby earrings. "What I showed you, it only proves you need to stay as far away as possible."

"He's my father. End of story." Luke stood and pushed his chair back into place. "I'm the only one who can save him—his words, not mine. I have to go."

Everyone at the table stared at him without blinking, but no one spoke. He knew they only wanted to protect him. But he'd been running from Annamaria his whole adult life.

Running—that was something his father had taught him. He needed to be better than that now, to be the person his father could never be.

"Thanks for breakfast." He turned to leave.

"Wait, I'm going with you." Marisa jumped out of her chair. "You'll need someone to watch your back."

"You'll also need money. And clothes. And anything else I can buy," Paloma said.

"More *migas*, too," Harry said. "You can have mine."

CHAPTER 20

Annamaria pumped her arms to the beat thrumming in her earbuds while she sprinted on the treadmill, her pace set at nine miles per hour, the incline at 7 percent. Noordhoek jogged beside her on his own machine. No one else occupied the executive gym at the Cleveland Metropolitan Hotel this morning. The Secret Service had secured every entrance for the next forty minutes.

She'd wanted to run in Wendy Park, but the agents had nixed that idea. Too dangerous, they had said. It wasn't easy hearing no as an answer. She needed her freedom, needed the ability to act when the situation called. Not to worry. The agents had won this round, but if she ever truly wanted to leave, no one could stop her.

She glanced to her left. Noordhoek looked terribly awkward in workout clothes. His lanky body jerked with each step, and his cheeks puffed out huge breaths. She might have laughed if she wasn't in such a foul mood.

Sleep had evaded her last night. Nothing she tried had worked, not even the Swedish massage she'd ordered at two A.M. When she closed her eyes, all she could see was her father exposing her secret in front of a camera—Psychic Nick using his final breaths to betray her one last time. She pulled out her earbuds and stomped on the treadmill as the program lowered the incline. Her stomach growled. She opened her mouth and scraped her fingernail across the surface of her tongue. Her father's chalky aftertaste still clung to the back of her throat no matter what she tried. She spat on the floor.

Noordhoek didn't seem to notice, or else he'd become an expert at pretending not to. Maybe he was focused on trying not to wipe out and embarrass himself. Anyway, she hadn't hired him to run on a treadmill beside her.

"Tell me about this internet clown," she said.

"Clyde Merritt, twenty-nine. Lives in Memphis. Rents a basement apartment on the east side from a retired couple. He travels often while filming documentary-style videos about"—he blew out two breaths—"strange or unbelievable stories."

"He makes a living doing that?"

Noordhoek wiped his forehead with a small towel. His blue T-shirt had turned three shades darker since they'd started running. "He seems to get by. Never missed a payment on his 2004 Mitsubishi Galant. But earlier this week the number of his subscribers jumped into the millions. It surges with each video he posts, along with the views. The man's set for a huge payday, and he knows it. He bought a new Mercedes yesterday in Houston."

"How many views?" she said.

"Fifteen million and counting—that's per video, not total."

Annamaria punched the treadmill display. This bushy-haired, skinny little twerp was making money while trying to destroy her life. She pounded the controls with the bottoms of her fists again and again. Finally the numbers went haywire, and the belt slowed to a stop. She grabbed a towel and slung it around her neck. "Has he posted anything new?"

"Not yet. We assumed he lost track of Lucian the same time we did. He's probably on his way back to Memphis."

"I don't pay you for probably."

Noordhoek stepped off the treadmill. He swallowed hard. "I'll confirm as soon as I can."

"I want to go see him," she said.

"In Memphis?"

"Wherever you find him."

"What about your debate?"

Dammit. She'd forgotten about that again, the only reason she'd ever visit a city like this. She rubbed her thumb against her index finger. Where was her bear when she needed it?

"I need to talk to him," she said. "Find out what he knows. Watch the footage he hasn't already shared with the world."

"And then?"

"Then we leave." She drew a long sip from her water bottle. "And he never posts another video."

Noordhoek stood at attention while she wiped her arms and neck. He'd shifted back into soldier mode, exactly the way she liked him best. If he wasn't so sweaty and gross, she might have touched his cheek. Instead she threw her towel over the broken digital display. "Get on a plane. Take Gilbert with you. Find him, take him. But keep him alive until I get there."

CHAPTER 21

Luke pressed the scan button on the Camry's radio, hoping for a music station with no static. He checked the speedometer—seventy-six miles per hour, held steady by the automatic cruise control. Marisa stared out her window through a new pair of sunglasses.

A sign on the interstate suggested they were ten miles outside of Big Spring, Texas. They'd reach Memphis in about ten hours. He shook his head. After sitting in three different cars and driving God-knows-how-many miles, they still hadn't crossed a state line.

The radio switched channels every five seconds, giving him a moment to either stay or pass. The singer Meat Loaf crooned about what he'd do for love, then dropped into silence. Alan Jackson sang about his favorite river. A news reporter interjected with a story about an upcoming vice presidential debate. Luke rolled his eyes. The thought of watching such a thing nearly put him to sleep.

A smooth, baritone voice poured out of the speakers. A man sang about heading out to San Francisco for a Labor Day weekend show. Luke didn't recognize the artist, but something about the melody seemed to calm him. He pushed the scan button again, to stay on the station. The voice kept singing, assuring an unnamed woman that everything would be all right.

Marisa reached over and turned up the volume. "Good choice."

"Might be the first thing we've agreed on," he said.

"Come on." She turned her shoulders toward him. "I didn't argue about going to El Paso. And I'm not complaining now—unless you want me to."

"Beats arguing with the radio." He reached to tap her knee, but his hand landed on hers. She latched onto it and curled her fingers around his. He didn't pull away.

"I really like Paloma," she said. "And Harry. He has such a genuine soul."

"She's an angel. Harry came to her as an orphan, and she accepted him as her own. Not many people in this world would do that."

"What happened? Did someone abandon him?"

"Not exactly, but it was a bad situation. I'd rather not talk about it."

"Have you ever tried to…you know?" She raised her eyebrows like she expected him to read her mind.

"Know what?"

"Have you ever tried to heal him?"

He shook his head. "There's nothing wrong with him."

"I know. But his condition."

"I can't change someone's genetic makeup. If I could, he wouldn't be Harry."

"You're right." She lowered her head and looked away.

He squeezed her hand. "Don't be embarrassed. This is new territory for you. It took me a while to figure out my limits."

"What are they?"

"I can't raise the dead, if that's what you're asking."

"Seriously."

He turned down the radio. "I can get hurt, like anyone else. And I can die. I've been close enough to know it can happen. I have to use my hands to heal. The power flows through them and into the person's body. But only if I concentrate."

"That's exactly what I felt."

"Pretty cool, isn't it?"

She pulled his hand toward her face and kissed his ring finger. "It's more than cool."

Warmth rushed to his cheeks. He had to admit there was an energy between them, one he'd never experienced before. When she looked at him, he didn't feel like an exhibit in a carnival show. She didn't stare at him like so many others had once they learned what he could do. Not anymore. She saw him as a person, someone who shared her calling to help others. Someone who needed to be loved.

"We're low on gas," he said. "You hungry?"

"I also need a bathroom." She let go of his hand. "Let's do the trifecta."

He laughed. Food, gas, and a restroom—those were the only reasons his parents would stop during the long road trips of his childhood. In that way maybe they hadn't been much different than other families. But then he remembered the night his parents left, the sound of tires spitting gravel at the motel siding, the glow of red taillights fading from their room's translucent drapes.

He chose a gas station connected to a burger restaurant and a sandwich shop, figuring one of those places might offer a restroom clean enough for Marisa's standards. She marched toward the sandwich shop while he prepaid for gas.

The automatic fill notches on the nozzle were missing. He leaned against the Camry and held the nozzle in place while the pump filled the tank. No other motorists were near him except a bald man in a bowling shirt three pumps away. Luke stared at the horizon in the direction of Dallas and listened to the gentle *whoosh* of interstate traffic. The sound reminded him of a shoreline he'd visited as a child, a distant Carolina beach where the problems of this world faded in the light of a blinding sun.

The roar of an engine drew his attention from the horizon. A late-model Mustang tore across two lanes of traffic and barreled into the gas station parking lot. It skidded into a parking space in front of the sandwich shop. A young man in a red T-shirt burst from the driver's door and waved his hands in the air.

"Somebody come quick."

Luke sprinted across the parking lot. "What's wrong?"

"My girlfriend." The man pointed toward the backseat of the Mustang. "She's having a baby."

The windows were too dark to see through. Luke rushed to the door and leaned inside. A woman no older than twenty lay across the rear bucket seats with her jeans around her ankles, her knees pointed toward the roof and squeezed together. The leather upholstery beneath her glistened bright red. "Something's wrong." She grunted through a few breaths. "It's ripping me apart."

A small but powerful hand gripped his shoulder and pulled him away from the door. Marisa pushed the driver's seat forward and climbed inside. She placed her hands on the woman's bare feet. "It's okay. I'm a nurse. How far apart are the contractions?"

"I don't know. It just hurts."

"Is this your first baby?"

"No."

"How many weeks?"

"Thirty-five."

Marisa turned toward Luke. "She's burning up. Go to the other side."

"It's coming," the woman said.

"Should I call 911?" the boyfriend said.

Luke ignored him and ran to the passenger side. He pulled the door open and leaned inside. The woman's short, dark hair was matted to her face. Sweat coated her skin and pooled at the base of her neck. Marisa was right—this woman radiated with fever. "What's your name?"

"Carrie."

"I'm Luke. This is Marisa. We'll help you get through this."

"It hurts so bad," Carrie said. "Not like last time. Something's wrong."

The man in the red shirt appeared behind Marisa's shoulder. "They're sending an ambulance. It's five minutes away."

"Too long," Carrie said. "Get it out. Get it out now!"

Marisa leaned forward. "Let's take a look." She reached for Carrie's underwear and pulled it over the woman's knees.

Carrie reacted like someone had stabbed her gut. She squirmed away from Marisa and raised her pelvis a foot in the air.

Marisa stared at Luke, then tilted her head. He didn't need a neon sign to know what she meant.

He placed his hands on the woman's head and rubbed her temples with his thumbs. "This will help you relax." He closed his eyes and concentrated.

Every cell in Carrie's body was in distress. Her temperature soared. Her muscles flexed and strained, and her nerves flared with sensitivity. He probed deeper, through her core, into her womb. Her baby was head-down, wedged inside the birth canal. Her cervical muscles clamped around the tiny body, forcing it downward. The umbilical cord encircled the child's neck. It strained with tension, pulling against the baby and the placenta.

And there he found the biggest problem. Carrie wasn't lying. Her unborn baby was ripping her apart. Part of her placenta had torn away from her uterine wall. Blood surged from the damaged uterus, draining both mother and child of oxygen.

"It's her placenta," he said.

Marisa blinked. "We need to deliver this baby now."

Carrie screamed so loud it made Luke's ears ring. She bucked her hips like she wanted out of her skin. He didn't blame her.

Marisa turned toward the boyfriend. "Give me your shirt."

The man pulled off his shirt, exposing a tattooed left shoulder, and handed it over.

"And your shoelaces."

"My what?"

"You heard me. Both laces. Now." Marisa turned her attention back to Carrie. She reached between the woman's legs. "Take short, deep breaths. Then push while I count to ten."

"Whatever. Just hurry," Carrie said.

Marisa directed Carrie through a round of pushing. Carrie screamed both during and after, a never-ending soliloquy of pain.

Luke focused on her bleeding, sent the warmth through his hands and into her uterus. Raw, open blood vessels closed and repaired themselves. The placenta absorbed his healing energy even faster, multiplying its cells and reattaching to the uterus at the same time. The umbilical cord grew and expanded, relieving the tension that had caused the placenta to tear from the uterine wall. Carrie's fever evaporated under the wash of his healing energy. Her breathing slowed, and her heart rate leveled off.

"I see the crown," Marisa said. "Just a few more pushes."

Carrie gritted her teeth. "I can't."

"Yes, you can. You're strong. You're a mother. And your baby's life depends on it." Marisa raked her hair out of her face. Sweat dripped from her nose. Her eyes bulged in their sockets. He'd never seen her more focused. "I'll talk you through it. Here we go."

Carrie pushed, Marisa coached, and Luke watched in amazement. The mother's face turned strawberry red, and her veins swelled. She contracted every muscle in her body, all at the same time. If he didn't know better, he'd think she was having a seizure.

Marisa barked orders with such authority Luke wondered how anyone could ever disobey her: "Come on, now. Chin to your chest, elbows out, bear down like you're going to the bathroom. Deep breath, now hold it and push. Two, three, four, more-more-more and six, seven—yes, right there—come on, just a little more. Harder, harder. Now let that breath go and another deep breath in. Push, that's it, two, three, here it comes, five, six, yes-yes-yes."

And then the baby was out. Carrie's whole body relaxed. Her mouth opened. She didn't scream or cry out in pain. Instead her lips formed a smile.

Marisa worked quickly between Carrie's legs. She wrestled with the umbilical cord and unwrapped it from the newborn's neck. She held the baby upside down, cleared the airway with her finger, and stimulated the bottom of its feet and its back.

But the baby didn't cry.

"What's wrong?" Carrie said.

Marisa cleared the airway again. She lowered her face near the newborn's and covered its nose and mouth with her lips. Her cheeks puffed once, twice.

The baby still didn't cry. And it wasn't moving.

"Why is it so blue?"

Marisa's eyes grew watery. Her nostrils flared. She pressed two fingers into the baby's elbow. She nodded, then wrapped the newborn in the red T-shirt and held it out toward Luke.

He grabbed the baby, still connected by the umbilical cord to its mother, and cradled it in one arm. He placed two fingers on the child's chest. Closed his eyes and concentrated.

"What's he doing?"

"Shh."

The newborn's heart was strong, but its lungs couldn't kick into gear. They were underdeveloped, not ready to handle the task of respiration. Its body was cool to the touch, its skin fading from blue to light gray. He flattened his hand across its tiny chest.

The warmth built inside him, then rushed into the newborn's core so quickly it made Luke shiver. The baby's lungs grew and filled its chest cavity. Its arms and legs twitched and flexed. Its skin turned purple, then reddish pink. It opened its mouth, drew its first breath, and let out a wail that could've broken glass.

Carrie screamed even louder, but not like before. She reached for the newborn. Luke lowered it onto her chest. Mother and child wailed in unison, a joyous cacophony that filled the Mustang's interior.

Marisa rushed forward with the shoelaces. She tied off the umbilical cord in two places near the newborn's belly. Then she backed off. He knew why without asking. The new mother needed this moment with her child. And she had earned it.

The shirtless boyfriend leaned inside the doorframe. "Is it a boy or a girl?"

Carrie dug inside the T-shirt and lifted one of her baby's pink thighs. "Oh, Johnny. It's a boy!"

"Hot damn." Johnny slapped the Mustang's roof.

Sirens sounded in the distance. Luke tried to locate the ambulance. A small crowd had gathered around the Mustang, blocking his view.

Carrie kissed the top of her newborn's head. Then she looked at Luke and Marisa like she'd seen a ghost. Her knees snapped together. "Who are you people? And what are you trying to do to my baby?"

Luke nodded at Marisa. "Time to go."

"Carrie, it's okay," Marisa said.

"Johnny, where are you?" Carrie raised her voice another octave. "Get these people away from me."

Marisa climbed out of the backseat. Luke did the same. He rounded the Mustang and grabbed her elbow, pulling her toward the edge of the crowd.

Johnny tapped his shoulder. "What happened in there?"

"Your girlfriend had a baby."

"You know what I mean." Johnny stepped closer. "All that blood, the baby not breathing—that's not normal, right?"

"I couldn't say. Maybe the paramedics can."

Carrie screamed Johnny's name from the backseat. But the man wouldn't stop staring at Luke. "Why is she freaking out?"

"Welcome to parenthood." Luke turned and pushed his way through the small crowd.

Marisa joined his side. Someone had given her three sheets of wet wipes. She scrubbed her hands as they walked toward the Camry. "You were amazing."

"Me? Did you hear yourself? You sounded like you've delivered a thousand babies."

"Almost." She jabbed her elbow into his side. "I worked in L&D for three years."

"Of course you did."

An ambulance zoomed past the fueling island and screeched to a halt next to the Mustang. Paramedics jumped out from three different doors and rushed toward Carrie and her baby.

Luke grabbed the filling nozzle and topped off the tank. Marisa climbed into the passenger seat. He leaned through the open driver's side window. "Still hungry?"

"Next exit. We need to get out of here."

"What about the trifecta?"

She touched the radio knob and smiled. "Two out of three ain't bad."

CHAPTER 22

Clyde sucked the last of the piña colada through his favorite straw and set the glass on his computer desk. The alcohol kept him relaxed enough to keep his eyes from crossing while he obsessed over each frame of his latest video.

His basement apartment seemed too small for him now, his desk too short, the carpet too dirty and cheap for a man of impending wealth and celebrity. He glanced at his email inbox. The number of new messages had grown impossibly large. Only someone with more patience than him could open and read each one. He scribbled the word *assistant* on a notepad in pencil. Next to it he added *attractive, young, smart*. He tapped the pencil against his front teeth, then returned to the notepad and struck through the last word.

He focused his attention back to the editing program. Garry the cremation tech would soon take his place among the internet stars *ShowMeClyde* had created in the last week. As soon as Clyde uploaded the video to YouTube, notices would pop up on millions of smartphones and tablets, alerting his subscribers that another episode awaited. They'd cringe when Garry shoved the body into the furnace, gag when he raked the charred bones into a pile, and cheer when he agreed to share the information in his files—conclusive proof Annamaria Gabor was more than just a character in the story Nicholas had shared before he died.

He zoomed in on the shot he'd captured of her signature. The cremation tech's resistance had folded once Clyde insisted his subscribers would demand visual proof. Clyde inspected the swirling loops, the bold lines, and the sharp angles used to create such a beautiful signature. A notary stamp from California guaranteed its authenticity. A cashier's check from a bank in Sacramento satisfied the balance owed. All of it proved an undeniable fact: Annamaria was a real person, probably living in California. Maybe she'd traveled to Memphis to find and kill the father who'd abandoned her. Maybe she'd done it in a way that had captured the fascination of millions of viewers. Or maybe not. But she'd definitely signed for the ashes.

So there it was. Annamaria was real. So was Lucian. But what about the rest? Three eyewitnesses with questionable motives all claimed to have witnessed Lucian's healing ability. And a dying man swore Annamaria had murdered him with a curse. Clyde folded his arms. Could it be possible? Could everyone be telling the truth?

He grabbed the empty glass, walked into his cramped kitchen, and poured another piña colada from the blender. He planted his straw into the center of the icy drink and smiled. Only one thing really mattered, and it wasn't whether the story was true. He needed more compelling footage, more content. And that meant finding Annamaria. Or Lucian. Or the third sibling, wherever he or she might be hiding.

He returned to his desk and reviewed the Garry episode one last time. He waved his mouse, clicked a few tabs, and released a new episode into the world. Never mind that it was well after midnight. The confirmation *ding* sounded like a cash register drawer popping open, its deep compartments waiting to be filled.

He closed the editing program and opened a search window. He entered as many keywords referring to Nicholas Gabor's daughter as he could think of: *Annamaria, Gabor, California*. Then he added a few words based on speculation, words Nicholas had used during the drive to the emergency room: *powerful, beautiful, deadly.*

The results looked like a random mix of social media profiles, PDF documents, and outdated web pages. He checked the online profiles. No one shared her exact name, but he didn't expect them to. If Annamaria was who Nicholas claimed, she'd never use her given name. But she might choose a similar one out of sentimentality or ego. Either way, it didn't matter. None of the profiles matched the age and appearance of the woman Clyde sought—midforties with a dynamite face and body.

He entered the name of the notary who had certified her signature. Turned out the man worked for a law firm based in Sacramento. The address was the same building as the bank that had issued the cashier's check.

Sacramento. That was where Annamaria was probably hiding.

He closed the search window and loaded his favorite travel app. He entered the destination airport code—SMF—and clicked on the first-class ticket option. The search icon spun in a never-ending circle while the results loaded.

A bright light flashed through the window above his desk. It stayed too long to be lightning. He glanced at his watch—3:35 A.M. No one drove through his neighborhood at this hour. He ran to the window and peered outside. A black SUV pulled to the curb in front of the house next door, turned off its headlights, but didn't kill its engine. A man in a dark suit climbed out of the passenger door. He didn't walk up the sidewalk toward the neighbor's porch. Instead he angled across the lawn, in a direct line toward Clyde's door.

Clyde ran to his desk, unplugged his laptop, and tucked it under his arm. He grabbed his phone. Rushed into his bedroom and jumped on top of the bed. He'd never opened his window before. Hopefully it hadn't been painted shut.

Something heavy thumped against the front door. The sound of shattering glass echoed into the bedroom. Clyde jumped a foot above his bed. Jesus, this was really happening. He worked the latch—pushing, pulling, grunting, cursing—until finally it un-locked. He slid the panel to the side and scrambled out the window.

He rolled under a bush and through a flower bed. Wet, sandy mulch clung to his shirt. He sat in a crouch and peeked back at his window. A tingle ran down his spine. The suited man stormed into the bedroom, a gun in his right hand. Clyde blinked. Sprawled across the bedspread were the two objects in this world he couldn't live without.

His phone and his laptop.

CHAPTER 23

Luke and Marisa rushed down the stairs of a budget hotel they'd found along Interstate 40 in northwest Memphis. He led the way, working his legs in a light-footed pattern so his footsteps would make less noise. The business center opened in less than a minute, assuming the sign didn't lie. He yawned. Six A.M. was early no matter what time zone they were in, especially the morning after a fifteen-hour road trip.

The smell of coffee and bacon greeted him when he strolled into the lobby. His stomach churned, but it needed to wait. He pulled open the door to the business center and held it while Marisa strode past. Automatic fluorescent lights blinked on overhead. They grabbed two chairs and fired up the computer.

"How many should we check?" she said.

"As many as it takes." He dragged the desk phone closer and read the instructions printed on a note taped to the desk:

LOCAL CALLS ONLY
PRESS "9" FIRST
PLEASE KEEP CALLS UNDER THREE MINUTES.

No problem. He figured he could keep each call under a minute. Marisa might be even faster, but she claimed to be better on a computer. He chose not to argue.

Her fingers danced over the keyboard. "Here's a good list with numbers. Ready?"

"Hit me."

Marisa scowled at the screen. "I forgot we're in Memphis. St. Jude's is first on the list, but I guarantee he isn't there."

"Probably not."

"Let's start with Methodist University." She read the number aloud. He dialed and waited. A soft-voiced operator answered. The woman's slow Southern accent defused the urgency in Luke's tone. She told him she was sorry, but no patient with the name Nicholas Gabor was currently registered there.

He called the VA hospital, because he couldn't rule it out. Nicholas appeared nowhere in their registry.

They tried St. Francis, the Regional Medical Center, Delta, Baptist Memorial, Methodist North and South, every hospital Marisa could find. His father didn't occupy a bed in any of them.

He slammed the phone in its cradle. "He's under an alias. That's got to be it."

"He used his real name in the video," Marisa said.

"Maybe he's afraid she'll come back for him. Or that she'll send her men." He folded his arms. "If he's hiding, we'll never find him like this."

"Remember how bad he looked. We don't have much time."

She didn't say it, but he knew what she was thinking. Time might have already run out. But he didn't want to admit that yet. They needed to try. Using his normal method of exploring a hospital, it'd take nearly two months and dozens of janitorial shifts. "We need to track him."

"And fast," she said. "I know where to search first." She clicked on the keyboard so quickly it sounded like sleet on a window. "Here he is—Clyde Merritt. *ShowMeClyde*. According to this, he lives in a residential area ten miles east of downtown."

"He's the guy stalking me with a camera," Luke said.

She turned from the screen and scribbled something on the hotel notepad. "That's why I'll take the lead."

"What's plan B?"

"Don't need one. I've seen all his videos. Believe me. I can handle this guy."

"I don't want you starring in his next episode."

"No worries. Only need to check one more thing." She spun back toward the computer. More clicks. YouTube's main page appeared. "Let's see if he's posted anything new." She typed the word *ShowMeClyde* into the search window, clicked the icon, and dropped the mouse on the floor.

"They're gone," she said.

"What do you mean?"

"The episodes. The channel. Everything—it's all gone."

Luke jumped from his chair and leaned over her shoulder. He stared at the screen. She was right. The search results listed a mix of lesser-known Clydes.

"You know what this means," she said.

He knew. A man like Merritt would only delete his account for one reason.

Annamaria was on the hunt.

CHAPTER 24

Annamaria wrapped her hair in an Egyptian cotton towel and paced toward the window of her suite at the Joule. She surveyed the streets of downtown Dallas below, then craned her neck to see part of the parade route John F. Kennedy's motorcade had taken in November of 1963. Several blocks away, in Dealey Plaza, America had lost its president when an assassin's bullet found its mark. She imagined the overwhelming sense of loss and fear the country must have experienced back then. Only 9/11 had pierced the nation's heart as deeply.

She marched back into the bathroom, removed the towel, and ran her fingers through her dark hair. She stared at her reflection and drew her lips into a smile. The country would soon suffer another shocking loss. A newly elected president would fall ill and die before taking office, leaving the people who voted for him feeling as abandoned as a thirteen-year-old girl who'd lost her father.

Someone would need to step up. Someone would have to pick up the pieces of a shattered administration, to heal the wounds of a country in mourning. She shook her head. The thought of her healing anything was absurd, a metaphor that had overplayed itself. But she wouldn't shy away from the opportunity to take Blair's place. Despite her lack of political experience, she'd learned more about leadership and motivation by the time she was twenty-five than the senator had during thirty-two years of public service.

She snatched her phone off the counter and dialed. Noord-hoek answered on the second ring. "Do we have him?" she said.

Silence on the other end.

"Oh God. What now?"

"It's not terrible news. We entered his apartment. In and out, no one saw us. We secured his computer and mobile phone. Deleted his videos, took his channel offline, and changed his passwords for every social media account. Everything related to *ShowMeClyde* has gone dark. The public will forget in a few days. The internet will move on without him."

She squeezed her phone until the plastic cover cracked. "Not good enough."

"We're working on the rest."

"Answer my first question."

A long pause. She clenched her teeth. Noordhoek was lucky she couldn't reach through the phone.

"He must have heard us coming. Looks like he climbed out a window as we entered. He won't get far without his technology. We'll find him within a few hours."

"I'm coming to Memphis," she said.

Noordhoek didn't reply.

"As soon as I can arrange it. Be ready. We need to make sure."

"I understand."

She ended the call and threw the phone on the bed. She un-zipped her purse and grabbed her yellow bear. All this time she'd thought her brother was her biggest threat. Now a whiny-voiced wannabe reporter had started making waves. Men with guns weren't the answer to every problem. Sometimes you needed a woman's touch. She stroked the bear's fur with her thumb. She brought it to her face and breathed its familiar scent.

She retrieved her phone from the bed and dialed again. Sen-ator Blair's cocky voice blared through the speaker. "You should send Governor Strack an apology bouquet. You destroyed that poor man last night."

"That's what happens when someone attacks me. I'm a counterpuncher."

He laughed. "I'm not sure those talking points were approved. But what the hell, they worked."

"I'm glad you're happy. Listen—"

"Catherine will send your schedule for the next week. You've made us competitive in several states Bobby and I had written off. So now we need to cover them."

"Like Tennessee?" she said.

A pause. "Not right now. We need to target larger states. Like Texas."

"We should squeeze in Memphis. It's basically in Arkansas—two states for one."

"Catherine will send it over. Hang tight. We need to trust the professionals."

She held the phone away from her head. The tenor of his voice made her temples throb. She brought it close again. Nothing but dead silence. The bastard had disconnected.

She squeezed her bear so tightly one of the seams ripped. Dull gray cotton poked through the opening. She tucked it back in, opened her purse, and laid the bear inside, making sure not to injure it further.

She dialed Noordhoek again. This time he answered on the first ring.

"Don't wait for me. Just do it."

A long pause. "We'll make sure this time."

"You'd better."

CHAPTER 25

Clyde escorted two police officers through his ransacked basement apartment toward the front door. He stepped over pieces of his shattered blender. The smell of rum and coconut rose from the carpet. "When will I hear from you guys?"

The lead officer slid his pen into his shirt pocket. "We'll file our report by the end of the day."

"Will I get my stuff back?"

"Depends which stuff you're talking about."

"My electronics. My files."

"Wouldn't hold my breath."

Clyde grabbed the man by the shoulder. "What if he comes back?"

The officer stared at Clyde's hand like it was radioactive, then looked around the apartment. "Looks like the guy took everything he wanted."

"He had a gun."

"They usually do."

"Maybe he was after me."

The second officer shouted from the top of the outdoor steps. "Invest in a security system with a camera. And get a dog that barks."

"Thanks."

The cops ambled toward their cruiser. One said something to the other, and they both laughed.

Clyde dragged a barstool toward the front door. The intruder had kicked the dead bolt through the doorframe, splintering the brittle trim. The door wouldn't stay closed on its own anymore. He propped the stool against the door, wedging it shut—a pathetic fix at best, but it would have to do until the handyman arrived.

He marched into his bedroom and lifted a section of loose carpet in the corner. He reached into a cutout section in the floor—the hiding place that until a few hours ago had held his backup hard drive. In its place were a handgun and two ammo magazines he'd purchased earlier this morning. The merchant had sold him a Glock 21, touting it as a reliable choice for home defense. Its .45 caliber rounds were bound to stop the next intruder from stealing his electronics and ruining his online momentum. He opened the case and wrapped his fingers around the gray metal grip. It felt heavy but comfortable. And it rarely misfired, according to the merchant. Clyde inserted one of the magazines and locked it into place. He stared at the trigger and wondered if the merchant had been lying.

A knock on the front door startled him. He nearly dropped the gun. What now? He steadied himself, held the grip firmly in his hand. Burglars and intruders never knocked—or did they?

A deep breath in, then out slowly, confidently. Everything would be okay. His big payday was still coming. He could afford a new computer, a new phone. Even a cloud-based backup service that would ensure he never lost data again.

The knock sounded a second time. A woman's voice called. "Anybody in there?"

Clyde strode into the living area, gun in hand. The door inched open. A head covered with dark, curly hair poked through the gap.

He pointed the gun. "Stop."

Their eyes met. The woman froze. Her skin was darker than his, her features sharper, more striking. And she didn't seem as scared as he'd expected. "Put that down. I'm not armed."

"Who are you?"

"One of your fans, checking to see if you're okay. Everyone's worried."

"Everyone?" he said.

"Can I come in?"

Clyde kept the gun aimed at her forehead. "Your name's not Annamaria, is it?"

"*Dios mío.* We need to talk." She looked at the blender pieces strewn across the carpet. "What happened here?"

"Home invasion," he said. "They got me once, but never again. This time I'm prepared."

The woman lowered her chin. "I'm not your enemy."

The pistol grew heavier in Clyde's hand. The muscles in his forearm twitched. Maybe she was a fan, maybe not. He didn't know what Annamaria looked like. But her birth certificate proved she was forty-two years old. This woman looked at least ten years younger than that.

"Are you alone?" he said.

"Yes."

He lowered the gun, stepped forward, and pulled the barstool away. The door creaked open. The woman stood just across the threshold with her hands on her hips. She looked past him, into the chaos of his ruined apartment. "You need to leave before they come back."

"Why?"

"You pissed off the wrong woman."

Clyde stepped back. He moved his finger to the trigger.

"Not me," she said. "The daughter of the man you interviewed."

"Annamaria?"

"She's more dangerous than you think. The people who did this are working for her. They erased your YouTube channel, but I'm guessing that wasn't good enough."

Clyde swallowed hard. "They did what?"

"Did you hear me?" she said. "Your life's in danger."

"Bullshit." No way this woman was just a fan. Clyde checked the nearest window to see if anyone was filming him. Nothing was there.

"Tell me who you are or get lost," he said.

"I'm a nurse from Houston. I saw the man you're looking for. He's running from the same men who did this."

Clyde reached into his pants pocket, the one that usually held his phone. Of course, it was empty. "You saw Lucian?"

"His name is Luke."

"You *know* him?"

"We don't have time for this. You need to get out of here. And you need to tell me where Nicholas Gabor is hiding."

"Didn't you watch my latest video?"

"I told you, they're all gone."

His arms dropped to his sides. The videos couldn't be gone. No one would go through the trouble of tracking him down, breaking into his apartment, and seizing his electronics just so they could delete a few digital files. Not unless they wanted to make sure the videos never surfaced again. Not unless those videos contained damaging information about someone important.

Who the hell was Annamaria, anyway?

He turned toward the door. The woman darted past him. She yanked his sleeve and pulled him with her, deeper into his apartment. "Get down," she said.

"What—"

A crack of gunfire from the doorway provided the answer. He ducked. The woman pulled him around his dining table, pushed it on its side, and crouched behind it. He knelt beside her.

His heartbeat pounded in his temples. Another shot zoomed over him and blasted through the dining room wall. Flakes of drywall fell on his head.

"Hand me that gun," the woman said.

The warm grip slid out of his palm, glistening with sweat. That was all he could focus on, the slick, wet grip. The handle of a gun he'd never fired, and probably never would.

The woman raised the Glock over the table's edge and pointed it toward the door. She fired twice. Blind shots. No way she'd hit anything. The sound pierced his eardrums and sent a ringing into his head. Another shot came in return. It struck the table inches from his face. The underside of the table splintered open. Jesus, why were they hiding here? And who was shooting at them?

She grabbed an iron candlestick and placed it in his hand. "Throw this into the living room, count to three, and run for the bedroom."

"What about you?"

"I'll follow. And you better not trip."

He wrapped his fingers around the candlestick. The metal was arctic cold. He hesitated. What good would throwing this do when the other guy had a gun?

The woman fired again. "Now," she said.

Clyde threw the candlestick as hard as he could. It ricocheted off the living room wall and crashed into his end table lamp. Another shot blasted from his own gun—covering fire, he figured. He crouched as low as he could and sprinted toward his bedroom door.

A sharp pain tore into his shoulder. He charged into his bedroom, leaped over the corner of his bed, and dove through his open closet door. He threw himself into the corner and sat on a pile of clothes. When he reached to close the door, his arm wouldn't work properly. His left shoulder throbbed with pain. He touched it gingerly and brought his hand to his face. His fingertips were coated in bright red.

Dizziness enveloped him. He braced himself against one wall of the closet with his right arm, trying to stay focused on the bedroom doorway visible through the opening. His shoulder burned from inside out. His stomach twisted into a knot. He couldn't catch his breath. His entire body wanted to shut down. But he kept his eyes open, kept watching.

The woman hadn't followed him into the bedroom.

More shots echoed through his apartment. A few sounded like cracks from a smaller gun, or one fitted with a silencer—the intruder's. Others were louder and carried a bigger echo. Probably his Glock. The woman must have been cut off. Maybe she'd been shot. Maybe she was making a final stand. He looked toward his window. Did he have enough energy to climb through it again?

Everything went quiet. Too quiet. He reached for the closet door with his right hand. No good. He couldn't get up without making a ton of noise.

Heavy footsteps, fast and frantic. Growing louder. Closer.

"Behind you," a male voice called out.

Two shots blasted from the living room—two explosions so loud Clyde wondered if they came from a cannon. He straightened. That wasn't his gun, and it wasn't the intruder's. A new weapon had entered the fray. All he could do was sit and wonder who'd used it.

"Where is he?" said a voice he hadn't heard before. A deep, male voice. Different from the one moments ago. Clyde held his breath and tried to remain still.

The woman marched through the doorway. Her hair was a mess, and she was bleeding from her forehead. She scanned the room, ran toward the closet, and pulled the door all the way open. "Found him."

Clyde held his left arm in place with his right, trying to keep his wounded shoulder immobile. He couldn't stop shaking.

A man walked into the bedroom—tall, dark hair, with a half-circle-shaped scar marking his cheek. He held a huge gun in his left hand but carried it like it was weightless.

The man rushed to the woman's side. He lowered himself and peered into the closet. "You can come out now. It's safe."

"Easy for you to say."

The man glanced at the woman and shook his head. He laid the gun on the carpet beside his feet.

"No one wants to hurt you," the woman said. "We need your help." She snapped her fingers. "*Andale*, before someone else starts shooting at us."

"Who are you people?"

"Clyde Merritt, meet Luke Johnson."

CHAPTER 26

Annamaria turned the lock on her bedroom door and paced in front of the bed. Her smartphone radiated heat into her ear. She'd burned through most of the battery life already this morning. Someone needed to charge it soon.

"Find anything useful?" she said.

Noordhoek paused before answering. Didn't he know how much that infuriated her? "Remember the note you gave us in San Francisco?"

"What about it?"

"We found your answer."

"Shut up," she said.

Noordhoek didn't speak. She rolled her eyes. Did anyone in this world operate on her wavelength? "Not literally. Keep going."

"We found a birth certificate and an adoption record."

Her fingertips tingled. Warmth rushed into her cheeks. "Nice work. Are you and Gilbert in position?"

"We're farther away than I'd like, but Gilbert has a visual." He paused. A muffled voice—probably Gilbert's—squawked in the background. Then Noordhoek spoke again. "The police are leaving. Target is alone."

"Wait three minutes, then go."

"Got it. Hold on."

Static erupted from Noordhoek's end of the line. Gilbert barked something again, but she couldn't make out his words. "What's happening? Answer me."

More commotion, more static. Noordhoek was probably covering the speaker with his sleeve. Her men were arguing. She picked up that much. But about what? She stomped toward her locked bedroom door.

The Secret Service agents knocked with transparent urgency. She shot the bird at the door. "I'm fine. Just need a minute."

The static on the line cleared. "Marisa Cruz is here," Noordhoek said.

"Shut—" Annamaria stopped herself. "Are you sure?"

"Confirmed. She walked down the stairs and knocked on his door."

Annamaria pressed her phone against her chest. What was the nurse doing in Memphis? Only one logical answer existed. Lucian must be nearby.

"Same plan. Two minutes and go. But I want her alive."

"What about Merritt?" Noordhoek said.

"I said same plan."

Noordhoek's voice muffled again. He was probably relaying the message to Gilbert. She clenched her free hand into a fist. Giving orders over the phone was so frustrating. Things would go much smoother if she could direct the assault in person. But no, the campaign couldn't wait. The Secret Service agents launched desperate soliloquies from the main room. She turned her back on the door. "Noordhoek, put me on Bluetooth. I'm going in with you."

"Stand by."

Three random clicks and two thumps later, Noordhoek's voice sounded again. "You there?"

"Thirty seconds. Get ready."

The sound of gun magazines locking into place made her pulse quicken. Her men had a chance at redemption. Two birds, as the saying went. They could still manage a satisfying end to an infuriating morning. If she couldn't be there to see it, at least she could hear it—the sound of another threat forever silenced, the possibility her brother would be next. She closed her eyes and envisioned the scene: Noordhoek and Gilbert loading and checking their weapons, readying for the assault. She blocked out her surroundings and focused on the noises coming from Noordhoek's Bluetooth.

"We go in three, two."

Annamaria pressed record on her smartphone. Some moments were worth reliving.

The sound of two car doors slamming. Then footsteps, heavy at first, then softer, like they were crossing a lawn or a flower bed. She held her breath. This would be over in seconds.

Noordhoek puffed out words like she remembered him doing on the treadmill. "Go, go, go." His footsteps grew louder and more patterned, like he was climbing or descending steps.

She expected to hear him force the door open. Instead gunshots rang out—slightly muted but still loud. Probably from the silencers her men always used. Two quick blasts, then three more. Maybe that was it—no. Another three shots, one close, two from farther away. Did her men have the nurse and the YouTube journalist cornered? Or were they firing back?

A thin layer of sweat dampened the back of her neck. "What's going on? Do we have them?"

No answer. She knew Noordhoek was still there. His hurried breathing filtered through the Bluetooth, but he didn't answer. Thirty seconds had passed, and this still wasn't over.

A crash of glass. Two shots. Then several more, so many she lost count.

Someone near the phone whispered, but she couldn't hear what he'd said. Noordhoek whispered back, "She's still there. Let's move."

The sound of hurried movement crashed through her speaker—several people moving at once, furniture knocked out of the way, a repositioning of players. She tried to imagine the scene. Impossible. Too many variables.

Noordhoek spoke again. This time he didn't whisper. "Behind you."

Annamaria shivered.

Two loud, echoing shots blasted through her speaker—so loud she worried the Secret Service agents had heard them through the door. That wasn't Noordhoek's gun. A silencer-fitted pistol couldn't make a noise that thunderous.

"Noordhoek?"

He answered with hurried breaths, like before. Noordhoek was running. She tracked each stride by the sound of his exhalations. What had gone wrong? Where was Gilbert? Did they silence the YouTube journalist or the nurse? Questions came to her faster than Noordhoek's gulps of air.

She waited until a car door opened and shut.

"Noordhoek, can you hear me?"

"He snuck in behind us. Didn't say a word, just started shooting."

"Who are you talking about?"

A car engine fired and revved. Gears shifted. Wheels screeched. Noordhoek spoke over the noise. "Your brother shot Gilbert in the chest."

Annamaria stiffened. "Is he with you?"

"He didn't make it."

A loud crack sounded from the door to her suite. The knob turned, and the door swung open. A Secret Service agent entered, weapon drawn, and scanned the bedroom.

She tucked her phone behind her back. "What are you doing?"

"We heard shots."

"I'm alone."

The agent held his gun with both hands, arms outstretched, the barrel aimed toward the floor. He angled toward the bathroom, pointed the gun through the doorway. A moment later he relaxed and holstered his weapon. "Diamondback secure. All clear."

Diamondback—her code name. As if she didn't know how they felt about her.

She glared at the agent. "Thanks."

"We need to leave, Ms. Varner."

"One minute."

"You're already late."

"I said one minute."

The agent pressed his lips together and walked out. Annamaria rushed to the door and shut it behind him. She aimed her voice into the phone. "Noordhoek?"

"Yes."

"What about our targets?"

"Negative," he said.

Everything about this day was maddening. Lucian had obviously changed his mind about running. The nurse and Merritt had proven to be more difficult targets than she'd thought. Gilbert was not only lost but also now a potential problem. And then there was her fucking campaign schedule. Why couldn't Senator Blair see she'd already done enough to help him win? The polls weren't even close anymore. Only a moron could let a lead this huge slip away.

"Did Gilbert carry identification?" she said.

"He knew better than that."

"I need you to take care of this."

"I'll call Sacramento."

A few trusted members of her first-lady staff still manned an office back home. They specialized in covering her tracks without asking questions. Gilbert's work history would disappear. His identity would revert to whatever it'd been before she started calling him Gilbert. No one would ever trace her dead aide back to her. But his death had created a void, one that needed immediate filling.

"Stay in Memphis," she said, "and stand by for more instructions. I have an event, but I'll be in contact soon." She ended the call and slid the phone into her purse, next to her injured teddy bear.

Enough was enough. Too much was at stake. Sometimes you needed to dive into the mud and wrestle the pigs yourself.

She opened the door and flashed a smile she'd perfected for the cameras. "Gentlemen, I believe we have somewhere to be."

CHAPTER 27

Luke gripped the steering wheel tighter than he intended, changed lanes quicker than other cars, and accelerated and braked through Memphis traffic with more aggressiveness than needed. He couldn't help it. The freeway couldn't provide a big enough distraction to make him forget what he'd done.

He was a killer now, just like his sister.

Marisa touched his arm from the passenger seat. "You had no choice. It was him or me."

She was right. He couldn't save the gunman this time. The man was already gone before he could check for a pulse. Marisa probably would've died if Luke hadn't acted, but her words didn't ease the tension coursing through his veins. "The cops will be after us. We fled a murder scene."

"That wasn't murder," she said. "You were protecting me. Anyone could see that."

He shrugged. "Not the police. They'll wonder why we left. They'll make assumptions, then call in a forensic team. We're screwed."

"We have an eyewitness." She pointed with her thumb toward the backseat.

Clyde rested unconscious across the bench seat. His soft purr matched the hum of the engine.

"You think he's okay?" she said.

"Probably."

"What do you mean? Did something go wrong?"

"Don't think so. The bullet came out in one piece."

"Then why wouldn't he be okay?"

Luke glanced in the mirror toward the backseat. Merritt's eyes remained closed, his snore still audible over the road noise. "Sometimes there are aftereffects."

Marisa stiffened. "What kind of aftereffects?"

"It doesn't happen often."

"Now you're scaring me."

"Don't worry," he said. "It didn't happen with you."

"What didn't happen?"

Luke stared at the highway. "Memory loss. Usually it's minor, only a few seconds or minutes before they're healed. Maybe the brain stops recording during the process. I don't know."

Marisa leaned back in her seat. "The young mother in the Mustang. She didn't recognize us after her baby was born."

"That's usually what happens."

"But sometimes it's worse, isn't it?" Marisa grabbed his knee. "Tell me."

Luke thought back through the worst cases. Thankfully they'd occurred so infrequently they easily stood out. "Sometimes people lose a day or even a week. They forget where they are or why they were admitted to the hospital."

Marisa nodded. "We see that in patients all the time, especially the elderly ones."

"Other cases are worse." Luke tightened his grip on the steering wheel. "A few forgot the names of their loved ones. Some even forgot who they were."

Marisa didn't say anything for a moment. She rubbed her arms and stared at the floorboard. "Regaining your health but losing your memories—makes you wonder if it's worth the risk."

"I think about it every time."

Marisa placed her hand on his shoulder. Her warmth helped soothe his nerves, but not completely. She leaned in close. "Thanks for taking the risk with me."

"I'm glad you didn't forget me."

"Impossible," she said.

Just ahead on the highway, a section of tread broke loose from a tire on an eighteen-wheeler and landed in their path. Luke swerved to avoid it. The car jerked to the right. His seat belt tugged against his chest and hips, keeping him stable.

He checked the rearview mirror. Clyde's eyelids flickered open. He sat up and looked around. "What happened? Where am I?"

"Relax. You're fine," Marisa said. "We got you out of there."

Clyde lifted his left arm and stared like it wasn't part of his body. "My shoulder."

"What about it?" Luke said.

"Somebody shot me."

Luke glanced at Marisa. "Are you sure?"

Clyde pulled at the collar of his T-shirt and stretched it wide, exposing the back of his shoulder. "I was shot right here, I think."

"How bad is the wound?" Marisa said. "I'm a nurse. Maybe I can help."

Clyde's fingers crawled under his T-shirt like they were searching for something. "I remember a pain in my shoulder. I thought it was a gunshot."

"You suffered a panic attack," Marisa said. "You freaked out and lost consciousness. I bet you don't remember us dragging you out your front door."

Clyde tilted his head like a dog watching a television commercial. "These aren't the clothes I was wearing."

"I certainly didn't dress you," Marisa said.

Luke couldn't tell if Clyde was buying this. He regretted having to fool the man, but they couldn't afford to treat him with bandages or take him to a hospital. Luke had no choice but to heal him. And Marisa was smart enough to suggest changing him into clothes without bullet holes or bloodstains.

Clyde leaned forward until his face drew even with the front seat. He stared at Luke. "You're Nicholas Gabor's son?"

"Yes."

"Do you have any special powers?"

"Of course not."

Clyde smirked. "What about your sister?"

"She's dangerous, but not the way you think."

"Did she murder your father?"

Luke stepped on the brakes and guided the Camry to the shoulder. He turned all the way around in his seat. "What did you say?"

"I thought you watched the video."

"Is my father still alive or not?"

Clyde's eyes bulged. Luke knew before the man spoke it was too late. His father had already passed—another victim of Annamaria's rage.

"I'm sorry. He died three days ago."

Luke faced the windshield again. He draped one arm over the steering wheel and made a fist. That was it. He'd never see his father again, never be able to share the stories about the people he'd helped. Never get the chance to tell him he wasn't mad anymore.

Marisa rubbed circles into the center of his back. "I'm sorry, Luke."

"I have to stop her."

"Stop who?" Clyde said.

Luke turned toward Marisa. "Now that my father's gone, she'll never stop. It won't end with me. She'll come after you, Paloma, Harry, Clyde, and anyone else she perceives as a threat."

"Who's Paloma?" Clyde said.

"What makes you think you can kill her?" Marisa said.

"Not kill. I said stop."

"You're ready to quit running?"

"Was never good at it anyway," he said.

"When was the last time you saw her?"

"Twenty-five years ago."

Marisa closed her eyes and drew a deep breath. "We don't even know where to start."

"Sure, we do." Luke motioned toward the backseat. "I bet he has a file on her an inch thick."

Clyde's stare jumped back and forth between Luke and Marisa. "That reminds me of something your father said before I drove him to the hospital."

"What's that?"

"He warned never to go looking for his daughter."

Marisa reached for Clyde's arm but missed. "We saved your life. You owe us."

"If she's the one who sent those men, I'm not going near her."

"You won't need to. But you'll help us find her. Before she finds you again."

"How?"

"You're a journalist, right?" Luke said.

"I'm so much more than that."

"Then share your research."

Clyde shifted into one corner of the backseat. "They took everything I had."

Luke closed his eyes. Of course Annamaria's men had swiped anything that might have led to her. She'd probably demanded to see the files in person before she threw them into a fire.

"What do you remember?" he said.

Clyde smoothed a wrinkle in his T-shirt. "California."

Marisa snapped her fingers. "¿*Cómo que* California?"

"She might live there. The papers she signed to collect her father's ashes were notarized by a law firm in Sacramento."

Luke swallowed hard. *Ashes.* He was never even close to saving his father.

Marisa said, "I'm not driving to California."

"What else do you have?" Luke said.

Clyde ran his fingers through his hair. "I hired a PI to do some research. Last time we talked, he hadn't found much. Nothing on Annamaria or you."

"When was that?"

"Two days ago."

"Is he close?" Luke said.

"Near Gaston Park," Clyde said.

Marisa unfolded a paper map across her lap. "Got an address?"

Clyde rolled his eyes. "Neither of you has a phone?"

"What about yours?" Luke said.

"Never mind. I know the way."

CHAPTER 28

Annamaria stepped off the stage to the sound of thousands of clapping hands and cheering voices. She dabbed her forehead with her sleeve. The lights she once craved now seemed to burn her skin each time she gave a speech, raising her body temperature to an uncomfortable level.

Two Secret Service agents escorted her through a narrow hallway backstage of whatever conference center they were in. She'd already forgotten its name. All she knew was she needed fresh air, space to breathe. The campaign circuit was harder on candidates than it looked on television. No wonder Senator Blair had developed a serious drinking problem.

The first hallway led to a narrower, darker one. The agents edged into her personal space. She elbowed one out of her way—the same agent who always stared at her from behind his dark sunglasses. Like that was a subtle way to hide his creepiness.

They reached the end of the hallway. A door opened. Morning sunlight seeped under the covered parking area beyond. She ducked her head and crossed the threshold. A black SUV waited, its rear passenger door held open by yet another agent. A fourth sat behind the wheel. The government provided layer upon layer of security even for a simple ride to the airport. And she wasn't even running at the top of the ticket. This was the future she'd chosen—being shoved into cars and planes by men with short haircuts and stern expressions. And it would only get worse. How many agents did Senator Blair have to put up with?

She approached the SUV, then stopped. She grabbed the hand of the agent holding the door. Unlike the other agents, this one had kind eyes. She stared into them, blinked, then whispered, "Grand mal seizure."

The agent went stiff, his neck muscles straining against his skin. His body convulsed and slammed against the SUV. Two other agents rushed forward and caught him before he could fall.

Annamaria sidestepped the melee. She raced around the rear of the SUV toward the exit. The fourth agent—the one from behind the driver's seat—met her there. He extended his arm like a traffic cop. "Ms. Varner, what are you doing?"

She reached into her purse, pulled out a tiny can of mace, and sprayed the agent's face.

The agent guarded his eyes with his elbow and charged. The impact nearly took her breath. He tackled her, fell on top of her, covered her with his massive torso. He peeled her fingers away from her mace can. Annamaria strained against him, but he was too strong. She stifled her gag reflex. The man smelled like allspice and cigarette smoke.

The agent spoke into his wrist. "Diamondback secure. Backup needed."

She reached for his exposed neck and dug her nails into his skin. This one deserved to suffer. With a blink and a whisper, she sealed his fate: "Asphyxia."

The agent wheezed in a breath. The sound confirmed her words had done the trick. The agent's neck turned red, then purple. The strength he'd used to hold her down dissipated like air from a balloon.

She pushed him off her chest and rolled him to the side. Climbed to her feet and raced toward the exit.

Another agent approached on her left. She stuck out her hand and pressed it against his face.

"Stroke."

The agent fell away. Annamaria kept running and didn't look back.

Out of the parking area, down the sidewalk of a busy street, past a small group of supporters who gasped and shouted her name. She raced into an alley and through a row of parked cars like they were part of an obstacle course. She turned one corner, then another. Stopped to check her surroundings. No taxis, no buses. No choice but to keep running.

A set of arms locked around her from behind. They squeezed so tightly she nearly threw up. "Where you going, Ms. Varner?"

She couldn't see his face, but she knew it was the last agent, the one she hadn't incapacitated, the one with the sunglasses who always stared. She twisted her shoulders. He only squeezed tighter, pressing himself against her lower torso. "We can do this the easy way or the hard way."

She knew the agent must be enjoying this. No doubt he'd secretly hoped she'd try something that would allow him to use physical force against her. She reared back her head and turned her face to the side. Pursed her lips in a way that couldn't be misunderstood. "What are you going to do with me?"

He didn't answer. Their faces were only centimeters apart. His chest expanded rapidly. He was sniffing her perfume, taking in the scent of her skin. She leaned closer, exposing the softness of her cheek.

Rough lips brushed against her skin. *That's a good boy.*

She blinked. "Myocardial infarction."

The thrum of his heartbeat knocked against her back, deep and irregular, slowing with each second. The agent's grip tightened, then relaxed. She stomped on his instep with her heel, bent forward, and broke free of his arms. She turned. The agent's sunglasses had fallen off, his pale blue eyes wide and focused on her.

She grabbed his throat and pushed him against a brick wall behind him. She brought her lips close to his.

"Not in a million years, kid."

Annamaria drove her knee into his crotch, then turned and ran across the street, disappearing into the heart of the city.

CHAPTER 29

Clyde wondered how big of a mess he'd gotten himself into. The story he'd been chasing had literally broken through his front door, destroying the sense of detachment he usually enjoyed. Like it or not, he was part of the story now.

Lucian Gabor guided the Camry into the parking lot of a two-story office building that had seen better days. Clyde had visited the PI's office only once, and now he remembered why. The building looked abandoned. A few exterior glass panels had been replaced with plywood sheets. Nearby trees looked like they hadn't been trimmed in a decade. Styrofoam food containers and beer cans littered the parking lot. No wonder the guy had such cheap rates.

This qualified as the weirdest day of Clyde's life, and it wasn't even noon. He hadn't been online in eight hours. Armed men had invaded his apartment not once but twice. Both times he'd barely escaped. The first time his own instincts and agility had saved him. The second, he still wasn't sure. He suspected he'd been shot while running into his bedroom—a phantom pain still ached deep inside his shoulder—but he couldn't remember. Luke and Marisa acted friendly enough, and they appeared to have saved him from the second attack. But they were lying to him. He reached inside his T-shirt and felt the roundness of his shoulder, the tautness of his skin. Something had happened to him, something he couldn't remember. He decided to stay silent on the subject until he figured it out.

Luke shifted into park. "You sure this is the place?"

"Suite 202. Hanlon Investigations," Clyde said.

Marisa slid Clyde's gun into her purse and reached for the door handle.

"You plan on returning my weapon?" he said.

"You plan on using it?"

He exited the car without another word. Standing in the parking lot, he realized how ridiculous he looked. His T-shirt was nothing but a tagless Hanes he'd purchased to wear under his new suit. His jeans were part of the slim-fit fad he'd abandoned the previous summer. And his belt was missing—he never forgot a belt. He closed his eyes, drew in a cleansing breath, and blew it out. He looked down. His Givenchy shoes shined like new, but they didn't match his outfit.

"You coming?" Luke spun the keys around his index finger.

"This is a waste of time," Clyde said. "He probably isn't here."

Marisa shut her door. "It's worth checking out. Just introduce us. We'll do the rest."

A marquee sign greeted them in the lobby, warning the elevator was broken, of course. Clyde led the way up the stairs. He ignored the smell of urine and avoided touching the handrail. Jesus, this place was disgusting.

Suite 202 was midway down the hall. At first glance he noticed something was wrong. The wooden door had been kicked in. An upside-down cardboard file box straddled the doorway. Someone had obviously stepped through it on their way out. He raised his arm and pointed toward the suite. Luke raced past before he could speak.

"Wait." Marisa rushed ahead of them, gun raised and ready.

Clyde braced himself against one wall. What was it with these two? Everywhere they went, they seemed to expect an ambush. He wasn't about to help. He wouldn't risk getting shot—possibly for the second time.

Luke and Marisa whispered something to each other. Clyde couldn't hear what they said. Then they rushed in, each motion fast and efficient, like they'd practiced the maneuver in the parking lot.

Clyde stood rigid and listened. One gunshot and he'd bolt for the parking lot. These two could fend for themselves. If they somehow got shot or killed, he'd be a sitting duck.

Rapid footsteps sounded through the office. A heavy thump silenced them.

"Show us your hands," Marisa said.

Luke's voice echoed through the doorway. "Do what she says, and no one gets hurt."

"Okay, okay. Don't shoot."

Silence.

Clyde's leg muscles twitched.

Luke's head appeared in the hallway. "Get in here."

"Why?"

"You need to identify this guy."

Clyde followed Luke into the suite. The office housed two separate rooms. The one on the left looked like a tornado had struck, but no one was there. Inside the one on the right, behind an overturned desk, stood the PI he'd hired a week ago. Hanlon's skinny arms reached for the ceiling, his elbows shaking. Marisa stood five feet away pointing Clyde's Glock at the man's nose. Hanlon's eyes grew larger when he saw Clyde. "Merritt, thank God. Tell them you know me."

Clyde blinked. "This is the guy I hired. What happened here?"

Marisa lowered the gun. Hanlon blew out a huge breath. "Was like this when I came in. My files are scattered, my hard drives are missing, and someone shot my monitor."

"Annamaria," Clyde said.

Luke stepped forward. "Probably her men. They know how to make a mess." He walked around the overturned desk, toward a set of open metal cabinets. "You had a file on us?"

Hanlon stared at Luke and Marisa. "Who are you people?"

"This is Nicholas Gabor's son," Clyde said. "And this is his friend." He didn't expect anyone to shake hands, but at least his PI could finally relax.

"So did you?" Marisa said.

Hanlon looked at Clyde, as if for support. "Merritt asked me to make files on all three Gabor siblings."

"Wait—all *three*?" Marisa said.

Clyde had never missed his video camera more than now. Apparently he wasn't the only person Luke had been lying to.

"I found birth certificates for three children," Hanlon said. "Lucian, Annamaria, and a third child—all born to Nicholas and Marian Gabor."

Marisa glared at Luke. "Did you know about this?"

"I didn't know he found the birth certificates."

She turned her back on him, focusing instead on the PI. "Tell me about this third sibling."

Hanlon shrugged. "The record is mostly unreadable. Someone obviously tried to obscure the information. I couldn't even make out the sex of the baby."

Clyde backed away. Marisa's body language had raised the temperature in the room. Something was about to explode, and he wanted to be outside the blast zone when it did.

She turned to Luke again. "Do you have another brother or sister?"

"Yes."

"Boy or girl?" she said.

"Doesn't matter."

"*Dios mío.* Are you kidding?"

Luke picked up a stack of folders and inspected the labels. He dropped them one by one on the floor. "We need to find Annamaria. That's all that matters."

"Bullshit," Clyde said. Everyone in the room stared at him like he'd spoken out of turn. Maybe they were right, but he couldn't help himself. "If what you guys told me is true, every member of your family is at risk." He zeroed in on Luke. "If you know something, you need to share it. This third sibling—she's probably after him, too."

"Or her," Marisa said.

"That person is safe. I promise." Luke's posture straightened, like he was trying to talk over everyone's heads. "I made sure of that long ago."

"I did find an adoption record," Hanlon said.

Luke spun around. "That's impossible."

Marisa rushed to the PI's side. "Show me."

"I can't find it again without my computer. But even that document was heavily blacked out." He massaged his eyelid with his index finger. "No dates, only the child's name—Horus Gabor. But I was able to make out the zip code of the adopting family."

"Let me guess," Clyde said. "California?"

"I don't remember the exact number." Hanlon looked at Marisa. "But I remember looking it up online. The adoptive parent lived in El Paso, Texas."

Now Luke looked like the one set to explode. "How'd you find that document?"

"Don't have much of a social life," Hanlon said. "So I developed a few hacking skills."

Clyde breathed a little easier. His instincts about this PI had been right all along. He made a mental note to interview Hanlon as soon as he bought a new phone.

"Harry," Marisa said. "He's your brother."

Luke stared at Marisa but didn't speak.

She placed her hand against his chest. "That sweet little boy—you saved him from your parents, didn't you?"

Clyde couldn't suppress his grin. This story grew more interesting by the minute.

"He's safe," Luke said. "Paloma will never let anything happen to him."

"If your sister ever found out…" Marisa's mouth hung open, like she'd forgotten what she wanted to say.

Luke pressed closer to the PI, invading his personal space. "Did you print a copy of those records?"

The look on Hanlon's face said it all. Clyde had never seen a man's cheeks turn so red.

"We need to find that file," Marisa said. "Everyone start looking."

Hanlon's office transformed into a flurry of activity, manila folders and papers shuffling from one stack to another. Everyone pitched in. Clyde suspected they already knew the file wasn't here. But Luke and Marisa needed to make sure.

Fifteen minutes later, Marisa threw the last folder against the wall. "That's it. She's got it. She knows."

No one disagreed.

"We have to get to El Paso," Luke said.

CHAPTER 30

Annamaria pushed through the exit door of the Irving Mall with her forearm, making sure to avoid touching the dirty brass bar with her hands. The bright Texas sun barely penetrated her sunglasses, but its heat quickly absorbed into her new wig—dark brown with long spiral curls.

She'd replaced every visible piece of clothing on her body in the last hour, shopping at places she swore she'd never visit again. The whole experience was disgusting. But she'd needed to kill time and find a disguise. This mall was the perfect place to do both.

Back when she was a governor's wife, she could easily venture out without being recognized. Those days were over. Her profile appeared on every cable news channel 24/7. Potential voters swarmed her events. She was the shiny new toy everyone wanted to own. A wig, dark glasses, and new clothes were her only option.

The Secret Service would be more difficult to avoid. Soon after she dispatched the last agent, she'd made a phone call, then removed the battery from her smartphone and threw everything into a dumpster. Her new burner phone worked just as well. As much as she detested the agents who protected her, she knew the agency commanded a tremendous amount of resources. She needed to keep her eyes open.

A small, box-shaped car pulled to the curb in front of her. The paint color looked ridiculous—avocado green with black trim.

The passenger's side window rolled down, revealing Noordhoek behind the wheel. His expression was as stoic as ever.

She approached, leaned into the window, and lowered her glasses. "Are you serious?"

"This was all they had."

She crinkled her nose. "What is this, a compact?"

"Kia Soul. It's popular with millennials."

"That doesn't help." She opened the door and climbed inside.

The air-conditioning felt only slightly less humid than outside. Noordhoek didn't seem to notice. He shifted into drive but didn't take his foot off the brake.

"Anyone follow you?" she said.

"No."

"What about your phone?"

"Scattered among several trash cans in Memphis International."

She paused. "Gilbert?"

"Handled."

Finally, someone who knew how to follow directions. She allowed herself to relax—a little.

Air travel was out of the question, especially from the same city where she'd escaped her protectors. No doubt more agents and maybe even US Marshals were staking out nearby airports. She laughed under her breath. The Secret Service must be going apeshit. All that training on how to spot threats and they never realized the biggest one was riding in the car with them.

"You know where to go?" she said.

"Take the interstate to El Paso."

"We need a gun."

He opened the side of his suit coat, exposing a holster and the handle of a pistol. "This is Texas."

She raised an eyebrow. Rarely did anyone surprise her anymore. She was glad Noordhoek had survived the shoot-out with her brother. It proved he was worthy to make this trip with her.

They'd screwed around long enough. Time to take matters into her own hands.

Senator Blair was probably pissed, but he'd welcome her back when this was over. She'd force him to accept her version of this morning's events because the truth was so inconceivable. No reasonable person could accuse her of causing a seizure, a heart attack, asphyxia, or a stroke. Blair's campaign staff would explain her canceled rallies as emergency personal leave. Given their influence, the media would accept her absence without question. The Secret Service, embarrassed at having lost her, would impose a gag order sure to keep the entire incident from making the news. Upon her return, she'd request a new detail with agents who knew how to behave. Then she and Blair would cruise into election night with a crushing lead in the polls. But she and Noordhoek had better hurry. They could afford only one day on their own, maybe two.

"Ready?" Noordhoek said.

She reached into her purse and found her yellow bear. She cradled it in her palm like it was a baby bird. "Let's go."

CHAPTER 31

Luke buckled his seat belt and claimed both armrests to the middle seat in the 747 bound for El Paso. Clyde had insisted on taking the aisle seat, and since he'd paid for all three tickets, Luke and Marisa didn't argue. Luke wouldn't complain if he'd been stuffed into an overhead bin. Getting to Paloma and Harry as fast as possible was all that mattered.

He watched Clyde's fingers dance over the screen of a new mobile phone. The man had acted like a kid on Christmas morning when he tore it out of the box hours ago. Luke knew it was dangerous to bring him along—a man who'd tried to expose his family secret in exchange for fame and money. But leaving him in Memphis would only prove more dangerous. While Clyde still didn't have any hard proof of Luke's ability, he was clearly suspicious. Then there was the prospect of Clyde running to the police, which would bring a whole new set of complications. Most likely Annamaria would take it personally and send another team, which meant Clyde was a dead man if he stayed in Memphis.

Luke glanced at Marisa. She'd tucked her elbows close to her sides with her hands near her face. Her fingers seemed constantly in motion, turning one of her rings over and back, then switching to another finger on her opposite hand and doing the same.

He hooked her left pinky with his. The corner of her mouth turned upward. "This is crazy."

"I know."

"You have a plan?"

"Of course," he said. But he didn't. Running had become his default reaction. He'd mastered the art of avoiding suspicion, of cutting losses and sneaking away before things came to a head. With no one to protect but himself and an ability that provided plenty of second chances, he'd always stayed just beyond Annamaria's reach. Now other people were in danger—people he cared about. And he couldn't risk using his ability in front of Clyde.

Healing a stranger was much easier than protecting someone he knew. It had taken every ounce of courage he possessed to kill one of the assassins shooting at Marisa. He didn't want to think about what he'd do if he needed to pull that same trigger on his own sister.

He reached into his back pocket and brought out his new ID—a Tennessee driver's license that looked like the real thing. He read the name: Dirk Henderson. It sounded normal enough. But the picture showed the face of a man who harbored a secret fear. He noted the scar on his cheek, his easiest identifier. One touch and he could wipe it away. Maybe one day he would, but not on this trip.

Clyde pointed at the ID. "How do you like it?"

Luke didn't respond.

"Told you my guy was good." Clyde pulled at the cuffs of his new button-down shirt. He'd insisted on buying clothes while they waited for his contact to print and laminate the ID. "He caters mostly to high school kids, but he's also a huge conspiracy theorist. His interviews were my most watched videos—until I met your father."

Luke couldn't believe people made a living doing what Clyde did. He might have respected it if the videos had struck a tone of either serious journalism or frivolous entertainment, but Clyde seemed to conflate the two while adding a heavy dose of sarcasm. Luke still wouldn't have cared as long as no one else took the videos seriously. But the numbers proved they did. His family secret had been placed at the fingertips of anyone with an internet connection. Part of him was thankful his sister had found a way to disable the channel.

Clyde leaned into Luke's space. "So everything Nicholas said to me, everything about you and your sister. That was all bullshit?"

"My father made his living by lying to people like you."

"So no paranormal powers?"

"Sorry to disappoint."

Clyde edged closer, so close Luke could see tiny patches of stubble on the man's face. "Then why did he want me to find you?"

Luke knew why. His father was never difficult to figure out. But he wasn't about to tell Clyde the truth. "The man knew he didn't have long. Maybe he wanted to apologize and make amends."

"For leaving you?"

"For giving him and his sister a crappy childhood," Marisa said. "They were abandoned as young teenagers. No money, no clothes. No place to call home. *Nada.* Imagine what that does to a kid."

Clyde closed his eyes slowly, then flashed them open, like he'd wished Marisa would disappear. "I'm trying to figure out why your dad seemed so scared of your sister."

"Remember what happened in your apartment?" Luke said.

"But Nicholas never mentioned anything about armed men." Clyde raised a finger. "He claimed Annamaria had killed him by herself."

"Did I mention my dad was a liar?"

Clyde squared his shoulders and stared at them both. "I've done enough interviews to know when someone is truly scared or just faking. Nicholas nearly jumped out of his skin when I mentioned trying to find Annamaria. I saw it in his eyes." He narrowed in on Luke. "And I see it in yours, each time I ask about her."

"She's dangerous," Luke said.

"Dangerous how?"

"Any way you can imagine."

"What about you?" Clyde's pupils sparkled in the cabin lights. "Are you dangerous, too?"

Luke noticed a subtle change in Clyde's pitch, like a performer on a stage. He glanced into Clyde's lap. The back side of the new smartphone was balanced on Clyde's knee, its camera aimed directly at Luke's face.

"What are you doing?"

"Nothing."

Luke snatched the phone from Clyde's hand. He checked the screen. The camera was in video mode. A timer near the top ticked forward, showing two minutes and counting. He pressed the stop button and slammed the phone against the armrest. "You're recording me?"

"*¡Que largo!*" Marisa said.

The color drained from Clyde's face. "I didn't mean it."

Marisa leaned across Luke's seat. "Are you saying you did it by accident?"

"No. Yes—I mean…" Clyde glanced down the aisle like he was searching for the nearest exit. "It's an automatic reaction when I smell a good story."

"Recording people without their knowledge?"

"It's legal in many states."

Luke turned to Marisa. "We should've left him in Memphis."

"Okay, I'm sorry." Clyde showed his hands like a poker player caught cheating. "You guys saved my life. I shouldn't have done that. It was dishonest and wrong."

Luke wondered why he ever agreed to let Clyde buy their tickets. They could never trust this guy. That much was clear. The man had just escaped two attempts on his life, and all he cared about was creating another viral video. Anything he heard, anything he saw, was sure to find its way online and into public view. Finding and stopping Annamaria was already a nearly impossible challenge. Doing it with the world watching would be even tougher.

Marisa still hadn't broken eye contact with Clyde. Her top lip rose high enough to show the tips of her incisors. Clyde's knees bounced nervously. A trickle of sweat worked its way from his temple to the edge of his jaw. His fingers flexed and relaxed like they were searching for a button to push. "I'm really sorry. It won't happen again."

Luke dimmed the screen on Clyde's phone, then slipped it into his back pocket. "I believe you."

No one talked for the next hour. Dozens of scenarios about what awaited in El Paso ran through his mind. He weighed the risks of each tactic and evaluated its chances. Then he settled on a plan, one he was sure Paloma and Marisa would approve.

Marisa's head rested against the cabin wall. Her eyes were closed. He touched her arm. Her skin still felt warm, but it didn't radiate heat like when she was angry. The dark, spiral curls that lay across her face highlighted the smoothness of her complexion. She was beautiful, but he doubted she'd ever looked in a mirror long enough to notice. He admired so many things about her—the way she cursed in Spanish; the calm, loving tone she used when she first spoke to Harry; the way she handled a gun; and how she'd grabbed his attention in the skywalk at MD Anderson. A grin spread across his face. He'd never met anyone who reacted as passionately as Marisa.

Not true, he reminded himself. Annamaria's image flashed into his mind—a younger, only slightly less dangerous version of his sister. The scar he'd given her vanished then reappeared like a scene in a psychedelic horror movie. He shook the image out of his head and tried to think about something else.

Twenty minutes later they landed in El Paso. Luke, Marisa, and Clyde marched through the baggage claim. Clyde paused to pick up his checked bag, then Luke led the way toward the rental car stations.

"Which company are we using?" Clyde said.

"The cheapest."

"I have a coupon for the one on the end." Clyde dug through his wallet and produced a yellow-and-white discount card. "Can you guys wait in line while I use the restroom?"

Marisa rolled her eyes.

"Fine," Luke said. "We'll meet you there."

Clyde handed Luke the card and strutted down a hall, his luggage in tow. Luke watched until the man pushed against a metal door and disappeared into the men's room.

"I need to go, too," Marisa said.

"Not now." Luke dropped the discount card and grabbed her wrist. "Let's leave before he gets back."

"We're ditching him?"

Luke touched the back pocket of his jeans. Clyde's phone rested safely inside. "We can't trust him, and we don't need him anymore."

"Isn't he in danger?"

"Only if he posts another video. Annamaria's after Harry and Paloma. And us."

Marisa glanced toward the men's room. "Okay. Let's go."

CHAPTER 32

Luke squinted through the sunlight pouring into the back of the cab. Apparently he and Marisa had found the only taxi in El Paso that didn't have tinted windows. The desert sun did its best to scorch every surface, but it didn't bother him at all. He closed his eyes and welcomed the sensation. This was a dry heat, not the humid, sweat-inducing kind that dominated the Gulf Coast.

The taxi driver stopped in front of a small restaurant. "Chico's Tacos," he said, then indicated the fare.

Luke handed the man a twenty. Marisa climbed out of the cab. He rushed past her, toward the entrance a few feet away. He pulled open the glass door and waved her inside.

"Is this your idea of fine dining?" she said.

"Give it a chance."

"When are we meeting Paloma?"

"Soon."

He'd always felt safe in El Paso, partially because his dark hair and olive skin helped him pass as a local. He and Marisa blended in perfectly with the other customers. Aside from one husky, red-haired man sitting in a corner, everyone looked like cousins.

Still, he studied each face, looking for signs of recognition. Now that his sister knew about Harry, his safe haven city was no longer safe. Annamaria's men could be anywhere, staking out Paloma's house, waiting for them to make a move. That was why he'd called before booking the flight to El Paso. He needed to give Paloma time to gather their things and to make sure she wasn't followed.

The restaurant seemed clear. No one gave them more than a casual glance. He and Marisa approached the counter. Luke ordered for them both. They carried their trays to a table on the far side of the restaurant and sat opposite each other. Large exterior windows offered excellent views in case Paloma and Harry arrived while they were eating. An ancient-looking tube television sat on a stand high in one corner. On the screen a local weatherman pointed at different parts of Texas and New Mexico while sporting a smile that must have cost a fortune.

Luke watched Marisa stare at her food. Cradled inside a small paper bowl were four finger-sized tacos. A pool of watery tomato sauce covered them. Piles of shredded yellow cheese rested on top.

"What exactly did you order?" she said.

"Chico's Tacos."

"People eat this?"

"Look around."

The same paper bowls decorated each table, each tray. A few customers broke apart their tacos with a fork. Most simply grabbed one with their fingers and dipped an end into a cup of green salsa before taking a bite.

Marisa reached for a fork. "I guess it can't be that bad."

Luke scanned the windows and checked the parking lot. Nothing. He noted the time—4:35 P.M. Five minutes late. Paloma was usually on time, but Harry could be a handful when he wanted to. Luke decided he'd wait ten minutes. After then he'd need to make a decision.

The sounds coming from Marisa's side of the table made him smile. She attacked her tacos with her fork, cutting and stabbing, then dipping pieces of the crispy rolls into the tomato sauce, then in the salsa, then back into the sauce before shoveling them into her mouth. She communicated only in grunts. Her hands and mouth never stopped moving until she reached the bottom of the paper bowl.

"Good?" he said.

"*Dios mío.* These are the best tacos ever."

"Welcome to El Paso."

A hand pressed against the back of his shoulder. "That's my line, *mi'jo.*"

He turned. Paloma greeted him with a warm smile and open arms. She wore a fancy green dress and a hat that would make any churchgoing lady jealous. He stood and welcomed her embrace.

Harry wrapped his arms around Luke from behind. The boy had a stronger grip than he'd imagined. "Uncle Luke, we snuck up on you."

"How about that?" he said. "No one ever does that to me."

"We're sneaky." Harry offered a toothy grin. "Mama says we need to be very sneaky now."

Paloma twisted her lips. "We had a talk."

"Of course," Luke said.

Paloma and Harry greeted Marisa, each giving a hug and a kiss. Luke cleared the trays and motioned toward the exit. "Everyone ready?"

"We're expecting one more, no?" Paloma said.

"Change of plans."

They headed for the door, first Paloma and Marisa, then Luke, with Harry still attached to his hip. A tiny set of bells hanging from the door jingled.

Luke felt a tug on his sleeve. "Uncle Luke. That lady looks like you."

He turned. Harry pointed at the television in the corner. The image on the screen stole the heat from Luke's body.

Annamaria stood on a platform decorated with American flags. He noticed the same dark hair, the long aquiline nose of his mother, and the soft, brown cheeks that made her look so charming when she smiled. A banner across the bottom of the screen announced that vice presidential candidate Anna Varner had canceled a rally in Florida.

"Don't you think she looks like you?" Harry said.

Luke couldn't stop staring at the screen. Little Annamaria, his younger sister, the most dangerous person he'd ever known, vying to become the next vice president? The muscles in his legs tightened. He read the news banner again. This close to an election, a canceled rally could mean only one thing.

"Luke, you coming?" Marisa let go of the door and paced to his side. "What's wrong? Did you see something?"

"It's worse than we thought," he said.

"What do you mean?"

"She's on her way here. And she's going to kill us all."

CHAPTER 33

Clyde opened his new laptop, settled into one of the comfy chairs that decorated the lounge area of the coffee shop, and sipped from his Caramel Frappuccino. Things weren't so bad at the moment. A cute barista had winked at him when she delivered his drink. The shop's Wi-Fi signal remained strong and clear. His YouTube channel was back online and earning more views each second. *ShowMeClyde*'s temporary absence had only made him more popular, more enigmatic, more mysterious. More—that was what his subscribers demanded. And he'd give it to them, as soon as he figured out where the hell Luke and Marisa had gone.

Getting ditched at the airport might have depressed him if he hadn't immediately taken several cleansing breaths and focused on the positives. He was alive, for one. His credit cards still worked. His new laptop made him feel like his old self. And soon he'd become richer than anyone in Memphis not named Elvis.

Luke and Marisa had done him a favor by taking off without him. Traveling with the pair had proven to be a smothering experience. He needed space to operate, to plan, to hunt down the story he knew they were hiding.

He checked the wall behind him—nicely decorated shelves featuring paintings from local artists and a few books with titles he didn't recognize. Foot traffic inside the shop was minimal, no loud talkers in sight. He positioned the webcam at a flattering angle, checked his teeth in the preview window, and adjusted the microphone. There, he was all set. He clicked the mouse and started recording.

"Clyde here. I know you're wondering why the channel went dark. There's a good reason. I promise. Turns out Nicholas Gabor's daughter is real after all, and she doesn't want me to find her. I can't confirm Nicholas's story, but I can tell you she's every bit as dangerous as he claimed. People who work for her broke into my home last night. They stole my files and hacked my account. Unfortunately, I wasn't there to stop them."

He glanced toward the counter, hoping the barista was watching his performance. She wasn't. He straightened his back and projected his voice even louder. "Early this morning they returned, this time with guns. Apparently Annamaria is a powerful woman. She wants me silenced. But I refuse to be quiet. The story of the Gabor family must be told."

The barista was definitely looking now. She covered her mouth and leaned toward her female coworker. Maybe she had finally put his name together with his voice.

He focused on the webcam again. "This time when her men came, I was ready."

A thought struck him. He'd better make this point clear. Otherwise his return to Memphis might not go as smoothly as he hoped. "To any members of law enforcement watching, this is not an admission of guilt. What I did was an act of self-defense. The dead man in my living room made multiple attempts to end my life. I had no choice but to shoot him."

Other patrons had taken notice now. Several stared in his direction, but no one approached. Surely they knew not to interrupt a professional at work.

"Later that day I tracked down Nicholas Gabor's son—Lucian the Healer. He's a real person, too. Turns out he had seen my videos, but not all of them. He came to Memphis to find his dad. Maybe he wanted to heal his father. Maybe he wanted to say goodbye. He wouldn't stay long enough to tell me."

A small crowd had gathered, still silent but rapt with attention. Why hadn't he thought of doing this in public before? He offered them a wink. "Once Lucian discovered his father had died, he left the city. He claimed his sister, Annamaria, was after him and anyone who helped him. Does he possess the healing power Nicholas described?" He rubbed his shoulder, which still ached from what might have been a gunshot wound. "I still don't have solid proof, but I suspect he's the real deal. I know you're counting on me to find out, and I won't let you down."

The cute barista joined the crowd. She wasn't smiling, but she was staring. That meant there was hope. He drew in a large breath. "I can't tell you where I am, but I'm busy tracking Annamaria and Lucian Gabor. They're both after the same thing now. One wants to kill, one wants to protect. It's a matter of life and death. And that life belongs to the third sibling in the Gabor family—a thirteen-year-old boy named Harry."

A few people shook their heads and left. The barista remained. She folded her arms but stayed quiet.

"Here's my promise to you, my dear fans. I'll find them. I'll expose their secrets. And I'll document what happens to this innocent child caught in the middle." He placed his hand over his heart and forced his eyebrows together. "May God protect him."

He ended the recording, convinced it was one of his best. No editing necessary. The upload would be available within the hour.

The barista walked toward him. This was it—a chance to use his new status to augment his personal life. He stood and grinned, waiting for her inevitable question.

"Sir, we need to ask you to leave."

CHAPTER 34

Luke rode shotgun while Paloma drove along Avenida de la Raza in downtown Juárez. Marisa and Harry peered out the side windows from the backseat. Harry provided a constant commentary on everything they passed, which helped distract Luke from the rush hour traffic.

"Look at those boys juggling bowling pins while the light stays red," Harry said. "Are they part of a circus?"

"*Sí. Circo Juárez,*" Paloma said. "The city can seem that way sometimes."

Crossing the border had been surprisingly easy. US Customs officials had waved them through. Paloma wasn't even asked to roll down her window. On the Mexico side, the inspection light had flashed green. The entire process unfolded exactly as Paloma had promised.

He suspected crossing back into El Paso might prove more difficult.

"How much longer?" Harry leaned into the space between the two front seats. His infectious grin kept Luke from noting this was the seventh time Harry had asked the question.

"We'll be there soon." Paloma handled the steering wheel of her Lincoln like it was an antique. Every movement was slow and measured, like she'd forgotten the urgency of their trip. Luke didn't let it bother him. After viewing the television screen at the restaurant, he had enough to worry about.

He'd assumed Annamaria had become rich enough to command a team of assassins, but he never thought she'd seek a position of power known only to a select few. Jumping into the national spotlight was risky for someone with her background. No wonder she'd killed both their parents and spent so much effort trying to find him. Anyone who might reveal her secret needed to be silenced. That included everyone riding in Paloma's car.

A quick internet search on Clyde's phone revealed the story of Anna Varner: born to missionaries who died mysteriously while overseas when she turned eighteen and educated at Harvard with the help of donor alumni scholarships, she forged an impressive career as a federal prosecutor—he couldn't imagine anyone challenging her in a courtroom—followed by a whirlwind romance with a US congressman who would become governor of California.

Unbelievable. His sister had served as first lady of California for the last seven years. He imagined her attending galas and balls, smiling for cameras, charming dignitaries, hosting business leaders and other government officials. No doubt more than a few had rubbed her the wrong way. How many had paid for those infractions with their lives?

Earlier this summer, Senator George Blair had picked Robert Varner as his vice presidential running mate. Luke remembered seeing the announcement on the front page of a newspaper one morning. Apparently Governor Varner had suffered a massive heart attack while on the campaign trail. The Wikipedia entry noted this was odd for a man in such reportedly good health. His sudden death had thrown the Blair campaign into chaos. Two weeks later the senator made the bold choice of asking Varner's widow to take his place. The decision vaulted the pair into the lead in the polls. Unless something major occurred, Anna Varner was set to become the next vice president.

Which meant she'd be one heartbeat away from the Oval Office.

"How long will we stay in Juárez?" Harry said. "I already miss my friends."

Paloma stared at Luke. So did Marisa. Both seemed like they wanted to ask the same question.

"Might be a while, Harry."

"Are there fun things to do here?" Harry said.

"Of course there are." Paloma smiled into the rearview mirror. "Your *primos* will be happy to show you around."

"What's a *primos*?"

"That means your cousins."

"Paco and Camila?" Harry bounced on his seat. "Ooh, I can't wait to see them again. We can play hide-and-go-seek."

Marisa tapped Paloma's shoulder. "Are these real cousins?"

"No," Paloma said. "They're the children of my friends, not family. She won't be able to track us there."

Luke smiled. Marisa was obviously worried Annamaria might find them. But driving to Juárez was their smartest choice. Disappearing into a foreign city with over a million people gave them a better chance at staying hidden.

They drove another twenty minutes through the dusty streets, past neighborhoods packed with tiny homes, past tire shops and bakeries and huge white buildings with dozens of loading docks. Every street looked flat, the sprawl seemingly never-ending. Only the mountains to the west broke the monotony.

Paloma pulled to the curb in front of a cinder block house painted the color of the sky. Two Hispanic children, neither of them older than ten, rushed toward the car before Paloma could stop the engine.

Harry burst out the rear door. "Hi, *primos*."

The boy and girl each gave Harry a high five. All three ran across the narrow strip of yard and into the house.

Luke and Marisa helped Paloma retrieve her bags from the trunk.

"You think this is safe?" Marisa said.

"As safe as we can manage, *mi'ja*."

Luke grabbed the largest bag and slung it over his shoulder. "I watched every turn, and I couldn't tell you how to get here."

"I don't want to put any more people in danger," Marisa said.

Paloma straightened her hat. "This *colonia* survived the drug wars by banding together. Everywhere you look, you're among family. *Andale*."

Two women with hair as white as Paloma's greeted them at the front door. The women spoke quickly in Spanish, so fast Luke couldn't guess at their meaning. Paloma introduced Marisa, who nodded and hugged her way inside. She seemed to understand everything the ladies said. A bright, warm smile emerged from her thin lips.

When it was his turn, he tried to listen carefully. Karina and Luna, apparently old friends of Paloma's, owned the house he'd entered. Luna's daughter, Rosana, also lived here, but she hadn't yet returned from the factory where she worked. Rosana was also the mother of Paco and Camila. The two kids' shrieks and giggles mixed with Harry's as they chased one another inside a small courtyard visible from the family room windows. The house looked overcrowded, with furniture and decorations packed against every surface, but at the same time, it felt comfortable and warm. Just like Paloma's home in El Paso.

The kids exited the courtyard and ran through the house toward the front door. Paloma raised her chin. "Harry, be careful in the streets. Watch for speeding cars."

"Okay, Mama."

Luke joined the adults at the kitchen table. Karina slid bowls of pasta and tomato sauce in front of the three of them. She smiled like she knew Luke couldn't understand her. "*Sopita*."

"*Gracias*." He dug into the pasta with a spoon, even though he wasn't hungry.

Paloma and her friends carried the conversation. Luke understood their tone more than their words. The women were catching up, discussing superficial topics, avoiding the reason for their sudden visit.

Marisa stayed quiet, too. She seemed engaged in a conversation with herself. He noticed her checking out the windows with her stare, glancing toward the doors every few seconds. The purse in her lap bulged—a Smith & Wesson 9mm Paloma had pulled from her glove box after they crossed into Juárez. Its identical twin rested in a holster under his jacket.

He hoped they'd never need to use them, but that seemed impossible now. Too much had happened. Too much was at stake.

Paloma nodded to her friends and turned toward Luke. "We've been invited to watch a wrestling match tomorrow."

"Animals or people?" he said.

She slapped his arm. "Don't be rude. It's *lucha libre*. The *niños* will love it."

He glanced at Marisa. She was busy inspecting her chewed fingernails.

"I don't know," he said.

"They only perform a couple of times each month," Paloma said. "I'm sure everything will be fine."

He thought about Harry—so young and innocent, with none of the childhood scars that marked his older siblings' past. Now that Annamaria knew about him, he could never live a normal life. He'd spend every moment like hunted prey, constantly watching over his shoulder, the same way Luke had spent the last twenty-five years. Maybe a wrestling match could serve as a good distraction—an opportunity to pretend they were normal people.

He drew his arms close to his sides and felt the firmness of the gun handle against his ribs. "Sure, why not?"

The children rushed through the house again. They huddled together on the family room couch. Paco and Harry poked at something Camila held firmly in her hands.

"I want to touch it," Harry said.

Camila pulled her hands closer to her chest.

"*Andale*. Give it, Camila." Paco grabbed at his sister's hands and pulled her off the couch. The young girl squealed in a pitch that hurt Luke's eardrums, but she didn't let go.

"That's enough," Paloma said.

Harry drew closer and wrapped his hands around Camila's wrists. He whispered into her ear. The girl stopped squealing, then calmly handed the item to Harry.

Luke marched into the family room and knelt on one knee. "What are you kids fighting about?"

Harry turned his back to everyone. Paco tapped the boy's shoulder. "Show him."

"I'll give it back. I promise," Luke said.

Harry sighed like Luke had asked him to clean his room. He turned and extended his open hands, presenting the object Camila had tried to hide—a shiny metal disc the size of a silver dollar. A company logo was etched on one side. The words and initials caused Luke's heart to skip a beat: *TrackMaster GPS*.

Marisa appeared over his shoulder. *"Dios mío."*

Luke stared into Harry's eyes. "Where did you find this?"

"It was stuck on Mama's car."

CHAPTER 35

Annamaria closed a manila folder labeled Horus Gabor and flung it into the backseat of Noordhoek's Kia. She'd memorized every word in the file stolen from Merritt's PI's office in Memphis. It held only two documents—a heavily obscured birth certificate and an adoption record—but both proved her intuition correct. Psychic Nick and psycho-mom had produced another child after they abandoned her. Nothing about that made sense. Why would the worst parents in history try to start another family? And why'd they give their new baby such a ridiculous name?

"Two more exits," Noordhoek said. His voice sounded weaker than usual, and his shoulders hung lower than at the start of their trip. No doubt he was tired from nine hours of driving, but it hadn't been a day at the spa for her, either.

She checked the clock on her phone. Six minutes after midnight—not an ideal time to conduct a home invasion, but some things couldn't wait. "Stay alert. We can't afford another mistake."

Surely things would go better this time, now that she was leading the assault. In and out in less than three minutes. She could silence all remaining threats and return to the campaign before sunrise. Noordhoek and her team in Sacramento could handle the cleanup while she focused on her future.

Part of her knew it wouldn't be that easy, especially if Lucian had rushed here to protect his baby brother. The condition of the adoption papers suggested he was involved. He'd managed to conceal his own identity for years, just like every other member of the Gabor family. And he'd rightly assumed when she learned of the boy's existence she'd want him dead. Shielding another Gabor from her probably seemed like a noble task to Lucian—his sacred duty to continue the fucked-up tradition started by their parents.

Noordhoek exited the freeway and turned left. He drove three blocks then pulled to the curb in front of a convenience store. A man walked toward the car wearing a brightly colored baseball cap and a dark suit. He waved, and Noordhoek pressed the automatic door locks. "This is our guy."

"You sure?" she said.

"He's the one your brother shot in Port Arthur."

Of course, the newbie. She'd named him Franklin when she hired him. No particular reason. He looked like a typical white millennial whose ancestors had probably arrived on the *Mayflower*.

Franklin hopped into the backseat. "Cool ride. How was your trip?"

"Do we have them?"

"Yes and no." He reached into his front pocket and produced a mobile phone. "I followed your directions to the word. 'Watch, but don't engage.' I even went a step further in case they tried to run." He swiped the phone screen and gave it a few taps. "I clipped a GPS signal on the adoptive mother's vehicle. Good thing I did, because an hour later the mother and the boy packed the trunk and bolted."

Annamaria shivered. *The boy.* Hearing those words somehow made him seem more real. Horus, her baby brother, the spawn of the two most evil people she'd ever known. "Where'd they go?"

"First they stopped at a local restaurant. They picked up your brother and the nurse. Then they drove toward the border."

Lucian, of course. She knew him so well. "You didn't follow?"

Franklin's eyes grew large. "Figured I'd better wait for you. Besides, we still have the GPS signal." He held out his phone like it was a trophy. "With this app, we can easily track them."

Annamaria snatched the phone from his hand. "Assuming they don't figure it out."

"It's an old woman and her kid."

"And my brother," she said. "He's good at staying on the run." She looked the newbie up and down. "And he knows how to use a pistol."

Franklin's face turned red. He pressed his lips together.

She glanced at Noordhoek. He stared straight ahead like he hadn't heard a word of her conversation. At least one of her employees knew how to behave.

"How do you work this thing?" she said.

"Just like a regular GPS app, but with a bonus. We're the blue dot. They're the red." Franklin relaxed into the backseat like he'd done something important. "Last I checked they were just across the border in Juárez."

Annamaria dug into her purse and retrieved a disposable wipe. She cleaned the touchscreen several times—no telling where this rookie had stuck his dirty fingers—then dried it with her sleeve.

A blue dot flashed in the middle of the screen. Only the surrounding streets showed on the display. She zoomed out. The Mexican border came into view. She panned south, surveying the tangle of narrow streets and wide avenues. No red dot anywhere.

She zoomed out again. The entire city filled the screen. Mountains dominated the west and forced the city sprawl to the east. Thousands of streets, and probably millions of people, slept under this satellite view.

But no fucking red dot.

She zoomed out again. Then again. Panned south along the only marked road on the map. Finally a red dot flashed along the line that marked the highway, miles into the dark desert, halfway between Juárez and the city of Chihuahua.

She threw Franklin's phone into the backseat. "You're an idiot."

"What?"

"They're on the move. And at least an hour ahead of us." She turned to Noordhoek. "Any issues with crossing the border?"

"Nothing a few dollars can't solve."

She reached into her purse, drew out her stuffed bear, and inspected the seam she'd stitched earlier. Not bad for someone whose mother never taught her to sew. She gave it a squeeze—but not as tightly this time. Firm, yet measured.

Noordhoek stared at the tiny bear like it bore a radiation warning sticker. She covered it with her hands. "What are we waiting for? Let's go."

CHAPTER 36

Darkness had swallowed the desert, except for where the pathetic twin headlight beams projected from Noordhoek's Kia onto the highway. Newbie Franklin snored in the backseat, testifying with each inhalation to his utter uselessness. Noordhoek drove with both hands on the wheel, his gaze steady, eyes alert, ready to obey Annamaria's orders no matter how big or small. Yet somehow even he managed to grate on her nerves.

She couldn't believe she'd spent most of the night tracking her brothers through a remote region of Mexico in a car painted the same color as the national fruit. Her muscles ached, even the ones in her fingers. She flexed and relaxed each digit. It didn't help. Each tiny movement brought new twinges of pain. She'd had enough of sitting in this car, of riding through this dirty, desolate country.

The mobile phone with the GPS tracker app rested in a cup holder between the front seats. She reached for it—and groaned.

A pleasant surprise flashed on the screen. She punched Noordhoek's arm. "Two miles and closing."

Noordhoek's facial muscles twitched. If she didn't know better, she'd have sworn he'd tried to smile.

She turned toward the backseat and slapped Franklin's knee. "Wake up. We're in range."

The newbie startled awake. His hand reached for the holster at his side. Nice reflexes. Maybe he'd prove useful after all.

She focused her attention forward. The road, a four-lane divided highway with more bumps and cracks than Senator Blair's face, stretched well beyond the reach of their puny headlights. Traffic was extremely light, and why wouldn't it be at three A.M.? No casual drivers operated this early, only those with a specific purpose.

Like hunting down the last people on earth with the power to ruin your life.

She didn't blame Lucian for taking everyone on the run. Crossing into Mexico was the smartest move he'd made in years. She wondered why he hadn't tried it sooner. The internet knew no borders, but most Americans didn't care about what happened in foreign countries. The farther he ran, the less interest his ability would generate back home, and the less likely she'd find him. For years she'd wondered why he stayed in the southern US, never venturing more than a few states away from Texas.

Now she knew.

Annamaria leaned toward Noordhoek and glanced at the speedometer. No need to speak. His foot pressed harder on the accelerator, and their speed jumped ten miles per hour.

How pathetic that her older brother, the one who'd proven so inept at protecting her, had chosen to devote his life to helping other people and hiding their youngest sibling from her. Like somehow *she* was the problem, a danger that needed guarding against.

Psychic Nick's words came back to her now, his prediction of a sudden change, a final judgment that would forever affect her future. She thought about the name of the orphan-turned-god who appeared on the final card—Horus. Was Psychic Nick trying to warn about her true enemy? Or was he just going with the cards, guessing like he always seemed to, playing on her internal fears and taking cues from her body language? She grabbed her half-empty water bottle and drained it in four gulps. Dammit, she still tasted him on the back of her tongue.

Red taillights appeared in the distance. She checked the mobile phone. Both dots flashed on top of each other.

"This is it," she said.

The taillights drew closer. Noordhoek slowed when the vehicle fell within range of the Kia's headlights. She squinted to make out the details.

The car was an early 2000s model sedan with Texas plates. Brown dust coated what looked like a white exterior. Four head-shaped silhouettes rode inside. Two in the front, two in the rear. Each rider appeared awake and alert. One silhouette in the backseat sat several inches lower than the others.

"Franklin, can you verify?" she said.

The young assassin leaned forward. "Same color, same body type. Must be them." His sleepy breath spilled across Annamaria's shoulder. Her nose caught a whiff of it. She nearly threw up.

"Should we stop them or follow?" Noordhoek said.

Annamaria stared at the smaller shadow in the backseat and pulled her hands into fists. "Just wreck them."

Noordhoek pressed the accelerator. The Kia's engine revved. He pulled into the next lane, edged the front fender close to the sedan's back quarter panel.

"You sure?" he said.

"Do it."

Noordhoek turned the steering wheel to the right. Their vehicle clipped the sedan's back bumper and caused it to fishtail. He stepped on the brakes. The sedan worked to regain control, but it was moving too fast. It spun a complete revolution and skidded off the shoulder, kicking up a huge cloud of dirt.

Annamaria tried to peer through the haze, but the Kia's headlights only made it worse. Noordhoek and Franklin threw open their doors and ran forward, pistols drawn. Both men charged into the dust cloud and disappeared.

She needed to see this, needed to make sure. The Kia's door caught when she pulled the handle. She kicked it open and sprinted toward the wrecked car.

A slight breeze blew the dust cloud away. The sedan rested in a barren, rocky ditch. All four wheels were still on the ground. Its headlights remained on. Noordhoek stood in a shooting stance near the driver's side window. Franklin covered the passenger side.

Someone inside the sedan screamed.

Annamaria strode past Noordhoek and stopped two feet from the driver's side window. A man cowered inside. His hands pressed against his large forehead—as if they could somehow stop bullets or the power of her touch. His skin was darker than hers, his body soft and pudgy. Not her brother. She looked past him. A large Hispanic woman filled the passenger seat, her index finger drawing an imaginary cross over her chest.

Annamaria glanced at Noordhoek. He shook his head.

She moved to the backseat. Another woman sat behind the driver—older, thinner, more frail. She held a handkerchief to her face, her entire body trembling. The woman drew back as Annamaria leaned close. A string of Spanish passed her lips, fast and desperate and completely unintelligible. Annamaria rolled her eyes. Lucian had definitely discovered the GPS device.

A fourth person's head rose into view. A young Hispanic girl with dark, curly hair sat up in the old woman's lap. Her brown eyes gazed at Annamaria—no fear behind them, only wonder.

The old woman tried to pull the girl back, but she held firm. Her mouth fell open, but she didn't make a sound.

Annamaria edged closer until her breath blew fog on the glass. The little girl never flinched, never moved. Like she'd been hypnotized by the encounter.

A metal click signaled Noordhoek was ready. Annamaria backed away. He stepped forward, his pistol aimed at the driver's head. One word from her and he and Franklin would execute them all, in order of threat level, from highest to lowest. Each passenger would receive two rounds. The little girl would die last.

The cries from the sedan fell silent. No one moved while Annamaria pondered her decision. She scratched the top of her wig. Her gut told her these people couldn't recognize her, but she needed to be sure.

Franklin broke the silence. "What are we doing?" He panned with his gun across the entire length of the sedan.

"Leave them," she said.

"But they saw our faces."

Annamaria stared into the backseat again. The girl placed her tiny palms against the glass.

"They won't talk."

"How do we know?" Franklin chambered the round in his pistol and aimed at the woman in the front passenger seat.

"I said leave them."

Noordhoek holstered his weapon. Franklin waited a few moments, then shook his head and broke his stance.

Annamaria turned and paced up the slope of the ditch. These people weren't threats. Someone—probably a person other than Lucian—had transferred the GPS device to their car without their knowledge. By the time they flagged down a tow truck, she and her men would be long gone.

Her brother had won this round. But the battle wasn't over. She still had options.

When she reached the highway shoulder, a shot rang out behind her.

She turned in time to hear the second shot, to see a flash from the barrel of Franklin's pistol. The fucker had shot the woman in the front passenger seat. Annamaria raced to the bottom of the ditch.

Total chaos erupted inside the car. Everyone screamed. The driver reached for his seat belt. The young girl in the backseat locked into an embrace with the older woman. Noordhoek drew his weapon but pointed it toward the ground. He looked at Annamaria. She shook her head.

Franklin rounded the front of the sedan and approached the driver's side window. The man inside scrambled across the dead woman and opened the passenger door.

"They would talk," Franklin said. "We have no choice." He sprinted back toward the passenger side. The driver climbed out of the car and threw his hands up. *"No dispáren. Mi familia—"*

Franklin shot the man in the chest. The blast echoed in Annamaria's ears. The driver fell and disappeared behind the sedan. Franklin stepped forward, pointed his weapon, and fired again.

Shrieks erupted from the woman and the girl inside the car. Annamaria couldn't look away. The little girl, who moments earlier seemed so calm in the face of danger, now wore a look of terror Annamaria could never forget. Her fingers pressed into the flesh of the old woman's back. Tears ran down her cheeks. She blinked, then her eyes locked onto Annamaria's.

"Franklin." Annamaria charged around the back of the sedan to where the newbie was standing. The driver's body lay sprawled across the sand between them. She acted like it wasn't there. "You were right. I don't know what I was thinking."

His finger moved away from the trigger, and his shoulders relaxed. "No problem. Want me to finish this?"

"In a minute." She edged closer and brought her lips close to his ear. She placed a hand on his shoulder. Extended her finger until it touched his bare neck.

She blinked. "Quadriplegia."

Franklin's pistol hit the ground first. His body followed with a deadening thump. His legs tangled with those of the man he'd shot. His arms lay at either side. Annamaria picked up his gun and stepped over him, straddling his torso.

Franklin lifted his head and stared at the rest of his body. His neck muscles strained and reddened. The rest of him didn't move. "What did you do?"

She pointed the gun at his chest. "I told you to leave them."

Franklin's chest rose and fell rapidly, pumping out large breaths. But no amount of oxygen could save him. "They were gonna talk."

She fired. His suit coat rippled at the impact. The bullet entered just under his rib cage. He groaned but didn't move. Because the fucker couldn't.

"They won't talk. And neither will you."

Franklin opened his mouth to answer, but her next shot silenced him for good.

Everything went quiet. A brisk desert breeze blew a wisp of hair from her wig into her face. She pushed it away.

Noordhoek appeared at her side. He stared at the two bodies, then straightened to attention. "What now?"

"Keep an eye on these two." She pointed toward the car. "I'll be back."

Annamaria raced up the slope of the ditch, across the shoulder, all the way to Noordhoek's Kia. She placed the gun under her seat, grabbed her purse, and returned to the wrecked sedan before she could count to ten.

The woman and the girl hadn't moved. Noordhoek stood outside their window, his weapon drawn but not aimed.

Annamaria approached the window. The little girl pulled closer against the old woman's neck. The woman's eyes were closed, and her mouth formed soundless whispers.

Annamaria opened her purse and reached inside. She drew out the tiny bear and showed it to the little girl.

The girl raised her head and stared at the stuffed toy. She released her grip from the woman's neck and reached toward the bear. But the glass was in the way.

Annamaria opened the driver's door, stuck her hand inside, and offered the bear. The girl snatched it and held it under her chin, her fingers rubbing against its yellow fur.

"Let's go." Annamaria turned to Noordhoek. "These two are no threat."

Noordhoek nodded. "What about Franklin?"

"Sacramento can handle it. Find the GPS device. I'll meet you at the car."

Two minutes later, Noordhoek climbed into the driver's seat. He dropped the GPS device into the cup holder. "You're sure you want to leave them here?"

"She'll be fine," Annamaria said. "You'd be surprised how tough young girls can be."

He started the engine. "Where now?"

"Back to Juárez." She grabbed the mobile phone and opened the GPS app. "That's where my brothers are hiding."

CHAPTER 37

Luke watched in horror as a masked man raised Harry's body high above his head. The man's muscles bulged underneath his spandex jumpsuit while he turned a tight circle in the center of the wrestling ring. The man sneered at the crowd, which numbered less than a dozen. Harry screamed, then giggled. "Uncle Luke, are you watching?"

Luke couldn't look away. He knew the entire scene was fake, that Harry was probably safer in the arms of this professional wrestler than while sleeping in his own bed back in El Paso. But the visual disturbed him. According to Paloma's friends, *lucha libre* had grown more popular than football in Juárez, especially with the kids. It reflected the struggle of good versus evil—or evil versus evil—so many of the city's youth had witnessed during the recent cartel wars. But in these shows, no one died.

Paloma's friends had arranged access to this private practice session before the evening matches. Later tonight this large tent would host over two thousand screaming fans.

Luke understood the appeal, but the display made his stomach turn. He'd seen enough real violence to last a lifetime, much more than he hoped Harry would have to witness.

Marisa touched his shoulder. "Stop worrying. He's fine."

He cracked a faint smile, but he'd never stop worrying. Finding the GPS device on Paloma's car had guaranteed a sleepless night.

He and Marisa had taken turns standing guard while the rest of the house slept. Paloma's friend Karina had insisted on delivering the device to her male cousin, who promised to send it as far from Juárez as possible before disabling it. Luke had reluctantly agreed. But secretly he wondered if he'd placed other innocent people in danger.

The wrestler whispered in Harry's ear, then gently pushed him toward a set of ropes that surrounded the ring. Harry raced across the canvas floor, bounced against the ropes, then sprinted toward the masked man. He stuck out his arm as he passed. The wrestler reacted like he'd been slammed by a wrecking ball. His massive torso smacked against the mat with a resounding thud. The small crowd shouted their approval. Harry raised his arms and projected a wide grin.

"Pin him," Marisa said.

"*Si*, pin him, *mi'jo*," Paloma said.

Harry rushed to where the wrestler had fallen. He dropped to his knees and draped his chest and arms across the man's body. Another man dressed in a striped shirt pounded the mat three times. A bell rang. The crowd cheered. Paco and Camila ducked under the ropes and charged into the ring. They each grabbed one of Harry's arms and raised it.

"Way to go, Harry," Luke said. For the first time since crossing the border, he let his shoulders relax. Seeing his brother acting so carefree and uninhibited warmed his insides. Paloma had given Harry the kind of childhood Luke had always longed for—days filled with love and attention, a home where he was encouraged to express himself without judgment, a life where he hadn't been forced to sleep on the floors of dirty motel rooms or collect money from people who couldn't afford to lose it. Harry didn't bear those burdens, didn't know the intense feelings of unworthiness that coursed through Luke's veins even now. The boy held a decent chance at living a normal life. But not if Annamaria found them.

The wrestler waved the children into one corner of the ring. He reached into a black duffel bag and pulled out a set of masks identical to his own. The children cheered as he passed out the masks. Harry's voice carried the loudest. "Thank you, El Matador. You're the best."

Marisa leaned against Luke's shoulder and slid her arm around his waist. "He'll never forget this."

"I'm glad you're here to see it." He reached behind her back. His hand met her purse instead of her hips. The bulky shape of the pistol inside brought him back to reality. "We're not safe here."

"What do you mean? In this arena?"

"In this city."

She pivoted in front of him and blocked his view of the ring. "No one showed up last night. The GPS signal is long gone. There's no chance—"

"What if she finds another way?"

"Like what?"

"I don't know. Maybe she's tracking us, waiting for the perfect time to strike."

Marisa tapped the side of her purse. "Whenever that is, we'll be ready."

He noted the confidence in her voice, the blind faith that whatever his sister threw at them, she'd be prepared to handle. But Marisa didn't know Annamaria. He touched the scar on his cheek, ran his finger along the jagged edges of his skin.

"We need to do something," he said.

"We already did."

"No, I mean bigger. We need to stop her from going after anyone, not just us."

"Too late for that. She's running for vice president." Marisa glanced behind her, then refocused on his face. "And it looks like she'll win."

"Not if we expose her."

"What are you saying? We should call Merritt and tell him the truth?"

An image of Clyde flashed into Luke's mind—that snarky grin, those shifty eyes. "Maybe a mainstream reporter would be better."

"And what would you tell them? Anna Varner kills people by touch?" She grabbed his hand and rubbed her finger against his palm. "No one will believe you. And anyone who does will be putting their lives in danger by speaking out."

She was right. Deep down, Luke had always known he could never expose Annamaria's secret to the media. Mostly because the secret didn't belong to just her. Theirs was a shared ability, equal and opposite, just like his father had explained on the video. It'd be impossible to reveal one power to the world without exposing the other.

Marisa said, "What about the cops?"

"They'd never believe us, either." He stared at his own hand. "Then there's the situation we left in Memphis."

Marisa blinked like she'd seen a disturbing image. She lowered her chin, and her tone. "Doesn't leave many options."

He didn't want to admit what he was thinking, didn't want to bring the words to his lips. His solution to most problems involved healing—the exact opposite of his sister. What if the only way to stop her was to become like her?

A tug on his arm pulled his attention from Marisa. Harry stood next to him, a shiny red El Matador mask covering the boy's head. The eyeholes formed sharp points on both sides, but Harry's beautiful almond-shaped eyes belied the mask's angry expression. "Don't worry, Uncle Luke. I'll protect you."

"I know you will."

"I mean it." Harry spun in a circle with his arms held high. He flexed his muscles like the wrestler had moments ago. "I won't let your sister hurt anyone else. Her heart is black, like midnight."

Harry's words stung deep inside Luke's chest. How much had this boy overheard in the past few days? He placed his hands on Harry's shoulders. "You don't need to worry. I'm here, and I'm not leaving this time."

"So we're staying in Juárez?"

Luke turned to Marisa. Tears formed in the corners of her eyes, but she was smiling. "Yes, Harry. We'll stay here for a while."

Paloma appeared behind Harry. Her bright red lips tightened before she spoke. "Could you do a favor for an old woman?"

"What do you need?"

She opened her purse and retrieved a small sheet of paper. "For dinner tonight. I made a list."

Luke scanned the items. Over half the ingredients he couldn't even pronounce.

Marisa leaned forward. "No problem. Where's the nearest *mercado*?"

"Two blocks east. We passed it on the way here." Paloma pointed across the wrestling ring like it didn't exist. "I can drive everyone there, but the *niños* would make it impossible to shop."

"We can walk," Luke said.

"*Gracias, mi'jo.*" Paloma crossed her index finger behind her thumb, then made the sign of the cross over Luke's forehead. He remained still as she blessed him in Spanish. She moved to his lips, then to his chest. When she finished her recitation, she smiled. "Now you can go."

"Thanks, Paloma."

Harry pulled at the hole in the mask that outlined his mouth. "Maybe you can get stuff for *migas*, too? You ate mine last time. Remember?"

"You got it, El Matador."

CHAPTER 38

Clyde pulled his luggage into the expansive lobby of the Hotel Americano. His rubber wheels clicked as they crossed grout lines between the porcelain tiles. He couldn't believe how clean everything looked, how stylishly the hotel interior was furnished. Modern sofas decorated the lounge, and granite slabs topped the concierge's station. Striking Mayan artwork hung in every nook. The employees dressed in dark blue suits and wore name tags embossed in gold. Each one smiled no matter how long Clyde stared. If it weren't for the overt southwestern theme and the strong smell of chlorine bleach, he would've sworn he'd landed in Manhattan.

But this definitely wasn't Manhattan. Every street sign and billboard he'd noticed from the backseat of his taxi reminded him he was no longer in the United States. He couldn't read Spanish. The squiggly lines above certain letters and the upside-down punctuation marks struck him as unnecessary and confusing. Venturing into Mexico meant leaping out of his comfort zone. But he had no choice. Luke and the nurse—and probably the youngest Gabor sibling and his adoptive mother—had taken the same route into Juárez the night before.

Maybe they thought leaving the country would make it harder for Annamaria to find them. Maybe they were planning on driving all the way to South America to avoid the men with guns. Clyde ran his finger along the starched cuff of his new shirt and nodded. It didn't matter why they were running, or even where. As long as

Luke carried the phone he'd stolen on the airplane, his location would never stay a secret.

The female registration agent offered a smile when she handed Clyde his room keys. She raised a perfectly drawn eyebrow when he asked her to repeat his room number three times. Then her smile disappeared. She'd probably heard that line before. He rolled his bag toward the elevator. No worries. He didn't come all this way just to fraternize with the locals.

On his fourth try, the electronic lock on his room flashed green. He pushed the handle and swung the door open. Whoever designed the pristine hotel lobby had never set foot inside this room. A flower-print polyester comforter and two flat pillows covered a low-lying bed. A framed print of a dandelion painting was screwed into the wall above the dresser. The tile floor looked damp with condensation—or maybe something less sanitary. He didn't want to think about it. He heaved his bag onto the bed, retrieved his laptop, and carried it to the small desk in the corner.

The Wi-Fi directions were in Spanish, of course. But he'd conquered more difficult situations than this. He drew in a cleansing breath, blew it out. He hissed in another, then released it. There, all was better. He found the hotel portal web page and typed in the odd string of letters exactly as they appeared on the directions. A new page loaded so slowly he thought he could hear the individual bytes filtering through the laptop's wireless adapter.

A word flashed onto his screen—*¡Felicidades!* No idea what that meant. But the stacked bars in the corner of the display told him he was connected.

He checked his email first. Another three hundred new messages waited. He scanned the list of senders and opened one from an online advertising company with *New Payment* in the subject line. He read the first line, skipped to the summary, and nearly fell out of his chair.

Thirty-five thousand dollars—the largest amount he'd ever received in one installment. A film of sweat coated his forehead. He wiped it away and checked the number again, counting the spaces after the comma to make sure. No mistake, that was how much he'd earned. The funds had already been deposited into his checking account.

He paced in front of the curtained window, pumping his arms and silently cheering. Then he remembered where he was. Who cared if anyone heard him? He let out a yell that would've made a cheerleader envious. He didn't care. The money meant vindication, a personal redemption. Proof what he was doing was both important and popular. He'd regained everything the men with guns had taken, and recovered from the shot to his ego that came after being ditched at the airport.

No one would take away this feeling again. He'd learned from his mistakes, knew he needed to play it smarter this time. Everything about the Gabor siblings proved they valued secrecy and deception above all. Much of their story still lay hidden beneath layers of denials and half-truths.

He rubbed his shoulder, returned to the desk, and scrolled through the subject lines in his email inbox. His subscribers demanded answers. Someone needed to strip away this blanket of lies to determine once and for all if Luke and Annamaria held special powers or if Nicholas was lying. Why had Annamaria killed her father and tried to silence Clyde's YouTube channel? The woman obviously had something important to hide. So did Luke, and so did the adoptive mother of the boy they called Harry.

Finding answers would require a change in tactics. No more internet searches, no more witness interviews. He retrieved his new phone from his front pocket, then connected the charger to the outlet and watched the power bar fill with energy.

On his laptop he opened an app he'd downloaded in El Paso. A map of Juárez loaded on the screen—painfully slower than last time. When all the data had filled in, he formed his lips into a sneaky grin. A blue dot flashed in the center of the display, its location a mere three miles from Clyde's hotel.

He locked his fingers behind his head and leaned back in his chair. He watched the blue dot.

And waited.

CHAPTER 39

Luke grabbed a set of tongs and waved them over a bin filled with prickly cactus pads. Marisa opened a paper bag a merchant had handed her and placed a plastic liner inside.

"Pick the greenest ones," she said.

"How many?"

"At least five."

Luke shoveled the pieces of cactus into the bag. The name on the bin had thrown him off, like it had when Paloma gave him the list. *Nopales* sounded more like a city than a fruit or vegetable. Thankfully Marisa knew every item on the grocery list. Even better—she also knew when the merchants' prices were too high.

This outdoor market was buried deep inside the city, dozens of blocks south of the border. No need to post English translations here. Few tourists perused the outdoor kiosks that crowded into the narrow city streets, so the merchants didn't seem to cater to them. A handful of vendors offered souvenirs, costume jewelry, and cheap handmade toys, but most sold staples for everyday living—produce and spices, meats and fish, bread that smelled like it had just left the oven. The walking spaces between kiosks were narrow and crowded. Other customers edged into his personal space. He pressed his hand against his back pocket. Clyde's phone was still there.

Luke paid the merchant then turned to Marisa. "What's next?"

"That's it." She crumpled the list into a ball and dropped it into a wastebasket. "Ready to head home?"

"As if there's such a thing."

Marisa smirked like she was preparing to scold a patient. "Things will get better. They always do."

"Maybe for some."

She stared down a long street that bordered the market, then focused on him. "Sooner or later you'll realize there are people who care about you. Wherever those people are, that's your home." She drew close enough for him to smell the shampoo in her hair. "Maybe one day you'll see yourself the way others do. I see an extraordinary man, and not because you can heal broken bones."

He couldn't escape her magnetism, the invisible energy that pulled them together. And he didn't want to. The sights and sounds of the market dissipated, leaving only her presence. Every part of her was beautiful—the roundness of her nose, the golden flecks in her irises, the smoothness of her skin. She pursed her lips. He closed his eyes and leaned forward.

"*¡Mira!*"

The entire weight of her body slammed against him. She grabbed his shoulders and pushed, toppling his balance. He back-pedaled to recover. Grocery bags flew from his hands. Three steps later he fell to the ground. Marisa landed on top of him.

He raised his head. A flash of metallic green shot across his vision. Tires screeched. People screamed. A car smashed into the kiosk that held the *nopales* bin, scattering produce in all directions and splintering the wooden structure.

Marisa rolled away and helped him to his feet. "You okay?"

He stared at the wreckage. A small car idled where they'd been standing, its front end pushed in and its hood slightly bent. The air smelled like rubber and antifreeze. The windows were too dark to see inside. A small crowd formed around the car. Two bystanders edged closer, then drew back when the passenger door opened.

A woman climbed from the car—tall and lean with dark, curly hair and a stare that could burn through metal.

Annamaria.

His sister.

He hadn't seen her in twenty-five years, but she looked exactly the same. Behind that molten stare hid the same seventeen-year-old girl who thought the world owed her a favor.

She'd finally come to collect.

The impact must have caused a scratch on her forehead. A thin red line traced across her brow. A bystander moved forward and grabbed her elbow. She pushed the man away, never breaking eye contact with Luke.

Marisa tugged on his sleeve. "Let's go." Her words barely registered. He couldn't process anything with his little sister standing ten feet away.

The bystander moved closer again. He said something in Spanish and offered a small towel. Annamaria extended her arm and pressed her fingers against the man's throat.

"Don't," Luke said.

She stared at him, then blinked. "Hypoxia."

The man's eyes rolled backward. He fell away, collapsing into the arms of another bystander.

"*Luke,*" Marisa said.

The driver's door swung open. A tall man in a dark suit appeared—the same man Luke had seen in Merritt's apartment. Twin streams of blood ran from his nostrils to his chin. He raised his arm. A shiny black object shimmered in his hand.

The crowd screamed.

Luke's body jerked to the right so violently he thought another car had hit him. He regained his balance when the first gunshot sounded. He tried to reach for his own gun, then realized Marisa held a firm grip on his wrist. She pulled at him again. "Luke, we need to run."

Chaos surrounded them. Merchants and customers fled in every direction, screaming words he couldn't understand. He still couldn't believe his sister had found him. Her presence seemed to paralyze him. But he knew Marisa was right.

The sound of another gunshot spurred him into action. He followed Marisa deeper into the market.

CHAPTER 40

Annamaria charged down the street in the direction Lucian had fled, her steps powered by a rage buried so deep she'd forgotten its potency. She'd finally tracked down the brother she used to fight with, the one who should have protected her but instead had caused her deepest wound. Twenty-five years of effort had led to this moment. And still her big brother was too scared to face her.

The narrow street emptied into an intersection connecting to four other pedestrian-only streets. Kiosks lined each one as far as she could see. She glanced back the way she'd come. The distance seemed about right. Lucian must have run down one of these streets after Noordhoek started firing. But which one? She paused while trying to decide.

Locals zipped past in both directions, each looking as clueless as the man who'd tried to move between her and Lucian. They'd never seen anyone like her, never witnessed the ability she held in her fingertips. No wonder they were running in panic. Their only hope of escape lay in their ability to stay clear.

She checked each street again. No sign of Lucian. Noordhoek appeared by her side. The blood from his nose streaked down his shirt and tie. His attention shifted left and right, then settled on her.

She pointed toward a street on her left. "Check that way. We'll meet at the car."

Noordhoek sprinted away.

Annamaria ran the opposite direction down the widest of the four streets, past an abandoned section of kiosks that held beets, potatoes, and radishes. An old man stumbled into her way. She pushed him aside, sending him into an apple bin. The man shouted, *"¡Bruja!"* She stopped and turned. His knobbed finger pointed at her as he lay sprawled over a sea of apples. The old man had called her a witch. Maybe she should show the bastard what a true witch could do.

No. Her brother was still close. She darted down the street, through the heart of the market.

Sweat streamed down her face. The bulky kiosks and tight streets seemed to hold in the dense, warm air. She tore off her wig and threw it aside as she ran. It didn't matter if anyone recognized her. Sacramento could handle the fallout.

At the end of the street, she checked the sidewalk that bordered the market. No sign of her brother or the nurse. Several people had fled, but a few moved back toward the market, their necks craned in her direction. Faint screams penetrated the air, but not as many as before. A police siren sounded in the distance. Dammit, she was running out of time.

She rushed along the sidewalk, checking each face she passed, searching for that telltale scar and those dark puppy-dog eyes. Nothing. They must've run another way. She kicked a trail of dust into the air.

Screeching tires caused her to turn. Noordhoek's Kia rounded the corner, busted grill and all, engine revving, heading her direction. She approached the curb. He skidded to a stop beside her.

She jumped inside and pulled the door shut. "You find them?"

Noordhoek stared straight ahead. A deflated airbag rested on his lap. His chin and neck were stained with blood. "Nothing."

"Circle the market."

"We don't have time."

"I said—"

The police sirens intensified, overpowering her words. Blue lights flashed in the rearview mirror. She slapped the center console with her palm. "Okay, let's go."

The Kia accelerated into traffic, its engine whining at the abuse. Seconds later they were clear. Noordhoek stayed silent, but for the first time, he looked upset.

She leaned toward him. "Is your nose broken?"

"Probably."

Annamaria said nothing. Words couldn't fix this. The never-ending string of frustrations they'd suffered since crossing the border gnawed at her insides. Things were supposed to go better with her calling the shots. She should've been back in the US by now, her energy renewed after settling the score with her brother and silencing all remaining threats. But no. Everything had gone wrong once she'd decided to trust the GPS app the newbie had shown her. That fucking red dot. The little girl. The mess they'd left in the desert. All of it caused by a program coded into a smartphone.

She glanced at the cup holder. Empty. She checked the floorboard, then reached between her knees and retrieved Franklin's mobile. The screen was cracked but still working. She pushed down her window control button. Wind blasted her sweat-soaked hair. She held the phone outside the car and stared at the display one last time.

She wanted to crush it, to throw it into the path of an oncoming truck and watch it smash into a thousand pieces. But her fingers wouldn't let go. She and Noordhoek had retraced the path of the GPS signal using the history function on the app, hoping it would lead them to Lucian's safe house. Along the way they'd spotted her brother and the nurse shopping at an outdoor market. Dumb luck, it had to be. A frustrating near miss.

Or maybe an opportunity.

She pulled the phone back inside, then studied the history map behind the cracked screen. "We don't know where they are now, right?"

"Right."

"But we know where they're going."

The corner of Noordhoek's mouth twitched—not quite a smirk or even a smile. Just enough to prove he was human. "Which way?"

"Take the next left." She tucked the phone into her lap. Her fingers searched unconsciously for her bear. Of course she'd never touch it again. She needed to find a different way to cope.

Not to worry. Her fingers would be busy soon.

CHAPTER 41

Clyde's eyes snapped open when his chin hit the space bar on his laptop. The screen saver flashed bright blue, jarring his vision. He rubbed his jaw and looked around. He still sat alone at the hotel bar. A skinny bartender busied himself wiping tables at the other end of the room. Clyde's half-finished piña colada rested exactly where he'd left it. The ice and coconut shavings had dissolved into a milky mess. No telling how long he'd nodded off.

He stared at the laptop display. The blue dot remained near the center of the digital map, but it was moving. Block by block it changed directions, working in a pattern that reminded him of the *Pac-Man* video game. He crossed his arms and nodded.

Luke was on the run again.

No other explanation would fit. The dot moved faster than a person walked but slower than a car. Jumping from street to street, turning left then right, zigzagging through city blocks. No way the man was just window-shopping. Someone was after him.

Probably the men with guns.

Maybe Annamaria herself.

Clyde shut his laptop and slid a twenty under his drink. He raced back to his room, threw his laptop on the bed, and yanked his newest phone from the charger. He'd loaded the same app on his phone, though the dot was more difficult to see. Yep, still moving. He noted the charge he had left—53 percent. Jesus, did anything in Mexico work like it did in America?

He dashed through the lobby and out to the street. At the corner he drew a large breath—then coughed. The air smelled like rotten fish. He looked down and discovered a sewer drain cut into the curb under his feet.

Cars and motorcycles zoomed by in large convoys, their hot exhaust spilling onto his new clothes. Street signs looked hopelessly unreadable, the billboards tacky and confusing. He couldn't wait to get back to Memphis. At least back home he knew which areas to avoid. Juárez represented a minefield on his path toward success. But he'd never create his next viral video by sitting at a hotel bar.

Stealth and cunning had worked against him so far. Now they would become his biggest allies.

He checked the phone again. His targets were ten minutes away, tops. Maybe this time he'd hit the jackpot. Luke and Annamaria would be too focused on each other to notice his presence. How many millions of people would click a link to watch the final showdown between brother and sister? And what if one or both possessed a special power? A tingle danced across his skin while he calculated the potential payout.

A horn blared in his ear. He didn't let it sidetrack his train of thought. This story was about to explode. The fallout could spread in any number of directions. Annamaria owned a secret identity—that much was certain. And she was willing to kill to keep it that way. Luke didn't want to be exposed, either. But he wasn't necessarily a bad guy. Airport ditching aside, he and the nurse had probably saved Clyde's life in Memphis. Clyde rubbed his chin. What if he saw an opportunity to return the favor? Would he put down his camera to save a life? He hoped it wouldn't come to that. Cover the story. Don't become part of it. That was what the experts said.

He wasn't so sure about that.

Only one thing was certain. Clyde needed to be in the right position at the right time in order to capture the moment. He waited for a gap in traffic, then stepped off the curb and dashed across the street.

CHAPTER 42

Luke and Marisa raced through the streets like marathon runners who'd veered off course. They sprinted down city blocks, paused at intersections, voiced their best guesses, then sprinted again. Luke had lost his bearings five intersections ago. Marisa still appeared focused, so he followed her lead. He didn't want to have to decide where to go next.

"This way," Marisa said.

"Are we close?"

"Don't know. But we need to hurry." She darted down an alley between a laundromat and a nightclub.

He struggled to keep up. With every step, he imagined Annamaria touching another innocent bystander, whispering illnesses into their body just for spite. How many people had she killed? How many thousands more would she wipe out as vice president? With the kind of access the position afforded, no one would stand beyond her reach. Not one of her crimes would be tied to her. And no one could ever stop her.

Not even him.

He couldn't stop her back at the market. Too much history, too much guilt. She was his kryptonite, the thorn in his flesh. The only person in the world he could never heal.

He stumbled into Marisa and nearly toppled over her. When they regained their balance, he noticed her hand pressing into her side. "You okay?"

"Don't tell me you never get cramps," she said. "I need a second."

He scanned the block. Nothing looked familiar. He hadn't seen any of these buildings on his way to the wrestling arena. They were lost and probably running in circles when they needed to get back to Paloma's friends' house and pack the car. He peered toward the sun. "Which direction are we heading?"

"East, I think." Marisa patted her side like she'd fixed herself. "Just a few more blocks."

They headed across the street. A car wheeled around the corner, its engine roaring. A flash of green zoomed in front of them. They stopped. The side mirror nearly clipped Marisa's arm as the vehicle sped past. He grabbed her shoulders, pulling her back. They both watched as the car sped away.

"Wasn't them," she said.

"The next one could be. Let's go."

They crossed three more intersections. Finally he recognized a building, a tire shop named Muela's. Marisa seemed to notice it, too. She stepped up her pace.

"Harry might get upset when we tell him," he said.

"He can visit his *primos* again after this is over."

Luke wanted to believe her, but his mind seemed locked into one moment in time—the sound of metal smashing into wood, the predatory look on Annamaria's face when she climbed out of the car.

Time to get out of Juárez.

He ran along the edge of the street beside Marisa. Bright sunlight on the windshield of Paloma's sedan caught his attention. He sprinted past Marisa, his legs and chest burning. When he reached the front door, it was already open.

A girl's voice wailed from inside. He drew his gun and rushed into the house, down a dark hallway, and into the living room. That was where he found them—Camila, Paco, Luna, and Karina—all gathered around the couch with their backs turned.

"What happened?" he said.

Camila faced him. Tears streamed down her tiny cheeks. She extended her hand. He grabbed it. She pulled him forward, into the circle of people surrounding the couch.

Paloma lay on the worn cushions, her body an emaciated shell of its former self. Her lipstick was smudged, her cheeks sunken and ash gray. Her floral-pattern dress no longer seemed to fit her. When she saw Luke, she raised a skeletal arm and pointed.

"Paloma," he said.

Everyone standing nearby had their hands on her, caressing her forehead, rubbing her legs, her arms. He understood why. She looked so vulnerable and helpless, so in need of comfort. It was the only thing they could do.

Someone gasped behind him. Marisa approached and placed her hands on Paloma's shoulders. "Dios mío."

Paloma lifted her head. Her neck muscles strained against her skin. She opened her mouth, but nothing came out.

"Luke, help her," Marisa said.

He cupped Paloma's cheeks with his hands. This sweet, selfless woman who'd been his only friend for so many years now looked two decades older. Her skin felt like sandpaper. Air wheezed in short spurts through her tiny nose. Her eyes held a look of agony he'd seen only in terminal cancer patients.

He closed his eyes and concentrated.

Paloma's entire body was in distress. Every area cried out for attention. Her liver was shutting down. Her kidneys throbbed with pain. Every organ in her body, every muscle, each cell suffered from a severe lack of hydration. Her blood pressure plunged. Her heart weakened. The neurons in her brain misfired and sputtered. Soon she'd slip out of consciousness, and possibly out of this life.

He went to work, sending the energy through his fingers. Her muscles trembled at the sensation, but he held her still. The blood in her arteries responded first, soaking up his power as fast as he could send it. He shivered. Marisa must have noticed. Her slender arms wrapped around him from behind.

The sensation should have eased his anxiety, but it didn't. Paloma's body remained in a critical state. Her bloodstream couldn't provide hydration fast enough to reverse the effects of going without. Her organs continued to fail. Her muscles seized. Her face jerked away from his hands. She bolted upright and screamed.

A half dozen hands pulled at her, but she wouldn't lie down. Instead she grasped Luke's wrists. "She took Harry. Your sister, she took my little boy."

Her words stung like a gunshot to Luke's insides. His arms went numb, and he lost his balance. Marisa's arms kept him upright. He blinked away the dizziness. Paloma needed him, now more than ever. She needed the power flowing through his body, the power even he didn't fully understand.

"Paloma, please let me heal you."

The purple veins in her forehead pulsed. "You have to find him. Bring *mi'jo* back to me."

"I promise I will, but you need to lie down."

"Save my *mi'jo*." Gradually her muscles relaxed. Everyone eased her torso back onto the cushions. "Save my *mi'jo*."

He brushed his fingers over her face, forcing her eyelids closed. Then he went to work again.

Heat surged through his hands and into her body. The sensation became so intense he nearly let go. Paloma's eyelids fluttered. Her mouth twisted beyond her typical smirk. He closed his eyes and focused deeper. Her bloodstream carried his energy throughout her body, but her tissues couldn't absorb it. Something was blocking the process.

"It isn't working," Marisa said. "Something's wrong."

Karina and Luna prayed together in Spanish. Camila and Paco wailed.

Luke doubled his concentration. His hands felt like they were submerged in boiling water. Surely Paloma felt it, too. But he wouldn't let go. The power shot through him faster than ever. But Paloma's tissues remained frail and shriveled. Her heartbeat started to fade.

"Save my *mi'jo*."

Her voice came as a whisper, but it silenced the room.

"Come on, Paloma," Luke said. "Don't leave us."

But she was already gone. Her insides relaxed. Her lungs released their final breath. A cool sensation rushed over his skin, like something irreplaceable had left him.

Luke opened his eyes. The lifeless body before him looked nothing like the Paloma he'd known. But at least she looked at peace.

He crossed his pointer finger behind his thumb, like he'd seen her do a hundred times. Though he didn't know the words, he mimicked her actions the best he could, marking the sign of the cross over her forehead, lips, and chest. Maybe that would help her, wherever Paloma was now.

Other voices sounded in his periphery, but he blocked them out. Paloma was gone, killed by his little sister. He'd recognized Annamaria's handiwork long before Paloma spoke. Only his sister's ability could have withered a body so quickly.

Beads of sweat had gathered on his brow. He wiped them away. All the energy he'd expended, all the concentration he'd poured into healing her body, and it wasn't enough. Paloma had served as his lone source of stability for the last fifteen years. She was the one he'd turned to after he rescued Harry. The only person who accepted him as he was, no matter what he did or didn't do, no matter what he said or didn't say.

Now she was gone.

And Harry was missing.

Karina ushered the children into a bedroom. Her sister, Luna, approached the couch with a blue bedsheet. Marisa made the sign of the cross, touched her fingertips to Paloma's chest, and turned away. Luke allowed Luna to take his place. She spread the sheet over Paloma's body and gently tucked in the sides.

The entire house remained still. Everyone seemed to be grieving in their own quiet way. Luke wanted to scream. He wanted to scream so loudly Harry would hear him, wherever that precious boy might be, and know Uncle Luke was coming to rescue him. He wanted Annamaria to know he wouldn't rest until he repaid her unspeakable crime. He wanted to break something, to punch and maul and shoot and kill. Respect for Paloma's friends and their household was the only thing holding him back.

Karina returned from the bedroom alone. She motioned for Marisa and Luke to follow her into the dining room. Luna followed as well. Once everyone had grabbed a chair, Karina closed a partition that separated the room from the rest of the house. Luke sat next to Marisa and placed his fists on the bare wood. He tightened them until his fingers ached. Marisa covered one of them with her hand.

Karina and Luna looked like they'd witnessed a plane crash. They joined hands and whispered something in Spanish to each other.

"Tell us everything," Luke said.

Karina's facial muscles twitched, like it hurt to form each word. "After we returned from the *lucha libre*, we heard a bang on the door. The *niños* answered before we could stop them." She squeezed her eyes shut and shook her head.

Luna patted her sister's hand. "They came in quickly, the man and the woman. He had a gun. She didn't. But she was the boss. They made us gather in *la sala*. Then she asked who everyone was."

Luke's blood ran cold. He couldn't imagine how terrified they must have been.

"We tried to lie. Paloma tried to trick them into believing they entered the wrong *casa*. Then Harry spoke. Somehow he knew who the woman was." Luna's eyes grew wide. "He called her by her name—Annamaria. He wanted to defend his mama. But that only made the woman more upset."

"What did she do to him?" Luke said.

Karina lifted her chin like she wanted to answer, but the words never came.

Luna said, "She pushed him to say which of us was his mama. Made the man point his gun at each of us. He's a brave *niño*, little Harry. He stood up to her. Didn't tell her what she wanted to know. He protected his mama. But when the man put the gun to Harry's head, Paloma shouted his name."

"That's horrible," Marisa said.

Tears fell from Luna's eyes. She spoke like it was the only way to stop the flow. "Your sister grabbed Paloma by the neck and talked into her ear. I didn't hear what she said. But Paloma was never the same."

Luke didn't need to hear any more. He turned away, climbed out of his seat, and paced along one side of the room.

"They took Harry and left. Then we comforted Paloma," Karina said.

"I'm so sorry." Marisa leaned across the table and hugged each of the sisters.

"Which way did they go?" Luke said. "We need to track them."

"*No sé.*" Karina shook her head. She dug into her pants pocket and produced a mobile phone. The screen was cracked, but it lit up when she touched it. "The woman said to watch for a message—a message for you."

Luke nearly stepped out of his shoes rushing across the room. He grabbed the mobile phone and inspected the screen. One message waited:

Brother—do you like the present I left you???

He typed as quickly as his fingers could move:

Where did you take him?

A gray text balloon with three blinking dots formed beneath his words. Ten excruciating seconds passed. Then another message appeared:

Waited 25 yrs for this. You can wait, too. Bye…

He slammed the phone on the table. "We have to find him."

Marisa read the text messages. She tucked the phone into her pocket, then approached Luke and placed her hands in his. "Listen, we're going to save him—together. But we need to make a plan."

He wanted to believe her, but a rash of urgency gnawed at his insides. "She has him right now. One word and it's over."

"But she wants you. The only way to get to you is to keep him alive."

Her touch sent a calming sensation through his body. And her words helped him focus. "You're right. We need to think this through. Dig into that phone. Maybe there's something we can use."

"What about Paloma?"

"I'll call Dr. Cisneros," Karina said. "He will know what to do."

"We can't tell anyone the truth about this," Marisa said.

Karina wiped her cheek with a linen napkin. "I know."

CHAPTER 43

Annamaria pulled her little brother through a huge abandoned factory on the southeastern edge of the city. The little twerp had fought her at every turn since she'd forced him into Noordhoek's Kia. He'd done the opposite of everything she said—stay quiet, don't touch that, get out, go through this door. The entire process reminded her why she never wanted children.

Upon first glance she'd noted Harry's distinctive physical features. The child obviously possessed an extra chromosome. No surprise. This living genetic mistake represented the last of her parents' epic failures.

Noordhoek led the way across the factory floor. No lights, no fans. Afternoon sunlight streamed through the windows thirty feet above, but precious little filtered down to where they walked. Heavy shadows blanketed their path. Harry stopped at a workstation equipped with dozens of tiny tools and clamps used to assemble small electronics and grabbed one with his stubby fingers. She slapped his hand. "Give that to me."

Harry tucked his hands behind his back.

Oh, this kid. She could think of a thousand words she wanted to say while pressing her finger against his throat. But she needed to wait.

"Noordhoek," she said. "Come handle this."

Noordhoek strode toward the workstation and pointed his gun at Harry's forehead. "Give it up, son."

"I'm not afraid of you," Harry said.

"Bravery doesn't stop bullets."

The boy stared at Noordhoek like he was trying to control his mind. Either that or the kid had trouble processing Noordhoek's meaning. After a moment he produced the stolen item, a tiny screwdriver that looked more like a toothpick than a tool.

She pointed a finger at him. "No more stealing, or I'll make sure you can't use your arms."

Harry jutted out his chin. Annamaria noticed the same tiny dimple that had made her father's face appear so charming. As if she could've hated him more. "Let's go."

They negotiated the rest of the factory floor in silence. Near the back wall stood a painted steel staircase leading toward a second-story office. She headed upstairs without looking back. The boy was Noordhoek's problem now.

A steady, rhythmic thudding sound proved her wrong. The vibrations reverberated through the handrail, up her arm, into her core. She turned. Harry stomped on each tread as he climbed. He returned her glare with a smile, the kind only simple-minded people like him could produce. It only infuriated her more.

She felt no regret for killing the woman he believed was his mother. Judging from his behavior, she'd probably done the woman a favor by ending her misery. Annamaria couldn't imagine trying to raise a boy this difficult. Just getting through these next few hours would test her limits of restraint. The only solace came in knowing everything would soon be over.

She retrieved her phone and checked the screen. No new messages. She'd expected to find a dozen or more desperate texts from her brother begging her to reconsider. Maybe she'd taunt him with a few more messages. Maybe she'd play with his emotions one last time and profess a change of heart. She shook her head. Not even Lucian was that gullible. She unlocked the door to the office and strode inside.

The factory belonged to one of her late husband's business friends, someone who'd leveraged the governor's political influence to secure a manufacturing contract with a mobile phone company. Unfortunately, the factories in Juárez weren't immune to worker strikes like those in other Mexican cities. The factory had closed its doors six months ago. Annamaria still remembered the day the panicked friend had shared the news. An accusatory tone had flavored the man's voice, like somehow his problems were their fault.

One call to Sacramento had revealed the address and the lockbox combination. With a secluded location and a lookout point high above the labyrinthine floor, she couldn't have hoped for a better place to lure her big brother into a showdown.

The office interior held all the comforts and amenities the rest of the factory didn't: a leather sectional, two televisions, a refrigerator, a sink, and a private bathroom. She flipped the light switch. Nothing. She marched toward a large window on the outside wall and pulled the blinds. Angled sunlight reflected off the side of another factory building on the adjoining property. Its parking lot was also empty. No one else would witness the fireworks show her meeting with Lucian was bound to ignite.

Harry plopped himself on the couch and grabbed the remote. He pointed it toward one of the televisions and punched the buttons furiously. She opened her mouth to scold him but decided against it. The little idiot could figure it out for himself.

Noordhoek scanned the room, then joined her at the window. An electronic buzz sounded from inside his jacket. "Sacramento keeps calling. Blair's people are growing restless."

"Tell them I'll be back tomorrow," she said.

"They want to know what you're doing."

"Resting before the homestretch."

Noordhoek typed a few keystrokes into his phone and put it away. "I need to check for other entrances."

"Go," she said.

"Should I take him with me?"

Annamaria stared out the window, into the golden Juárez landscape. "I'll handle him. Just go."

Footsteps. A squeak of hinges. Then the sound of a door latch locking into place. They were alone now, she and her brother. The baby boy her parents had created after abandoning her in a motel room. A living reminder of the shittiest thing her parents had done to her.

She strode toward the couch. Its surface looked dirtier than the one in Psychic Nick's lobby. She sat on it anyway, a few inches from Harry. "We need to talk."

He threw the remote over her head. It smacked against the window and broke apart. The batteries rolled across the linoleum floor.

She smirked. This kid definitely shared her blood. "You know who I am?"

"You're my uncle Luke's sister."

"Don't call him that."

"Why not? His name is Luke."

"Don't call him uncle." Her mouth twitched when the word passed her lips. "You don't have an uncle. And you don't want one. Believe me."

"Yes, I do."

Her nails scraped across the leather armrest as she drew one hand into a fist. "If he's your uncle, then I must be your aunt, right?"

Harry said nothing.

"Relax, you're with family." She tapped her finger on his knee. "And family never hurts each other."

Harry shifted his legs away from her. "I saw what you did to Mama."

"What do you think I did?"

"You made her sick with your fingers. And your mouth."

Annamaria leaned in close. "She hid something from me."

"What was it?"

She waited until he closed his mouth. "You and your brother."

Tiny sparks flashed in his eyes. "Uncle Luke is my brother?"

"Yes."

Harry leaned back against the cushions and folded his arms. The gears in his head must have been turning at maximum speed. She expected him to cry, but instead the little shit grew a smile. "I have a brother."

"And a sister." She patted him on the head. "Let that sink in." She rose and walked back toward the window. In the distance, a huge rust-colored cloud rolled across the desert. The cloud grew as it moved, swallowing thorny bushes and power lines and anything else that stood in its path.

Harry's voice filtered into her ears. "My brother will come and save me."

She unlocked her phone and began to type.

"I'm counting on it."

CHAPTER 44

Luke ejected the magazine from the Smith & Wesson Paloma had given him. He checked the chamber, dry fired once, then set the gun aside. One by one he dislodged each round from the magazine and set them in a line on Luna's dining room table. Then he reloaded the weapon and the other spare magazines, ensuring everything fit perfectly.

His hands would never fit comfortably around something so deadly, but he touched it anyway. It was all he could think to do while Marisa explored the phone his sister had left behind.

"Any new messages?" he said.

Marisa shook her head. Her stare never left the lighted screen.

"Any clues?"

"Not many places to hide one." She bit her bottom lip. "No email accounts, no text messages except the ones you read earlier. No downloaded apps. There aren't any pictures or videos. She must have recently bought this, or else she wiped it."

"What about the location history?"

Marisa tapped the screen several times. "She must have turned it off."

A deep chill passed through his body, like he'd lost something more than just heat. Annamaria had outsmarted him again. She must have checked the location history on the GPS tracker they'd found on Paloma's car, which might have shown an extended stop in front of this house. After she lost them at the market, she'd headed straight here. He squeezed his eyes shut. His supposed quick thinking yesterday evening hadn't even bought them twenty-four hours of protection. Worse, it had cost him the life of his closest friend.

Now they had no choice but to wait for another message from Annamaria. Each excruciating second drained more of his hope his little brother hadn't been harmed.

Marisa laid the phone on the table. "Your sister is good at covering her tracks."

"She's been running longer than I have."

"What do you mean?"

Luke rested his hands flat on the table, on either side of his gun. "She disappeared when she was seventeen. After our parents left, the state placed us with a relative in North Carolina. For four years we lived what most people considered a normal life, but it seemed strange to us. We attended high school, made friends, and pretended the history with our parents had never happened."

"But your sister couldn't forget," Marisa said.

"She never forgot anything." He closed his eyes for a second. "We made a pact to hide our abilities, to blend in and not make any waves. But Annamaria was still upset. She never let anything go. Every time someone slighted her, that person would miss a few days from school. She was smart about it, and subtle. The diseases were never life threatening but often embarrassing."

"Embarrassing how?"

"She gave the prom queen a bad case of cold sores," he said. "A half dozen broke out across the poor girl's lips moments after Annamaria congratulated her."

"Aye, dios mío."

"I tried to minimize the damage when I could. I'd visit the people she cursed and try to heal them without them noticing. But often that proved impossible. The prom queen went into hiding for two weeks. She wouldn't show her face until she'd recovered."

"And no one suspected Annamaria?"

Luke slid the gun toward the edge of the table, out of his immediate vision. "Some people noticed she never expressed concern when a classmate got sick. More than a few suspected she wasn't as nice as she pretended. But no one ever guessed at the truth. How could they? She never left any evidence—only a whisper and a touch."

"She must have been a holy terror," Marisa said.

"Actually, most people liked her. She was pretty—and popular."

"Did she have a boyfriend?"

"She dated but not seriously," Luke said. "My sister never had much use for men."

Marisa leaned forward and checked the phone. She shook her head, then settled back into her chair. "Why did she run away?"

"That's a long story," Luke said.

"We have time."

Another chill passed through him. This one settled into his chest and lingered like a houseguest who'd overstayed his welcome. The same sensation crept into him each time he thought about the night his sister left.

"Annamaria tested out of the eighth grade, so we graduated high school the same year. We threw a small party the evening we received our diplomas. Uncle Jack—that's what we called him, though he was actually a distant cousin—spared no expense in celebrating. He served pulled pork shoulder with a vinegar barbecue sauce I can still taste. Everything was great until Uncle Jack stumbled into a table and knocked over the cake. I'd never seen him that drunk before. Neither had Annamaria. She shouted at him, and he shouted back. The party guests disappeared soon after."

"I bet that made her furious."

"She didn't care about the cake. But her uncle had embarrassed her. She waited until everyone had left, then confronted him in his bedroom. I heard screaming and decided to stay clear. Then it got quiet. So I ran to the door."

"What did she do?" Marisa said.

The chill in his chest surged through his bloodstream and spread to his fingers. He blew out an unsteady breath. No use denying what he'd seen. Telling the story differently wouldn't change what had happened.

"I wanted to blame it on the drinking or the late hour. But there's no excuse for what Uncle Jack did." Luke stared through the table like it wasn't there. The scene in Uncle Jack's bedroom flooded his senses. "When I opened the door, he was on top of her. His hand covered her mouth, and his belt was unbuckled. It clanged against the metal bedframe like an alarm bell no one would answer. Her screams were muffled. His grunts weren't. The bastard didn't even notice I'd come in."

Marisa's facial muscles tensed. "Tell me you stopped him."

He held his breath and pondered his next words. Maybe if Paloma hadn't died, maybe if Harry was still safe and playing in the next room, then he might have skirted the truth. But he knew Marisa was committed to staying by his side. She'd grab her gun and follow him whenever the phone vibrated with a new message. She'd risk her own life to save Harry's. So she deserved to know why Annamaria hated him.

Luke stared into her eyes. "I froze for a few seconds, maybe half a minute. I just stood there while he attacked my sister. I can't say why. Maybe I was scared or in shock. It doesn't matter—there's no excuse. Annamaria saw me. Our eyes locked. I'll never forget her expression. The terror, the absolute fear."

Marisa squirmed in her chair, but said nothing.

"Finally something clicked inside me, and I rushed across the room. I pulled Uncle Jack away. He immediately cinched his pants and chased after me. He kept shouting that I didn't understand, he was just trying to calm her. I knew it was bullshit. I didn't want to touch him. So I ran to my room."

"What about Annamaria?"

"We left her in his bedroom. I know, that sounds horrible. But I figured if he stayed focused on me, then she could get away. Uncle Jack was a big guy. Part of me thought he wanted to kill me for what I'd seen. Instead he knelt in front of my bed. His hands wrung against the folds of my comforter as he pleaded, 'You have to believe me, Lucian. Your sister was out of control.'"

"What a monster," Marisa said.

"I sat on my bed listening, but all I could think about was my sister. Uncle Jack started crying, blubbering between his words. He smelled like stale beer and vinegar. And he looked like a huge, sweaty mess. Words spilled from his lips, all jumbled together and mixed with inebriated logic. I listened for the sound of the front door closing, but it never came. Instead Annamaria appeared in the doorway."

"*Dios mío.*"

"Her makeup was smeared, her hair disheveled. The skin around her mouth looked raw. She stayed as silent as I'd been while Uncle Jack assaulted her. But she never froze. She crept up behind him and slapped her palms against his cheeks."

Marisa sat back in her chair.

"Uncle Jack never saw it coming. The curse exploded from her mouth like a shotgun: 'Brain hemorrhage.'

"He reached for her hands, but it was too late. Uncle Jack shrieked like someone had stabbed him. Deep blue veins bulged across his forehead. His muscles seized. His skin turned a deep crimson. Then his eyes rolled back into his head, and he collapsed."

"She killed him," Marisa said.

"I wasn't sure. I needed to check. But before I could move, Annamaria attacked. She launched herself across the bed and wrapped her hands around my throat. She cursed me with a dozen diseases—typhoid fever, malaria, leprosy, you name it."

"But you were able to heal yourself, right?"

Luke shook his head. "Didn't need to. Nothing she said worked. Somehow I was immune to her ability, which made her more upset." He drew his arms inward, recoiling at the memory of the attack. "She punched and kicked, tried to bite me on the arm. I had to fight her off, just like when we were kids. Ten minutes of fighting, and she wouldn't give up—punching, scratching, and screaming until she couldn't lift her arms.

"Finally she backed away. She stood over Uncle Jack's body and glared at me. 'You watched him! You let him do that to me!' Then she ran out the door. I never saw her again until today. That's why I hesitated at the market." He pressed his hands against the table until his muscles shook. "My sister is a killer. But I helped make her that way."

Marisa walked around the table and sat next to Luke. She draped one arm around his shoulder. "You've never told this to anyone, have you?"

He closed his eyes and lowered his head. Every part of his body seemed to shake at the same time. Heat rushed to his cheeks.

"Then it's very important for you to hear this. You did the right thing. You saved your sister."

"I froze," he said.

"No, you acted. You pulled that monster away from her. You stopped the attack. That makes you a hero."

Luke didn't believe her. He knew something was wrong about his reaction that night. Heroes didn't hesitate when someone was under attack. Something inside had caused him to wait—the darker side of his personality, a side he didn't want to explore.

Annamaria had seen that part of him. And she'd never forgotten.

"I made her this way," he said.

"She's a grown woman." Marisa rubbed the center of his back. "She makes her own choices. Your sister suffered an unspeakable attack, but so have thousands of other women. And very few became killers."

Soft voices echoed from down the hall. The people Luna had called after Dr. Cisneros arrived were quietly handling the transport of Paloma's body. Luke strode to the dining room door and opened it. He anchored himself in the doorway as the gurney rolled past. A long blue bag with a silver zipper now held the remains of his friend. No one but the people inside this house would ever know the true cause of her death. He made the sign of the cross and said a silent prayer.

Marisa edged beside him in the doorway. She waited until the gurney was out of the house before speaking. "I know you feel like you owe your sister something, but you owe Paloma more."

"I know."

She grabbed his hand and held it between hers. "Whatever it takes to get him back. No exceptions, no hesitation. Agreed?"

Blue lights flashed through the tiny glass windows near the front door—no sirens, just lights. Paloma's body would receive a silent escort to its next destination.

He blew out a short breath. "Agreed."

A buzzing sound erupted behind them. The phone's screen glowed with electronic light. Luke ran toward the table.

"What does it say?" Marisa said.

The message resembled one sent by a seventeen-year-old.

Come join the party, Brother!

He read it aloud. Marisa opened her mouth, but the phone vibrated again before she spoke.

He handed Marisa the phone. "It's a link to a map location."

She tapped the screen twice, then pinched and zoomed. Her facial features tensed in a way that reminded him of Paloma. "They're inside a *maquiladora*."

"A what?"

"It's a factory owned by a foreign company. Luna's daughter works in one. They're bigger than a warehouse and usually buzzing with workers around the clock."

Luke grabbed his Smith & Wesson and slid it into the holster behind his back. "You navigate. I'll drive."

Marisa stared at the screen. "This doesn't make any sense. Why would she pick a place filled with potential witnesses?"

"We'll figure it out when we get there." He gathered the spare magazines and slipped them inside his jacket.

Marisa's fingers tapped furiously on the screen. She placed her palm to his chest when he tried to walk past. "The satellite view is dated two months ago. It doesn't show any cars in the parking lot. Maybe it's abandoned?"

"She'd never pick a place like that at random," Luke said. "She has something planned."

"We know there's at least one hired gun backing her up."

"Guns we can handle." Luke offered Marisa her weapon. "Just don't let her touch you."

CHAPTER 45

Clyde stretched his arms as far outside the taxi window as he could reach, held his smartphone still, and snapped a picture. He pulled himself back inside the cab and reviewed his work. After only five attempts, he'd captured the perfect shot. This image would serve as the opening still frame in the video he'd produce later tonight.

The house resembled every other home on this street, but the large van with blue flashing lights parked out front signaled something extraordinary had occurred inside.

He'd arrived just before the van and directed the taxi driver to park one block away. The wording on the van was in Spanish. He didn't have a clue what it meant. But the three men who'd gone inside definitely didn't look like policemen.

A stucco wall joined the side of the house to the next building and protected the backyard. Clyde estimated its height at five feet, max. He could probably scale it without scuffing his new shoes.

His confidence brimmed. Even if he somehow got caught, what would Luke and the nurse do? They owed him a favor after leaving him at the airport. He'd earned the right to tell their story now, with or without their permission.

"Stay here, *señor.*" He reached for the door handle.

The front door of the house swung open. He let go of the handle and settled deeper into his seat, lowering himself until he could barely see out the window. The three men who'd arrived in the van rolled a gurney through the doorway and across the sidewalk. None of them looked hurried. A closed body bag rested on top of the gurney.

The taxi driver made the sign of the cross over his chest. Clyde shook his head. Somehow he'd arrived too late. The confrontation he'd hoped to capture must have already taken place. The zipper was already closed; he couldn't even identify who'd died. The men started the engine and drove away. Clyde gritted his teeth. This story was leaving him behind. He needed to act before the witnesses dispersed.

A strong desert gust slammed his chest when he exited the cab. He sprinted against it as he crossed the street and approached the house from the side. The stucco wall sparkled in the late-afternoon sun. When he drew closer, he realized why. Shards of embedded glass stuck out from the surface. The pieces resembled fragments of broken soda bottles, some green, some clear. Each looked as sharp as a surgical blade.

He surveyed the property next door. Its backyard wall featured the same embedded glass. Even the windows of both houses were protected with black iron bars. Similar bars adorned the homes across the street. What kind of neighborhood was this?

A thought occurred to him—the police were probably no strangers to this area. The van with lights belonged to a medical team of some kind. They'd arrived and left quietly, staying no more than ten minutes. Someone had obviously died. But why hadn't any policemen arrived?

Any shooting required police involvement. You couldn't just call an ambulance and explain it away as an accident. Did Mexico operate differently? He doubted it. Whatever had happened wasn't the result of a violent confrontation—or at least it wasn't reported that way. He needed to get inside and find out. And hopefully get it on video.

There had to be another way in. What if he knocked on the front door? He'd lose the element of surprise, but at least he'd get inside.

Or maybe he wouldn't. Luke and the nurse had ditched him for a reason. They didn't want him or his camera anywhere nearby, didn't want him filming the next battle in their war with Annamaria. But his subscribers demanded he press forward. The advertisers who'd pay him obscene royalties needed him to discover whose body was on that gurney and why. There had to be another way in. And he needed to find it now.

The taxi driver waved at him from behind the windshield. Clyde gave the driver a thumbs-up. He wondered if the gesture meant the same thing in Juárez.

Voices echoed from the front of the house. The front door closed with a thud. Clyde peered around the corner. Luke and the nurse marched toward a white sedan parked on the street.

Clyde pressed closer to the wall. A sharp pain bit into his forearm—the stupid broken glass again. He raised his sleeve. A small hole and a tiny red stain ruined an otherwise spotless designer shirt. So much for surviving the day unscathed. He covered the sleeve with his hand and squeezed.

Two car doors closed. An engine fired. Clyde risked another peek. Luke and the woman appeared locked in an intense conversation, probably about the person who had died. Luke shook his head. The nurse nodded. Then the car shot forward like it was in a race. Trails of exhaust lingered in the air.

Clyde angled across the street and rushed back to his taxi. He jumped inside. "Did you see that white car?"

The driver threw up his hands. "¿Automóvil blanco?"

"Does that mean white?" Clyde tapped the back of the seat. "I need you to follow it—not too closely, but don't lose it."

The driver stared at him through the rearview mirror. The man's bushy eyebrows lifted.

Clyde gazed through the rear window. The sedan had already disappeared. "Forget it." He retrieved his phone and opened the tracking app. The flashing blue dot streamed away from his location, traveling much faster than the last time he'd checked.

He leaned forward, keeping the phone display mere inches from his face. "Just drive. I'll tell you where to go."

The driver shifted into gear, and the taxi surged forward. Clyde divided his attention between the streets ahead and the map on his phone. The blue dot could run, but it couldn't hide—not from ShowMeClyde.

The unintended rhyming of his thoughts caused him to smirk. Maybe he'd use that line when he edited the video later. He checked his battery—37 percent remaining. The Gabor family reunion had better happen soon, or else there'd be no video to edit.

CHAPTER 46

Annamaria pressed her hands against the factory office window. With the dust storm's arrival, the desert view had disappeared. The ambient light had also darkened noticeably, even though nightfall was at least another hour away. She checked her phone. Half an hour had passed since she'd sent the text. Lucian should arrive any minute.

The office door swung open. Noordhoek marched inside. His lanky profile was barely visible from across the room. "Sacramento needs to talk to you. They say it's an emergency."

"I'm busy."

Noordhoek glanced at Harry, who'd stretched out across the couch like he was taking a nap. "The Secret Service is onto us. We can't delay any longer."

Her aide's body language worried her more than his words. Noordhoek, who'd never before wavered in the face of difficult circumstances, fidgeted nervously as he dug into his jacket and retrieved his phone. Despite the cool temperature, his forehead shimmered with sweat. He wiped it with his sleeve, then handed her the phone. "It's been ringing nonstop."

She noted the display—area code 916, the Sacramento office. These were people on her payroll, people she could control. She answered the call.

"What the hell are you doing in Mexico, Varner?"

Senator Blair. She'd recognize that chauvinistic tone anywhere. He'd obviously found Noordhoek's new number. But why was he calling from Sacramento?

"I needed some time alone," she said.

"Veep candidates don't get that luxury, especially not two weeks before an election. Have you lost your mind?"

"I'll be back tomorrow."

Blair blew a long stretch of static through the line. She imagined his alcoholic breath. "The Secret Service claims you attacked their men."

"There was a misunderstanding."

"Four agents are *dead*, Anna."

The veins in her temples throbbed. "I don't know what happened. We were leaving an event. One of them had a seizure, then everything went haywire."

Silence emanated from the other end. Harry sat up on the couch and stared at her. Noordhoek backed away. She drew the phone to her chest and clenched her teeth. She didn't have time for this. Blair was overstepping boundaries by forcing her to explain before she was ready.

When she returned the phone to her ear, Blair was already speaking. "…they admit no one knows what happened, but your absence makes you look guilty."

"I don't see how that's possible. I didn't attack anyone."

"One of the agents was covered with pepper spray."

Damn, she'd forgotten that detail. Still, each agent had suffered a naturally occurring medical event. The timing was suspicious, but they could never pin it on her.

"Has the story leaked to the media?"

"Not yet," Blair said.

She drew a deep breath. "I didn't want to mention this, but one of the agents attacked me. I got scared. I used my pepper spray—the man gave me no choice. Everything after that is a blur. I was in an unfamiliar city with no protection. The people I'd trusted had attacked me. I didn't know what to do, so I followed my instincts and ran."

"Why haven't you returned my calls?"

She knew the words she needed to say, but giving them a voice caused her stomach to turn. "I don't know if you've ever been a victim of a physical assault, but it takes time to recover. I needed to spend a day alone to regroup and heal. Just a little time away from the bright lights and the strangers paid to protect me." She swallowed hard. "Don't worry. I won't press any charges. I just need until tomorrow. Then we can put this traumatic event behind us."

Muffled conversation filled Blair's end of the connection. Surely he was talking to someone else—about her, no doubt. At least she wasn't on speakerphone. Or was she?

"Anna, you're too important to be running around unprotected in a foreign country. This isn't a negotiation. You're one of us now. I need you to stay at your current location until the US Marshals and Secret Service arrive. When you get back, we can—"

Annamaria threw the phone on the floor and stomped it with her heel. The screen cracked, but the glass didn't shatter. The display still showed an ongoing call. She marched toward the kitchenette and grabbed a heavy pan from the stovetop. She rushed toward the phone, dropped to her knees, and swung the pan like a sledgehammer. Shards of glass scattered across the floor. The frame deformed, the battery bounced away like someone had flipped an ejection switch. She kept swinging. The sound of each impact echoed like the blast of a shotgun. She imagined Blair's face on the other end of the line. With each blow she pushed herself further from his grasp.

She stopped when nothing but pieces remained.

Noordhoek stood at attention. His focus seemed aimed toward the window, away from what she'd done. His mouth remained closed. Strangely, he no longer seemed nervous.

Harry's pudgy face appeared above the back of the couch. "Whoever that was, he sure made you angry."

She ignored the little twerp. He'd be dead in a matter of minutes, anyway.

"We need to finish this quickly," she said, "then move out before Blair's people arrive."

"Understood."

"And disable the rental's GPS system."

"Already done."

She climbed to her feet. "How big is the cargo area?"

Noordhoek's facial muscles twitched. "Why does that matter?"

"We need to take the bodies with us."

CHAPTER 47

A dust storm washed across the hood of Paloma's sedan three blocks from the *maquiladora* where Annamaria and her men were keeping Harry. Blinding sand pelted the windows in relentless waves. Luke tried the wipers. They didn't help. He had no choice but to slow down and guide the car toward what he hoped was the side of the road. He cut the engine.

Marisa opened the glove compartment and searched through its contents. She drew out a long turquoise scarf and ripped it in half, then offered him one piece. "Tie this around your nose and mouth like a *bandido.*"

"A what?"

"Like this." She stretched her half of the scarf across her nose and tied the ends behind her head. "The *maquiladora* is just ahead. They'll never see us coming."

Luke copied her technique. The scarf smelled like apricots and roses—Paloma's favorite perfume. He sensed she was watching them now, willing him toward her precious son.

"Ready?" he said.

Marisa glanced at the phone and tucked it into her pocket. "We need to stay close. I'll get us there."

When they opened the car doors, the sand blew in. Each gust stung like birdshot against the exposed skin on his face and neck. He hurried toward Marisa's side and followed her down the road, into the prevailing wind. The only way he could see was to tuck his chin against his chest and squint toward the ground. He assumed Marisa was doing the same, but he couldn't tell. She grabbed his hand and pulled him into an asphalt parking lot. They angled across empty parking spaces and through an unmanned security gate. Five steps later Marisa stopped. He lifted his chin and peeked ahead. A metallic-green Kia with a smashed front grill sat parked near the corner of a huge white building.

The *maquiladora*. He squeezed Marisa's hand. Not even a raging sandstorm could blunt her sense of direction.

"How do we get in?" Marisa said.

"Let me check something first." Luke rounded the Kia, peering through each window. No blood had stained the upholstery in the backseat—a good sign. The doors were locked. He didn't see any weapons, but he did notice something else.

A sudden gust knocked him against the car. Paloma's scarf blew upward, exposing his open mouth. Fine grains of sand and dust embedded themselves between his teeth. He spit out as much as he could, then pulled the scarf back down. The salty, gritty taste remained.

Marisa tapped his shoulder. "This is brutal."

"We need to go around back," Luke said.

She pointed to her left, toward a set of steps. "The closest door is this way."

"They're watching that one," he said. "We need to find another way in. They can't cover every entry, so they'll only monitor the obvious ones."

"How do you know?"

Luke indicated the Kia. "How many people rode in this car?"

"No more than five."

"I say three." He pointed into the passenger's side window. "Only one of these rear seats has been used. The floor mat on this side is dirty, but the other side is clean. Harry must've sat alone in the back. They probably engaged the child locks to make sure he stayed put."

"What if they have another car?"

"You see another car?"

"I can barely see this one."

"My sister's on the run, just like us. Her team would need to be small. I'm betting there's only one hired gun—the one we saw at the market."

"The man who attacked us in Memphis," she said.

"This way." Luke took the lead, edging along the side of the building in the opposite direction of the steps. The *maquiladora's* footprint looked massive, probably a hundred yards by fifty. Apparently the owners had built this structure with no frills. The thin metal siding rattled under the dust storm's assault. The wind and sand pounded even harder this close to the building. The gusts seemed to change direction, whipping back and forth, testing his balance. He powered through the gales until they reached the corner.

The storm intensified as they trekked along the next side of the building. He checked on Marisa. She gave a thumbs-up. They kept moving, taking short, deliberate steps. The temperature dropped, making the wind feel even heavier. The dust seemed darker than before. Large pellets showered against him. He raised his arm near his face. Mud drops speckled his jacket.

"This is crazy," Marisa said. "Let's hurry."

"Almost there." He doubled his speed, knowing she'd keep up. Mud and rain kept falling, but the visibility improved. A door stood just ahead. He ducked under the small, built-in window in the door and passed by without even checking the handle.

Marissa followed. Once they were both clear, she said, "What was wrong with that one?"

"Too obvious. And it's probably locked."

"What do you want, a welcome mat?"

"Don't worry. I have a plan."

The mud storm gave way to driving rain. In seconds their clothes were soaked. He didn't let it bother him. Harry wouldn't hug him any tighter if his jeans were dry.

They turned another corner. The back of the *maquiladora* featured a wide loading dock with a dozen bays, each large enough to load a cargo truck. The roll-up doors were closed but battered. More than a few looked like they'd taken a shot from a truck bumper or a forklift. The wind and rain beat against them like an onslaught of archers' arrows, creating a thousand metallic echoes.

A gray eighteen-wheeler trailer rested in a loading spot three doors away. Two of its tires were flat. A rear door of the trailer was open, swaying on its hinges as the storm winds pushed and pulled.

"What are we looking for?" Marisa said.

"Follow me." Luke rushed across the loading dock to the back of the eighteen-wheeler. The trailer and the building were separated by two feet. He peered through the gap. The cargo area looked mostly empty, but it was too dark to be sure. He climbed on the bumper and stepped inside. Marisa extended her arm through the gap. He leaned forward and helped her up.

Her face was barely visible in the darkness. He retrieved the phone he'd taken from the YouTube journalist and activated the flashlight feature. Deeper inside the cargo area, two wooden pallets lay under a pile of loose strapping and cellophane sheeting. A discarded empty box showed a picture of a mobile phone on the outside.

He pulled Paloma's scarf down to his neck. "I bet the local *bandidos* marked their calendars when this place announced it was closing."

Marisa scanned the cargo area, then shook her head. "I don't get it. Is this part of your plan?"

"The trailer isn't, but that is." He aimed the phone's light toward the building's roll-up door. A large section in the middle looked like a bull had charged into it. Near the bottom was a ten-inch gap between the door and the concrete.

Marisa pulled down her scarf. "How skinny do you think I am?"

"Don't worry. I'll go first." He shut off the flashlight feature and slid the phone in his pocket. "We can squeeze our way through. The key is not making a bunch of noise."

"And not getting shot."

"Wish me luck." He started to kneel, but she grabbed his wrist and pulled him close. She kissed him before he could react. Her lips held a warmth that passed through his entire body.

When he tried to kiss back, she pulled away. "You won't need it. This is what you do—you save people."

"Promise me something."

"No time. Harry needs us. Let's go."

She was right. He dropped to his knees and peered under the roll-up door. Darkness covered everything inside. He didn't hear any sounds of movement, only the dull roar of the storm winds lashing against the exterior. This was their best entry point—far enough away from the other doors to reduce the chances of anyone seeing them.

He lowered himself to a horizontal position on the narrow ledge extending from the *maquiladora*. Raindrops fell through the gap and splattered against his face. He pressed his eyelids closed. Nothing about this would be easy.

A moment later, the rain seemed to pause. He opened his eyes. Marisa stood over him. "Hurry up. It's raining."

He grabbed the bottom of the roll-up door for leverage and scooted his body under it. His lower half passed through easily, but his chest posed a problem. He forced the air out of his lungs. It helped, but he needed another inch. He pushed against the roll-up door. The gun in his holster pressed into his lower back. Something inside the building popped, sending a deep echo through the interior. At the same time, the door inched upward, just enough so he could wiggle through.

He rolled free from the door and jumped to his feet. He reached for his gun and scanned the area nearby. All was quiet, but he couldn't see much. Gradually his eyes adjusted, and the *maquiladora's* interior came into focus. Light from the windows above penetrated just enough to show a few details. The area near him was clear. A forklift sat parked against the wall close to where he'd entered. Twenty feet away stood several rows of mini-workstations that seemed to span the entire floor. To his far right, more than a hundred feet away, he noted a stairway leading to a second-floor office—an excellent vantage point for bosses to observe workers below. With the lack of lighting, he figured no one up there could see him now.

Movement near the door caught his attention. He rushed toward Marisa and pulled her inside. After she climbed to her feet, she also reached for her gun. "Hear anything?"

"Nothing."

They spoke in whispers. The echo from the driving rain outside ensured their words wouldn't travel far.

"Where are they?" she said.

Before Luke could answer, the door to the second-story office opened and a figure marched onto the walkway. The slender form gave away her identity. Annamaria leaned against the steel handrail and projected her voice across the factory floor. "Brother, is that you?"

Marisa drew close to him. "Don't answer."

Luke agreed and stayed quiet. The only advantages they held were their guns and their silence. Still, part of him wanted to answer his sister, to let her know he was here.

"Lucian," Annamaria said. "Are you hiding? Or are you just watching again, like you did the night of our party?"

She wasn't looking in his direction, but her loathing stare still penetrated Luke from a hundred feet away.

He couldn't trust his accuracy to take her out from this range. Most likely he'd only give away their location and make them vulnerable to the hired gun he suspected was nearby. He tapped Marisa's arm then crept toward the workstations, careful not to make any noise. Marisa followed.

"Time is short, Brother. Harry's feeling sick. He looks pale and weak. Someone should probably take him to a doctor."

Marisa grabbed his free hand and squeezed. "Don't fall for it."

"Or maybe he needs a faith healer like our father." Annamaria shifted her weight. "Oh, I forgot. He's not around anymore."

Luke couldn't stand still any longer. Each second he didn't act left Harry vulnerable to his sister's ability. He wanted to race up the stairs and save his brother, but he knew he wouldn't make it to the first step before her gunman started shooting. They needed to flush the man out of hiding before he went for Harry.

"Let's clear each row, one by one," he said.

Marisa nodded, and they moved deeper into the current row. After twenty yards, he motioned for Marisa to stop, then he continued another twenty. Her silhouette was barely visible from that distance. They couldn't risk operating any farther apart. He led with his gun and squeezed between two workstations and into the next row. He checked both directions for signs of movement. Nothing. Farther down the row, Marisa copied his technique. She raised her gun, a sign all was clear and she was ready for the next row. He moved forward.

Annamaria's voice echoed above his head. "After I killed his mother, I wondered why anyone would leave such a cute little boy unprotected. But now I understand. He's quite a handful. Thankfully your brother is too dumb to realize he's about to die."

Another voice streamed from the second-story platform—higher in pitch and more intense than Annamaria's. The office door swung open and a second figure rushed onto the platform. Harry yelled as he charged toward Annamaria, swinging what looked like a frying pan toward her head.

Luke couldn't do anything but watch. Annamaria blocked Harry's blow with her forearm. The frying pan tumbled away and clanged against the platform floor. She pushed him backward, pinning him against the wall. Harry went silent, but he didn't give up. His arms flailed and punched at Annamaria, but nothing landed. She held him at a distance with one arm. "See what I mean? The little shit doesn't know how to behave." She reached behind her back and drew a pistol, then pointed it at Harry's chest.

Luke shouted, "No!"

Annamaria's head snapped in Luke's direction. Even in the low light, he recognized her snarky grin.

Movement to his left caught his eye. He swung his pistol in that direction as a gunshot sounded. A gunman stood twenty feet farther down the row in a shooting stance. His first shot had missed. Luke ducked and rolled into the next row. Another shot sounded. A plastic workstation divider above his head shattered.

He rolled forward again, then stayed low, his gun aimed toward where he'd last seen the flash of gunfire. His senses sharpened while he watched and listened. No movement, no noise. Maybe the gunman had sprinted several rows ahead, trying to outflank him.

"Uncle Luke!" Harry's voice sounded weaker and more distant.

Luke ached to answer, but he stayed quiet. He squeezed his eyes shut to block out the image of Harry with a gun pointed at him. Annamaria looked mad enough to kill. But he couldn't think about that now. Gunman first, then save Harry.

When he opened his eyes, a shadow moved in the next row.

The movement was so slight he almost convinced himself he hadn't seen it—a shift of weight, a quarter turn of a leg. Dark pants. Dress shoes.

Luke rose and aimed. The man's eyes flashed wide. His hands flew into the air. A mobile phone clattered against the floor. "Jesus, don't shoot."

Clyde Merritt, the YouTube journalist. Luke couldn't believe it. "What are you doing here?"

"Chasing your story," Clyde said.

"Get out."

"I'm—"

A staccato of gunfire silenced them. Thirty yards away, several mini-flashes interrupted the darkness. The flashes came from two different places. Both were near where Marisa had been standing. Luke raced toward the gunfire.

Things happened so quickly his mind had trouble keeping up. Harry screamed something unintelligible from the platform above. Clyde shouted behind him. Luke ignored them both. He trained his focus on the scene ahead, the rapid gunfire, the swarm of movement. He glimpsed Marisa's profile and noted her two-handed grip on the Smith & Wesson. She kept her arms straight while her body swept across the row and into the next. He darted through a gap between workstations and found her again, still advancing through the rows, obviously in pursuit of the gunman.

And the gunman was shooting back.

Luke tracked the returning fire. The gunman stayed three rows ahead of Marisa, moving on a path toward the bottom of the stairs. He raced forward, but his weapon stayed aimed back at Marisa, firing wild shots as he ran. She'd probably surprised him as he tried to circle around Luke. Now she had him on the run. Still, she took a big chance chasing after the gunman like this. Luke readied his gun and charged ahead.

The gunman reached the end of a row and hesitated. Marisa fired. The gunman groaned then darted left, back into the maze of workstations, angling on a path directly toward Luke.

Luke ducked behind a workstation and waited. The gunman kept firing as he ran. Marisa returned each blast. Thirty feet and closing. The man sprinted forward, then glanced back. He fired once more. Fifteen feet. The man ran two steps, then looked back again.

Luke stepped into the row, set his feet, and aimed. The man didn't see him until the gun fired. Luke sent two bullets into the man's chest, dropping him instantly. The blasts echoed with a note of finality the other shots were missing. Luke stepped forward. Annamaria's gunman lay unmoving on the floor, two dark blooms growing across his already bloodstained shirt.

The factory went silent. Even the rain outside must have paused. Then a thudding sound resonated from the stairs. Luke checked the platform. Harry and Annamaria had disappeared.

Someone approached from behind. Luke ducked and turned, bringing his weapon in front of him.

Clyde's head appeared from behind a workstation like a groundhog emerging from its hole. "Did you get him?"

Luke knelt and checked the gunman's pulse. "Yeah."

Clyde's skin looked shiny and pale, even in the low light. "What about the boy?"

"I'm going after him. You stay here. I'll—"

He stopped himself. Where was Marisa? She hadn't been too far behind the gunman. Surely she would've appeared by now. He stared down the row—nothing. Maybe she'd taken off after Harry. Or maybe she hadn't.

"Stay here and stay quiet. If my sister finds you, you'll end up like him."

Clyde glanced at the dead gunman, then made a face like he needed to throw up. "Do I have to?"

"Hold this." Luke retrieved the assassin's gun and offered it to Clyde. "In case you need it."

"Why?"

"It'll protect you better than a camera."

Clyde handled the gun like it was a nuclear weapon. He stared at the barrel like he expected it to explode at any moment. Luke doubted Clyde possessed the nerve to pull the trigger. But he couldn't leave the man defenseless in such close proximity to his sister. He turned to leave.

"Where are you going?" Clyde said.

"To save my brother."

Luke ran down the row, retracing the gunman's footsteps. Something wasn't right. Marisa should've joined him soon after he put down the gunman. He slowed and listened. The storm's passing had left an eerie silence inside the factory. The sound of his footsteps echoed louder than before. He stopped. The sound of distant footsteps replaced his.

Other people were nearby. More than one set of feet shuffled in the darkness, maybe ten rows away. Maybe closer. He peered over the workstations. Nothing. But someone was moving in the darkness. He knifed into the next row as soundlessly as possible and held his gun ready.

A shadow moved to his right. He peered down the row. Fifteen feet away, Marisa sat with her back leaning against a workstation support, her legs spread at an angle. Her Smith & Wesson lay abandoned on the concrete floor. Her chin rested on her chest, but her eyes were open. He rushed to her side.

"It's not that bad," she said.

Blood streamed from a wound in her thigh. It passed through the fingers of both her hands and pooled on the floor. He moved closer and touched her shoulder. She shivered. "The guy's a terrible shot. He got lucky."

"Let me see," Luke said.

"No." She pressed her hands against the wound. Both were coated in dark red. "He's still down here somewhere."

"Don't worry. I got him."

"Good. Now you need to get upstairs."

"Let's fix you first."

"I'm *fine*."

Something moved in Luke's periphery. Clyde's high-pitched voice announced his approach. "Don't shoot. Is everyone okay?"

Marisa hissed in a breath. "You've got to be kidding."

"I told you to stay there," Luke said.

Clyde slipped into the row and drew closer. "Dead bodies freak me out. What's—oh Jesus. Are you all right?"

Clyde couldn't have arrived at a worse moment. Marisa had lost a lot of blood. Despite her protests, Luke needed to act quickly before she lost more. "Get out of here, Merritt."

"I want to help."

"We don't have time for this." Marisa stared into Luke's eyes with an intensity he hadn't seen before. "Go save Harry."

"But your wound—"

"Use Paloma's scarf," she said.

Luke untied his section of the scarf and quickly wrapped it around Marisa's leg. The scarf pressed tight against the denim of her jeans, but a small amount of blood still flowed from her wound. "This isn't enough."

"Go," Marisa said.

A gunshot sounded from several yards away. Two loud metal bangs followed. Then another two shots. Harry screamed, but one final bang silenced his cry.

"Go now," Marisa said.

A jolt of adrenaline raced through Luke's body. He grabbed Clyde by the collar. "Stay here and do exactly what she says. If I'm not back in five minutes, get her to a hospital."

CHAPTER 48

Annamaria forced her little brother down the metal stairs. He fought her on every step, but the handle of her gun proved a deciding force each time she thumped it against his head.

Noordhoek was gone. She knew he'd been killed even though she couldn't make out the identities of anyone below. At least three different people were moving among the rows, maybe four. He'd probably run into a cross fire. Noordhoek might have fired the first shot, but he definitely didn't shoot last. She shook her head. This was a mess even Sacramento couldn't fix.

Her only hope was that Noordhoek had taken out a few of them as well. In case he hadn't, staying on the platform was no longer smart. She needed to move.

Harry stopped at the bottom tread and anchored himself to the handrail. The pudgy runt wouldn't let go even when she pushed as hard as she could. She lifted her leg and kicked into the center of his back. The boy let out a grunt, then tumbled to the factory floor.

She thought about running into the maze of workstations and sneaking up on Lucian. Harry's insolence would make that impossible. She had no other choice but to run.

Near the bottom of the stairs was an exterior access door. She turned the handle and pressed against it, but the door wouldn't open. She surveyed the jamb. Apparently Noordhoek had done his job well. A dead bolt with a keyed latch was still engaged—no way to turn it without the key. She stood next to Harry and drew her gun. Her first shot was dead-on. When she turned the handle and slammed her shoulder against the door, it held. She backed up and gave it a kick. Nothing.

Another kick. The damn dead bolt still held.

Harry tried to crawl away. She grabbed his jacket and pulled him next to her. With her other hand she aimed her gun at the dead bolt. Two quick blasts opened a blade of ambient light near the jamb.

Harry covered his ears and screamed.

One last kick and the door swung open. Annamaria yanked Harry through the doorway like a rag doll.

A blast of cool drizzle splattered her face—remnants from the passing storm. She powered through the mist into the truck loading area with Harry in tow. Even with the light rain, visibility had improved since she'd last checked. On the other side of the loading area and beyond a chain-link fence, the raw Mexican desert waited. Sand and bushes formed a landscape that seemed to run past the horizon. She hurried in that direction.

The fence lining this side of the property looked to have suffered several raids by vandals, a few of which had been armed with wire cutters. She noticed a four-foot gash in the fencing to her immediate left. She pulled the fencing open and shoved Harry through the gap. Part of his jacket ripped as it scraped against the exposed links. She followed him through and headed into the desert.

If Lucian was still alive, he'd follow them. After she made sure no one else was with him, she'd exact her revenge and walk out of the desert alone, back into the waiting arms of the Secret Service. They might balk at her story of how she'd been stalked by her estranged brother to this hellhole of a city, but in the end they would accept her version, burying the details of both how they'd lost her and how she was found. The campaign would resume as if nothing had happened, and the public would never know how much she'd risked to earn her office.

If Noordhoek's aim was accurate and her brother had died before he could save himself, she'd still walk out of the desert alone. Only one Gabor sibling would survive this day. Only one story would be told of what happened here.

Harry clawed at her arm as she tugged him across the sand. "Let go of me."

She thumped his crown with the butt of the pistol. The little brat's head must have been made of titanium. The gun bounced out of her hand and fell into the sand. She stumbled and kicked it forward before finally scooping it up. Dirty, wet sand clung to the barrel and handle. She'd clean it off later.

Fortunately her blow seemed to work. Not only did Harry shut up, but he also covered his scalp with his hands, abandoning his attack.

"I'm bleeding."

You'll do more than that soon.

Twenty yards. Fifty yards. Seventy. The sand grew softer the farther they marched. She turned and looked back. The access door remained partially open, exactly the way she'd left it. The tracks she and Harry had forged in the desert were unmistakable. Even a Cub Scout could follow their trail.

She spotted a slight rise in topography just ahead. The rounded dune peppered with spiny bushes would provide just the cover needed to gain the upper hand.

"Uncle Luke," Harry whispered, like he was talking to himself.

"Yes, Uncle Luke." Annamaria shoved her little brother toward the dune. "He's coming to save you."

CHAPTER 49

Luke darted through the rows as quickly as he could, the sound of Harry's scream still reverberating in his mind. He remembered the expression on Annamaria's face when she'd looked over the factory floor. He'd seen that look twenty-five years earlier, just before Uncle Jack had met his end.

He reached the end of the row. The staircase stood on his left. To his right, an exterior metal door hung one-quarter open. He drew closer and inspected the jamb. Gunpowder and shrapnel on both the doorframe and the latch confirmed the noises he'd heard a minute ago. He clasped both hands around his gun and held it ready. Pushed the door open with his shoulder and rushed outside.

Part of him suspected she'd blasted the door open to fool him, but he brushed the thought aside. Annamaria hated playing hide-and-go-seek. She was all about confrontation. The partially open door was her invitation, her way of demanding he witness her next act of vengeance.

Outside, the storm had passed. Heavy clouds blanketed the sky, but only remnants of the downpour hung in the air. He charged through the parking lot and scanned his surroundings. Thoughts of Harry and Marisa pressed into his mind, but he kept his focus. No cars were in sight. They couldn't have run far. But in which direction?

Barren desert spread to the southeast as far as he could see. A chain-link fence topped with barbed wire marked the border of the property. He studied the fence line and noticed an opening in the chain links. He ran in that direction. Someone had pried open a section large enough for an adult to pass through. Rain had pockmarked the sand beyond, leaving a uniform texture. Two sets of shoeprints disturbed the landscape, forging a trail into the desert. He darted through the fence opening and followed the tracks.

One set of imprints occurred at steady intervals. A second, smaller set included twice the number of prints, many out of line and disjointed. A few resembled drag marks more than actual shoeprints. His pulse quickened. Harry was definitely still alive. And fighting.

Luke chased after the trail, stepping over shin-high sticker bushes and around barrel-sized scrub bushes. He imagined how Annamaria might react to his brother's resistance. Given the day's events, it wouldn't take much to set her off. He doubled his pace.

Their tracks led into the desert for nearly a hundred yards, then curled to the right behind a small ridge. He chased their steps as quickly as he could, pausing only to scan ahead for signs of either Annamaria or Harry.

Halfway into the curve, he spotted them standing side by side next to a set of bushes. They weren't hiding; the trail of shoeprints led directly to where they stood. Annamaria held a fistful of Harry's jacket, forcing him close to her hip. Her other hand gripped a pistol. Harry looked angry and defiant but otherwise healthy. His scowl dissolved when his gaze met Luke's, but he didn't call out or cry.

"That's close enough," Annamaria said.

Luke had taken three steps since he caught sight of his sister. He stopped. Twenty feet still separated them—too far to risk rushing her.

Annamaria pressed the barrel of her pistol against Harry's temple. "Lose the gun."

"Don't kill him, Annamaria."

"I said lose the gun."

Luke extended his arm and held the pistol by the end of the handle. He dropped it into the sand.

"Kick it clear," she said.

Annamaria was nothing if not smart. He kicked the gun under a sticker bush a few feet away.

"That's how I remember you, Brother. Standing all by yourself, helpless and defeated, of no use to anyone—especially a member of your own family."

Anger bled into her words. He could almost taste the bile from her throat. Harry must have sensed it, too. His eyes grew larger, and his chin quivered.

"Who came with you?" she said.

"Just Marisa."

"That's the nurse, right?" She blinked. "Where is she now?"

"Your gunman shot her."

"Is she still alive?"

"Barely."

"You should've healed her while you had the chance. I would've waited."

He thought about Marisa bleeding out on the factory floor with no one but Clyde to comfort her. Annamaria's plan was working to perfection.

"On second thought, I probably wouldn't have waited. But now I don't need to." Annamaria waved the gun in the air like it was a toy. "Where do we start?"

Harry jerked away. She caught him and pulled him closer. "Let's talk about this little runt who calls you Uncle Luke. How long have you been hiding him?"

"Since he was a baby."

"Smart move." She glared at Harry. "You wouldn't have lasted long with our parents."

"He isn't part of this." Luke stepped forward. "He doesn't even know who you are."

Annamaria returned the barrel to Harry's temple. "Tell me, Harry. Who's holding this gun to your head?"

Harry leered back at her. "A very bad lady."

"Harry," Luke said.

"Shut it." She placed her finger on the trigger and spoke into Harry's ear. "Who am I?"

"You're my sister."

She turned to Luke. "See? He's not as dumb as he looks."

"He's just a kid." Luke took another step forward. "He doesn't deserve this."

"Don't tell me what people deserve." Her expression darkened. "I didn't deserve to be abandoned by our parents. I didn't deserve what Uncle Jack did to me."

The burden Luke had carried since childhood grew heavier on his shoulders. But he stood tall. Harry needed to see his strength now. He needed to believe they still had a chance.

"I deserved a brother who could protect me," Annamaria said. "I deserved to be loved by my family. But instead you watched him. You just stood there and *watched* him."

"Annamaria, I'm sorry—"

She waved off his words with her gun. "Who do you love, Brother? Who do you cherish? Was it that nurse? Your little brother?" She cinched the collar of Harry's jacket so tight his neck turned red. "What about your sister? Did you ever love me?"

Luke wanted to answer, but he knew it was a trap. It wouldn't matter if he told her he still cared. She wouldn't believe him anyway. Bitterness had eaten away the sister he once knew. His next response would spur her into action, no matter the words. He risked another step.

She pointed the gun at him. "Step back."

Luke did as she told him.

"You can't talk your way out of this, Brother. Not this time. You took everything from me that night. So now I'll take something from you."

"You've already done that," Luke said.

"That woman doesn't count. She wasn't family."

Harry threw a punch at Annamaria's stomach. "You need to shut up."

She thumped Harry on the head with the butt of the pistol. "Do that again and I'll splatter your brains in the desert."

"Annamaria, wait."

"I've waited long enough." Annamaria trained her weapon on Luke and fired. His right thigh exploded with pain, dropping him to his knees. He pressed his hands against the wound. It burned like a branding iron.

"Your brother is going to die," she said, "and you're going to stand there and watch, just like before."

"Uncle Luke!"

"Shut up," Annamaria said.

Harry sneered at his older sister. Her words didn't seem to scare him anymore; instead he looked energized.

Luke's heart hammered against his rib cage. His leg felt like it was on fire. But his focus stayed on Harry. This wasn't supposed to end this way. He couldn't let it end this way.

"Our little brother deserves something special, doesn't he?" Annamaria said. "A special end for a special boy."

Luke struggled to his feet. "Annamaria, no."

She extended her index finger until it touched Harry's neck.

Luke charged.

Annamaria blinked.

Harry's finger pressed against Annamaria's lips. "Shh."

She knocked his hand away and opened her mouth. But no words came out.

"You shut up now," Harry said.

She tried to speak again—not even a whisper escaped her. Her face twisted into a snarl. She pointed the gun at Harry's chest.

Luke slammed into Annamaria's side so hard he heard her ribs crack. He pushed off with his left leg, threw his weight against her, and tackled her into a sticker bush. She winced but didn't let go of the gun.

He stuck his finger behind the trigger and wrestled her for control. She bared her teeth and hissed, squirmed like a serpent under his weight. She dug her fingernails into his arm and scraped deep tracks in his skin.

Luke ignored the pain. Only the gun mattered now. He grabbed the barrel and twisted. She wouldn't let go. Instead she pulled hard on the trigger, crimping his finger like a vise.

They fought like when they were kids—fists and elbows flying, teeth gnashing, legs kicking. Annamaria had never stopped back then. And she wouldn't stop now.

She lifted her head and bit his wrist. Her teeth tore like razors. He pulled his arm away and punched her in the face.

She opened her mouth. Again, no sound came out. Drops of blood stained her teeth. She bucked her head wildly and spit on his chin.

Luke refocused on the gun. Both hands worked to wrench it away, but she held on. She squeezed the trigger so hard he thought it might shear through his knuckle. Pain flashed up his arm. He tried a quick move, pulling his finger from behind the trigger and grabbing the barrel. Annamaria shoved the gun toward his stomach and fired.

The blast rocked his eardrums. Pain stormed through his gut, and his strength drained from his core. Annamaria glanced toward his wound. Her eyes grew wider, and a faint smile formed across her face.

Luke's adrenaline surged. He forced the gun away from his body, out toward Annamaria's side. The gun fired again, its report echoing through the desert. He slammed her hand against the ground, pressing with all the force he could muster. She fought back, twisting the gun with her wrist and firing another shot. The bullet missed his ear by only a few inches.

"Uncle Luke!"

"Stay back." Luke couldn't see where Harry was standing, but he hoped neither of the last two shots had hit his brother. His stomach burned like he'd been stabbed with a white-hot spear. He couldn't move his right leg. Breathing now required effort. Keeping her pinned beneath him proved more difficult by the second. He wouldn't last much longer.

Annamaria bucked her hips and pushed so hard he thought she might wiggle free. The metallic scent of blood filled the air between them. She crinkled her nose. He pressed harder against her chest, then slid his free arm toward her neck. His forearm settled against her throat. She gasped, then mouthed a silent scream.

He knew what he needed to do. Annamaria would never surrender, and he couldn't fight much longer. How many chances had he given her? How many times had she proven him wrong?

The lower part of his body felt numb. He forced his torso higher, leveraging more of his weight on his forearm, pressing it against her windpipe.

She pulled the trigger again. The shot plunged into a nearby dune. She tugged against his forearm with one hand and aimed her gun with the other. He fought to push the gun away, but she'd found a new reserve of energy. The barrel angled slowly toward his head. He lowered his face toward hers. Another blast sounded, and a bullet whizzed overhead.

She jerked the gun closer, wedged it between her shoulder and his. The gunshot sounded much louder this time, and the bullet ripped through his clavicle. His ears rang. His shoulder bloomed with pain. He lost his balance, and his forearm slipped. Annamaria heaved in a large breath before he could return pressure to her neck.

He couldn't fight her off any longer. His left arm was useless now. All he could do was press his weight against her throat with his right arm.

She drew the gun toward his neck and placed the barrel under his chin. The hot metal burned against his skin.

"Annamaria—"

She pulled the trigger.

Metal clicked against metal, but no blast followed. The magazine had finally emptied.

Their faces were inches apart. Her cheeks turned cherry red. A deep crease formed between her eyebrows. She shoved the barrel harder against his chin and pulled the trigger again and again.

Nothing happened.

She stared at the gun like it had betrayed her. Rage emanated from her eyes. Luke sensed another wave of strength rising within her. Soon he'd lose his leverage, then she'd turn him over and finish him.

The wounds to his leg, stomach, and shoulder had sapped his energy. Even if he managed to subdue her, he wouldn't be able to save himself—much less Marisa or Harry. Sweat and sand blurred his vision. He blinked it clear and watched his sister struggle to breathe. She bared her teeth and flared her nostrils like a lioness preparing to strike.

Luke couldn't let her leave this desert alive.

He bore the full weight of his torso on his forearm. The cartilage in her throat crunched under the pressure. She pulled at his arm with her free hand, her fingernails digging into his skin. He felt nothing. The adrenaline in his veins had subdued his nerve endings. The pain in his wounds fell away, and nothing remained but Annamaria and her struggle to catch her breath. He pressed harder. More cartilage collapsed under his weight. Her bony knees slammed against his back. Her shoulders jerked left and right. Luke grabbed a fistful of her blouse and held his forearm in place.

"I'm sorry, Annamaria."

She beat him with the gun, slamming the hard metal against his temple as her body struggled for oxygen. He tried to raise his left arm to block her, but it wouldn't move. The blows came quickly at first, but their intensity soon ebbed. A pulse of air escaped her mouth with a sickening rattle. Dark blue veins bulged near the top of her neck.

His strength was still fading, but so was Annamaria's. Her head settled back against the desert. Her hateful expression dissolved. Tears pooled in the corners of her eyes, just like they had the night their parents had left. Luke wanted to wipe them away. Instead he pushed harder against her throat.

"I'm sorry, Sister."

She blinked several times. The crease between her eyebrows deepened. She seemed to stare past him, into the darkening sky.

Tears clouded his own eyes as he pushed one last time. "I'm sorry."

The tension in her body gradually relaxed—first her legs, then her arms, then her torso and shoulders. Her jaw went slack. The crease in her forehead disappeared.

She was gone.

Luke released his arm from her neck and rolled onto his back. Low clouds rushed past overhead. He was too exhausted to follow them with his gaze. Pain returned to his wounds, but only in dull waves, like gentle reminders from his mind. He thought back to the night in Port Arthur when he'd been shot in an alley, how he'd wondered then if he'd seen his last star. He didn't wonder tonight. Even if he had time, his arms were so weak he could never bring his hands to his wounds.

He thought about Marisa. God, how he'd miss her. Hopefully Clyde would get her to a hospital before she bled out.

Darkness came for him, seeping through the periphery of his vision, chilling his bones. Soon it would envelop him and he'd join his sister, wherever she was now.

The shadows above him took form. Two cold hands pressed against his chest.

"Get up."

An unknown force surged through his body. His muscles flexed, and his limbs jolted into motion. Before he could think, he had risen from the sand. Harry stood before him, his cheeks streaked with tears. "You can't die, Uncle Luke. You have to heal yourself."

Luke wanted to answer, but he was frozen in shock. Part of him was convinced if he tried to move on his own, he'd collapse.

Harry grabbed Luke's hand and pressed it against his stomach. "Do it now. Heal yourself."

Luke blinked, and his mind went into a dream. In it he saw his insides repairing themselves, the bullets exiting like he'd directed them dozens of times before. A wave of warmth overtook him. Strength returned to his core, his shoulder, and his leg, all at the same time. He opened his eyes.

Harry's eyes were still closed. He pressed his own small hands against Luke's and mouthed a few silent words.

"Harry. What did you do?"

Harry opened his eyes and released Luke's hand. "I made her shut up." He threw his arms around Luke's waist but didn't squeeze. "You feel better now, Uncle Luke?"

Luke stared at his little brother in disbelief. What kind of power coursed through this boy's veins? And how long had it been hiding there?

His gaze moved past Harry, toward the ground near his feet. Three bloodstained bullets littered the sand. His entire body hummed with a resonance he'd never experienced before. "Thank you, Harry."

"I told you I'd save you."

"Yes, you did." Luke turned toward where his sister's body lay. Her limbs were splayed at unnatural angles. The gun was still in her hand. Her blouse was dirty and wrinkled, the side and lower half stained red from where he'd bled on her. Her eyes were still open. He wanted to reach down and grab her, to hold her close now that she couldn't fight back. But he knew Harry wouldn't understand.

"She can't hurt us now, right?"

"That's right, Harry."

"What do we do now?"

Luke pointed at the factory in the distance. "We need to get back inside."

CHAPTER 50

Luke bolted through the access door and charged into the *maquiladora*. Harry followed close behind. When they were both inside, Luke shouted Marisa's name.

Clyde's high-pitched voice answered. "Over here!"

Luke and Harry raced across the darkened factory floor. The energy Luke felt when Harry had touched him still resonated throughout his insides, powering him forward. But with each step he grew more worried he'd taken too long fighting Annamaria, worried those precious seconds he'd lost in the desert might've cost Marisa her life.

Clyde kept calling for help, each cry more desperate than the one before. When Luke and Harry reached them, Luke fell to his knees next to Marisa. A phantom pain shot through his thigh. He ignored it.

Even in the dim light, he noticed her ghostly complexion. Her eyes were closed. She wasn't moving.

"We need to get her to a hospital," Clyde said.

"No time." Luke grabbed Marisa's hand, which was covering her wound. It felt unnaturally cool. He checked for a pulse. Couldn't find one.

"She won't answer," Clyde said. "Please tell me she isn't…"

"Marisa, can you hear me?" Luke said.

No response.

Luke placed his hands on her wound. He closed his eyes. Concentrated.

"What's he doing?" Clyde said.

Harry said, "Shut up and watch."

Marisa was still alive but fading. The assassin's bullet had severed a major artery. The makeshift tourniquet stemmed the flow, but with each pulse a small amount of blood still escaped. The slug rested deep inside her muscle, but it was the least of her problems. The rest of her body suffered from a severe lack of blood. Every organ was in distress. Her brain and heart were close to shutting down.

Warmth built in Luke's hands and surged into her wound. The bleeding stopped. The artery wall formed a new layer, even thicker than before. The bullet receded from her muscle and worked its way out of her body. He pulled it from the opening as the flesh around it healed.

"Holy shit," Clyde said.

Luke doubled his concentration. "Come back to us, Marisa." He placed one hand on her forehead and one on her chest. Sent his warmth deep into her flesh. Her heart and brain absorbed the healing energy. Red blood cells divided and multiplied. New cells carried fresh supplies of oxygen to her tissues. Her blood pressure recovered. Her heart pumped faster, stronger. Her lungs expanded and contracted. Her natural skin color returned.

Her eyelids flickered open.

"Holy shit," Clyde said.

Luke removed his hands. Marisa looked lost and confused. Her gaze jumped between Clyde, Harry, and Luke. She blinked. "Where am I?"

A chill ran down Luke's back. He held her hand between his. "Marisa, it's okay. You're with us."

"We're in Mexico," Harry said.

Marisa explored the hole in her jeans with her finger, then she stared at Luke. He searched for a sign of recognition in her eyes, but her expression remained blank.

"Who are you?" she said.

The chill spread to his extremities. "You don't remember?"

"What's going on?" Clyde said.

Harry pushed Clyde back a step.

Marisa reached out and touched Luke's cheek. "Your face looks familiar. Aren't you the night janitor?"

"Yes."

The corner of her mouth drew upward. "No, you're much more than that." She leaned forward and kissed him. Her lips were warmer than he remembered, and sweeter than he'd hoped.

"You scared me," he said.

"I scared myself." She kissed him again, then drew back. "Why are you covered in blood?"

"Long story."

She grabbed his hand. "Your sister?"

"It's over."

"I'm sorry."

He looked at the floor. "It had to be done."

Harry approached and wrapped his arms around them. "Uncle Luke saved us."

Luke and Marisa joined their hands behind Harry. Feeling his little brother's arm around his neck and seeing the smile on Marisa's face filled Luke with a deep sense of relief. But their joint embrace would never feel complete. Paloma would always be missed.

After a moment Luke noticed Clyde standing a few feet away. The man's face had turned as pale as the moon.

"What the hell was that?" Clyde said.

Marisa untied her tourniquet, stood, and faced him. "What do you mean?"

"He healed you." Clyde rubbed his left shoulder. "Jesus, he can really do it."

"You can't tell anyone," Harry said. "If you do, he'll get in trouble."

"We'll all be in trouble if we don't get out of here." Luke climbed to his feet. "People will be looking for my sister."

"What do we do?" Marisa said.

"Merritt, help her find the gunman and bring him to our car."

"What about you?" Clyde said.

"I'll meet you there." Luke placed his hand over the hole in his shirt. "After I get my sister."

CHAPTER 51

Luke spread a final layer of sand over his sister's grave. He planted the borrowed shovel in the ground, grasped the end with both hands, and surveyed his work.

He'd done his best to match the original terrain. The area they'd chosen lay miles from any structure and hundreds of yards from the nearest road. The steady night wind promised their tracks would be covered before dawn.

She probably deserved a marker, something to declare Annamaria had once existed, but he couldn't afford the risk. So he'd buried her deep in the desert beside her hired assassin, along with the guns and disassembled mobile phones.

Harry held Clyde's phone high above his own head. Its flashlight function provided enough light for Luke to work but not enough to draw attention from anyone driving the winding roads southeast of Juárez. Harry had proven himself more than useful all evening, though Luke hated having to ask him to help Clyde carry the assassin's body a quarter mile into the desert.

Clyde stood nearby with his arms folded. Luke hadn't asked for help while digging, and Clyde never offered. Instead he'd served as a witness to Luke's solemn task.

Marisa wrapped her arms around Luke from behind. Her warmth defied the effects of the brisk desert winds. "You okay?"

"Maybe someday," he said. He drew his finger to his face and traced the outline of his scar. "She deserves better."

"No, she doesn't." Harry shifted the phone to his other hand and sneered at the ground.

Luke placed his arm on Harry's shoulder. "You're right. I'm sorry."

His little brother blinked through tears. "Who'll take care of me now?"

"I will," Luke said.

"Promise?"

"We'll take care of each other." Marisa grabbed the phone from Harry's hand. She offered it to Clyde.

"Does this mean you guys are done?" Clyde said.

"Not yet," Marisa said. "You're more than a witness now. You're part of this."

Clyde snatched his phone and smirked. "I know."

Luke stepped forward. "If you share any of this, the police will come looking for you. Not just the police—the Secret Service, the FBI, US Marshals, anyone who owns a federal badge will want a piece of you."

Clyde shook his head. "This is the best story I've ever discovered. It offers everything my viewers want—powerful people, family secrets, paranormal abilities, and mysterious deaths. I'd be crazy not to share how it ends."

Luke and Marisa looked at each other.

"But I won't." Clyde tucked his phone into his pocket. "You guys are good people, aside from what happened at the airport. I've interviewed a few of the patients you've healed, but I never understood why they wouldn't come clean on the details. It never made any sense."

He paused and rubbed his left shoulder. "Now I understand. Your father was a gifted showman, but he never helped anyone. He was a fake. You're the real thing. You can heal people." He blinked several times. "You healed me back in Memphis, didn't you?"

"Yes."

A spark of electricity danced behind Clyde's eyes, but he still looked confused. "Why can't I remember?"

Luke glanced at Marisa. "I don't know."

Clyde seemed to study Luke's face before continuing. "I guess it doesn't matter. I don't need proof to know what I felt. And what you did for Marisa—I couldn't describe it with a million words. You possess an amazing gift, Luke Johnson. And you need to keep using it."

"I have a gift, too," Harry said.

"Shh," Luke said.

Clyde motioned toward the unmarked graves. "I'll never tell anyone what happened today. The world needs people like you running around, not locked away in a federal prison."

Luke offered a handshake. "Thanks."

"It needs people like me, too." Clyde's sarcastic grin reappeared. "I expect you to watch all of my videos. And if I ever get really sick, I'll expect a visit."

"You got it."

"Can we get out of here now?" Clyde said.

"We'll meet you at the car."

Clyde trekked through a maze of sticker bushes back toward the road. Luke, Marisa, and Harry turned their attention toward Annamaria's grave. Luke didn't want to think about how many people might be looking for her or what they might do if they found this place.

He missed her. As strange and wrong as the idea seemed, he missed his sister nonetheless. No one could ever tell him not to love her. Annamaria would forever remain the secret he'd never talk about, the subject he'd refuse to discuss.

Marisa pulled Harry close and drew herself to Luke's side. "Can we trust him?"

"I think so."

"He doesn't want to get in trouble," Harry said. "He's a big scaredy-cat."

"You may be right," Luke said.

Marisa said, "What do we do now?"

"Find a place to lay low for a while. Someplace quiet."

"I hear New Mexico is nice."

"What do you think, Harry?"

"Is it anything like old Mexico?" Harry said.

Luke's chest filled with warmth. Raising his younger brother would offer a new kind of adventure. "It's much better."

"Good."

Marisa acted like she hadn't heard Harry's question. "We'll need new identities, all of us."

"I know a guy," Luke said.

"Do I get to pick my name?" Harry said.

Luke smiled. "Anything you want."

"I want to be David Copperfield. He does magic tricks like me."

"What's he talking about?" Marisa said.

"I'll tell you later."

"*Dios mío.*" She grabbed Harry's hand and led him toward the road. After a few steps, she turned. "You coming?"

"In a minute."

Marisa and Harry followed Clyde's trail back to the car. After a moment Luke was alone. The cool desert wind lashed against his clothes. He didn't waver as he turned toward Annamaria's grave one last time.

He knelt and drew a large letter *A* in the sand, then stood and admired his work. It would have to do.

He wanted to tell her how he felt about Marisa, how she'd become the partner he never knew he needed, how Harry was so much more than a boy with Down syndrome, that together they'd create a life marked with love, acceptance, and service to the sick and dying, that their days would be filled with miracles forged from goodwill. He wanted to say he was sorry they'd both known such horrible parents, that he should've acted faster when he walked into Uncle Jack's bedroom, that the horrors she experienced as a teenager didn't necessarily define who she'd become.

But it was too late to talk to the dead. He was tired, and Marisa and Harry needed him.

CHAPTER 52

Clyde planted his elbows on his new desk and peered out the window of his new high-rise apartment. The thick laminated glass was rated for sound, but live music from the Beale Street bars still filtered into his living room. The driving beat reminded him how trendy and relevant his new online persona had become.

The memory of his bullet-riddled apartment had nearly disappeared. So had the fear and anxiety that kept him from sleeping those first few nights after his return from Juárez. The cops in Memphis had left him alone. They never discovered any signs someone had been injured or killed in his apartment, which seriously lowered their interest in the case. But Clyde knew the truth. He'd decided to move out before the contractors finished repairing the walls.

Despite his worries, no member of federal law enforcement had ever knocked on his door. News reports about Anna Varner's disappearance never mentioned the city of Juárez. There were no arrests, no clues, and no theories that came within a mile of the truth. All of it confirmed Clyde's suspicion that nobody buried their mistakes deeper than those at the highest levels of power.

Now, four weeks and two huge advertising company deposits later, he could finally breathe easier, though he'd never stop looking over his shoulder. People recognized him now. They stopped him in the street and asked if he'd ever found Annamaria or if

Lucian really possessed the ability to heal. His inbox overflowed with emails from people all over the world who swore they'd found evidence of the paranormal.

He didn't let it go to his head. These were his fifteen minutes, as the saying went. If he didn't produce another viral video soon, his fame and notoriety might fade like so many who'd come before. The Anna Varner story would forever be too hot to touch. If he even hinted at her connection to Annamaria Gabor, he risked spending the rest of his life in a federal prison.

But he had other options.

He fired up his new laptop and perused his files. The green check mark in the lower right corner of the screen ensured his data would never disappear again. He smiled, then clicked on a file named MEXICAN_JACKPOT.

A video editing program loaded the file and showed the opening frame in the display window. The lighting was horrendous, the image grainy and dark, even after Clyde had spent hours manipulating the video controls. He could barely make out Marisa's profile as she sat slumped on the factory floor, her chin resting on her chest. Also barely visible: Luke kneeling in his bloodstained clothes, pressing his hands against Marisa's thigh. Clyde clicked the play button. On the screen, Lucian the Healer closed his eyes and went to work.

Using the program's digital zooming capability, Clyde had focused on Luke's face as he concentrated on Marisa's wound. The scar on Luke's cheek tightened when his jaw muscles tensed, revealing the urgency of the situation. The video zoomed out when Luke pulled the bullet from Marisa's thigh. The shiny metal caught just enough ambient light to sparkle on the screen—a detail Clyde had worked to enhance using the editing software.

After another moment of concentration, Marisa's eyes fluttered open. She spoke a few words, then leaned forward and kissed Luke on the lips.

Capturing that moment made every minute of Clyde's suffering worth the effort. This was his million-dollar video, the footage his followers had been craving since he'd posted his interview of Nicholas Gabor.

Of course the scene still required a detailed narration. Clyde also needed to erase the audio of his off-camera cursing and the part where little Harry told him to shut up. If he worked through dinner, he could upload by midnight.

A twinge of guilt passed through him, causing him to shiver. Exposing Luke's ability meant going back on his word to a man who'd probably saved his life twice within twenty-four hours. Soon after this new video aired, dozens of investigative journalists would join the search for Lucian the Healer, ensuring Luke and his younger brother would never enjoy a moment of peace.

Then came the question of fairness. Luke had done the world a huge favor by killing his sister in the desert. Anna Varner had revealed herself as dangerous and remorseless in the brief moments Clyde had observed her. He didn't want to imagine what might've happened had she been elected vice president. So was it fair to double-cross the man who'd stopped her?

Probably not, but it also wasn't fair to ditch someone at the El Paso airport. Luke had schemed to exclude him from his final showdown with Annamaria. He'd accepted a free flight to the border and stolen Clyde's phone, leaving him with no leads and few options. And he certainly hadn't thought twice about asking Clyde to forgo a huge payday by sitting on the biggest story he'd ever chased.

This video showed no identifying details linking it to Juárez or Anna Varner's disappearance. For all anyone knew, it could've been filmed in a Los Angeles soundstage. Posting this footage wouldn't expose anyone to federal prosecution—especially not himself. So what was he waiting for?

He pushed away from his desk and strode into the kitchen. He filled his blender with ice, a tablespoon of maraschino cherry juice, two shots of coconut rum, and a frozen piña colada mixer. While the blender worked its magic, he surveyed his new living space. The cabinets were custom, the floors hand-scraped and stained in dark ebony. The panoramic view of downtown Memphis was stunning. But how much more impressive might it look from the penthouse three stories above?

He poured the blender contents into a tall glass and planted a straw in the middle, then drew a quick sip. The coconut rum made his tongue tingle. Warmth rushed to his cheeks. He smiled, then drew another sip.

Best to take it slow for now. He had a long night ahead of him.

ACKNOWLEDGMENTS

I have to admit, I enjoyed every minute I spent writing this story. Each character stormed onstage and took control as soon as I created them. Writing this book was its own reward.

That said, many people helped make this story better. When I brought it to workshops and critique groups, the feedback I received gave me much-needed insight into what needed to improve.

Thanks to Ann Hood, author of the amazing novel *The Obituary Writer*, for acting out the scene from chapter 2 in front of me, showing exactly how ridiculous the body movements I had injected between lines of dialogue actually looked in real life. She taught me a lesson that day I will never forget. Thanks, Ann.

Robert Dugoni is not only one of the most talented authors on the planet, but he is also a great teacher and a true friend. As part of the Novel Writing Intensive retreat he hosts along with Steven James, Bob commented on the first fifty pages of this manuscript and offered priceless suggestions. Imagine receiving over a hundred comments from a *New York Times* best-selling author challenging every aspect of your story. Bob's input proved invaluable and spawned another much-needed rewrite. I'll never forget the note he added in the margins of chapter 3: "You know, using 'Janitor' in the title might not be a bad idea." I hope you're right, Bob.

Many other talented people provided helpful feedback. The monthly critique sessions organized by DiAnn Mills provided regular checks and balances. I'm thankful to everyone who offered suggestions—sometimes changing just one word in a sentence can make all the difference.

Special thanks to Stephanie Campbell for her expert advice as a labor and delivery nurse. The information she shared gives the scene in the Mustang more authenticity than I could have created on my own.

Jill Marr and her reader, Derek McFadden made significant contributions to the second draft with many deft suggestions. Again, Jill fought valiantly to sell this book to New York publishers. I couldn't have asked any more from one of the most talented literary agents in the world. I appreciate your faith in me, Jill.

Jennifer Zaczek at Cypress Editing has the sharpest eyes in the business. Thanks to her for saving me from including a thousand minor mistakes in this book and others. Amanda Kruse provided a thorough final proofread that smoothed several rough edges. Rob Siders at 52 Novels took a beaten-up Word document and transformed it into a professional-looking novel. Jeroen ten Berge created a dynamic cover that captures my vision of this story. The collective efforts of these four individuals helped me create a work of art I can be proud of.

Luzmarie Alvarez Allen is, and always will be, my first reader. I judge so much of what I write by her reactions. I couldn't do this without her, and I'm not sure I'd want to. Thanks for everything, and so much more.

Finally, thanks to you, dear reader, for selecting a book by an unfamiliar writer. I hope the story didn't disappoint. If you liked it, please consider posting a review. A review on Amazon or Goodreads is the best present an author could receive. Thanks again, and please turn the page to read a sample of my previously published stand-alone title, *The Keeper*.

AN EXCERPT FROM
THE KEEPER

T. F. ALLEN

CHAPTER 1

If anyone ever saw me, they might call me a spirit, or an angel, or a ghost. They would try to describe me, but they'd be wrong. Even I didn't know what I was. I only knew one thing—I needed to keep Michael safe.

I chased him through the museum's darkened hallway, screaming for him to drop the knife. If I lost him, there'd be nothing left—everything would go black. I ran as fast as I could.

We sprinted past a Picasso, a Kandinsky, a Matisse, a Brancusi. Michael ignored them all. Nothing could distract him tonight. Not until he did what he came here to do.

We stopped when he reached the next painting. It showed the image of a woman some considered strikingly beautiful. Others thought she was hideous. But everyone agreed the dark crimson scars painted across her face meant she belonged in a museum. Like Leonardo's *Mona Lisa*, the image looked smaller than most people imagined. But it never disappointed the thousands who viewed it each day.

Jolene was the reason most admirers packed into this hallway—and the reason the artist who'd created it had carried a knife into the Art Institute of Chicago.

Michael stared at his most famous work, face reddened, shoulders shaking, eyes focused on the scars that marked Jolene's face. He raised the knife and nodded, like he'd given himself permission.

I shouted, but Michael didn't hear me. He'd tuned me out again. I lunged to hold him back, pulled with all my strength. But I was no match for his rage.

The blade slashed through the canvas so deep it dug into the gallery wall. An alarm sounded. Michael raised the knife again. One slice wasn't enough—I knew this as soon as he thought it. Even a thousand cuts wouldn't be enough.

Drawing from the same energy that powered his famous brushstrokes, Michael murdered his painting.

We spent the rest of the night in a Chicago jail. Typical Michael, he hadn't planned his escape from the Art Institute. It turned out he hadn't planned any of it. I'd left him alone too long, and he went off again without thinking. His crime surprised me as much as it did the police. But Michael didn't care. Getting arrested, going to jail, seeing his mug shot splashed across every television in the country, setting off a firestorm in the art world—none of that mattered to Michael. The painting was gone now, along with his anger. And somehow that made it all worth it.

I sat on his bunk while he paced along the bars in a traffic-cone-orange jumpsuit, awaiting his turn with the judge. Thoughts stormed through his mind. I couldn't avoid hearing them. All he worried about was how long it would take before he could return to his studio in San Francisco. Only when he placed his hands on his paint tubes, his marble palette, his saw, his brushes, and his easel would he feel comfortable again. He hadn't slept all night, and it showed. His dark curly hair stuck out at weird angles, and bags had formed under his eyes, making him look much older than twenty-nine. He'd been running on adrenaline too long, and I knew he'd crash in front of the judge if he didn't rest soon.

I rushed to his side and touched the back of his neck. A tingling sensation pulsed from my fingers and raced down his spine, letting him know I was there. He walked to the bed, lay where

I'd been sitting, and fought to quiet his mind. I knelt beside him and stroked his hair the same way I had when he was a young boy scared awake by a nightmare. "Thank you," he said, letting me comfort him, and soon he fell into a brief but much-needed sleep.

Michael was far from perfect, but I loved him anyway. He saw the world with different eyes than anyone else. Colors were brighter and deeper, and people were darker and colder. Even though he couldn't see me, Michael was the only one who knew I was here. He was the only one who heard my voice, the only person who'd ever said a word to me. I never had anything of my own—not even a name. Nobody ever told me who or what I was, but with Michael, I found an identity and a purpose. He could act moody and antisocial, and sometimes he'd completely tune me out. But I could never abandon him. That was the last thing I'd ever do. Leaving Michael to fend for himself seemed more impossible than making myself visible to a Cook County judge.

The arraignment supplied no fireworks for the reporters who'd snuck into the courtroom, except for a brief debate over whether an artist could be charged for destroying his own painting. Michael couldn't avoid some kind of punishment, but by creating that gray area, his lawyers—hired overnight by Michael's richest collector—promised they could negotiate the charge down to a Class C misdemeanor. He would pay a fine and maybe serve probation but wouldn't spend any time in prison. This definitely wasn't a deal the district attorney would offer a typical vandal, but most vandals didn't attract a following like Michael Delacroix.

Having been deemed a threat only to his own artwork, Michael made bail and walked free. He grabbed his possessions and headed to the nearest taxi stand. I walked with him, of course.

The last stubborn leaves of fall clung to their branches as brisk winds swept through the courtyard. All he wanted was to leave this place, to get as far away as possible from the memory of *Jolene*.

When he reached the street corner, a blond woman holding a digital recorder called out to him. "Mr. Delacroix, just a few questions."

The nearest taxi stand now seemed too close. He rushed down the sidewalk toward the next intersection without looking back.

"Why'd you ruin your best work?" The clicking of her heels on the concrete punctuated her urgency. "Why destroy something so amazing?"

He still had a buffer of fifteen feet, but she closed in fast. He waved his arms at a taxi heading his way and grabbed the door handle before the car could stop. "O'Hare, and hurry." He slammed the door behind him.

The opposite passenger door opened, and a cold November gust blew into the cab. The woman with the recorder followed the wind inside and sat next to us. "I'll pay the fare to wherever you want to go. And you don't even have to answer my questions. Just let me ride with you."

"Please get out," Michael said.

"I'm not the only one looking for you." She glanced toward the courthouse. "It's about to get crowded if we don't get moving."

A tall man in an Italian suit ran down the sidewalk toward them. He waved his microphone at another man carrying a television camera, motioning for him to hurry. Three other reporters trailed behind, each adjusting their ties and coughing into their fists.

"Are we doing this or not?" she said.

The driver looked at Michael, then drummed his fingers on the seat back.

I watched the battle in Michael's head. He needed to get out of Chicago as quickly as possible, but he hated the idea of a half-hour cab ride with a pesky reporter who probably wouldn't shut up. He wondered if he could talk her out of this taxi and fight off the others at the same time. But then he caught a view of her midnight-blue irises glinting in the light coming through the back window. They were the color of his favorite tube of oil paint, the same shade as the sky on the last day he remembered being happy. And of all things, they were enough to win this fight.

The four of us sped past the crowd of reporters, then we rode in silence. This gutsy reporter had impressed us both, but I was the only one who wanted to hear her speak. As tense seconds stretched into uncomfortable minutes, she seemed to study Michael's body language instead of launching questions. Her mouth would open then close quickly, like she was rethinking her approach.

Michael refused to look at her. The Chicago sprawl outside his window kept his eyes occupied while he worried about what she might say.

When the taxi passed the first sign for the airport, the reporter cleared her throat. "I'm Hannah Klein, *Sun-Times.*" She flashed a smile, but Michael never saw it. "I'm not here to make you look bad. It's just that so many people loved that painting, and they can't understand why you attacked it."

"I'm not a freeloader," Michael said. "I'll answer one question for the ride, but you need to decide which one."

The reporter grabbed the crystal charm hanging from her silver necklace and rolled it between her fingers. "Everyone wants to know why you did it."

"Is that your question?"

"Not exactly. Some think this was the move of a modern genius, more savvy than cutting off your own ear. People love their artists mad and self-tortured. They say you doubled the value of your other work with the blade of that knife, but I don't think money was your motivation. This comes from a deeper place." She held out her recorder. "I want to know what made you hate that painting."

Her question pulled Michael out of his staring match with the city. "I didn't hate it when I painted it."

"Not at first. But when you added those last brilliant brushstrokes, you certainly did."

"You don't know what you're talking about."

"I wouldn't get far in this job if I only looked at the surface." She nodded, and her shoulder-length hair bounced back into place. "That piece was such a contrast to itself—beautiful and horrific, peaceful on one level, violent on another. I bet you painted your masterpiece during two different stages of your career. Am I right?"

She was right, but I figured she was only guessing. This nosy, aggressive reporter had great instincts. She seemed to read him like a mentalist, noting his reaction to each bullet point of the theory she kept pushing. And Michael's silence only made her push harder.

"I want to know who this woman is. And what made you hate her."

"I *never* hated her!"

The cab swerved as everyone inside reacted to Michael's words. Hannah grabbed her crystal again and held it like a cigarette. "Fine. Then you must have loved her."

"Terminal One," he said to the driver.

Michael neared eruption now. I could tell. He gripped the door handle and leaned his head against the glass as we approached the terminal. The reporter only had a few seconds left with us, but I feared she might glimpse a side of Michael few had ever seen—one she definitely wouldn't like.

The reporter must have sensed it, too. She leaned back against her seat and softened her tone. "You might not believe me, but I hope you find peace one day. Maybe your next painting will provide some healing."

"I'll never paint again."

"What—why?"

Michael threw open his door when the taxi stopped in front of the terminal. He tossed a twenty into the front seat. "Or maybe I'll destroy a few more. Thanks for the ride."

CHAPTER 2

The next morning I rode with Michael in his silver Hyundai down Sea Cliff Avenue in northern San Francisco. Every house on this street reflected a different architectural style, and each seemed to battle for its own space on the skinny lots that backed up to the Pacific Ocean. But to Michael they blended in with each other, creating a never-ending string of excess he had no interest in studying. He slowed as he approached a powder-blue fire hydrant, the only landmark on the street he'd cared to memorize, and parked along the curb in front of Grant Thatcher's house.

A woman in a yellow bikini answered the door. She squealed and threw her arms around his shoulders. "Graaant, he's here."

Thatcher bounded into the foyer dressed only in a heavy cotton bathrobe. The thick, curly hairs on his chest were wet, but his smile was as dry as ever. "My shining star finally returns." He draped a hulking arm around Michael's neck and pulled him away from the woman. "Keep the hot tub warm, Tiff. It's time for our planning session." Together we walked down a long hallway toward his office.

The inside of Thatcher's home looked like an art gallery, with Michael's paintings featured as the main attractions. To our left hung an image Michael created while studying at the San Francisco Art Institute, one of nearly a dozen decorating this long wall. Most came from Michael's studio, but Thatcher also had hung a few painted by younger emerging artists, though he rarely mentioned their names in front of Michael.

"This old gem." Thatcher pointed to an abstract with ribbons of gold leaf running through it. "Remember that one? Your stunt in Chicago just tripled its value—assuming you don't have a knife in your pocket." He slapped Michael's back and laughed.

The art world considered Thatcher one of the most successful dealers of the post-internet age because he knew how to handle people, both the artists he recruited and the super-rich collectors he kept happy. He'd mastered the ability to make people feel like they were the center of the universe, but Michael never believed much of what the man said. And neither did I.

"You don't have a knife in your pocket, do you?"

"Not today," Michael said.

"Good to know. Come, let's talk." Thatcher ushered Michael into his office. Everything that wasn't a piece of art was white—the computer, the desk, the curtains, the filing cabinets, the walls, even the leather beanbag chairs thrown into the corner. The idea was to wash out the details of everything else to highlight the colorful artwork, and the effect was stunning. No one could walk into the room and not notice the paintings—all of them Michael's, of course—which explained why Thatcher used this room to close his biggest deals.

"Pull up a seat." He motioned toward one of the beanbag chairs before sinking into his own white leather recliner. "We need to talk about Chicago and what we can do to capitalize on the fallout, but first I need to know something. Sorry for having to ask, but what the hell were you thinking?"

I could easily know what Michael was thinking at any moment. We stayed so connected all I needed to do was listen when I was near him. With anyone else, I needed to be inside their head, which took a lot more effort. This was one of the few abilities I'd discovered about myself while trying to protect Michael, but I rarely used it with others.

If Thatcher hoped to get a straight answer today, he needed to share my ability, because Michael wasn't about to tell him the truth. "Just one of those things."

"One of which things?" Thatcher said. "I've never felt anything that would make me stick a knife through my favorite painting."

Michael stared at the beanbag chairs in the corner. He wondered what kind of person would agree to sit in one of those. "I can't explain why, but it had to be done. If you're worried about the money—for the lawyers and the painting—I'll pay you back. Just know I needed to do this."

Thatcher locked his fingers together behind his head and leaned back in his chair. "Jesus, if you didn't want it to hang there, I could've had it moved. I know three other museum curators who would have killed to add it to their collections. *Jolene* drew larger crowds than *La Grande Jatte*. Do you know how huge that is?"

It surprised me how little Grant Thatcher knew about his most famous client. He had no idea how tightly Michael's insides clenched each time he thought about *Jolene*. If he'd been paying attention during their seven-year business relationship, he would have known Michael stayed purposefully blind to the popularity of his work. He never painted because people might find his work pretty and want to pay Thatcher more than an average mortgage balance to own it. He painted because it was the only way he could make any sense of the world he saw.

"Forget about it." Thatcher swatted at the air between them. "Today's a new day, right?" He grabbed a sheet of paper from his desk and held it out to Michael. The printout revealed a spreadsheet filled with names, phone numbers, and email addresses. "I have five A-list celebrities and two financial execs all begging me to presell your next painting. We're talking seven figures each. And they don't even care what it looks like. You could take a shit on the canvas—it doesn't matter, as long as you sign it. What do you think?"

"If you're asking me to paint, I do that already."

Thatcher laughed again. "I need you to paint your ass off. I'm talking nine or ten a week. We need to make the most of this before people forget." He climbed out of his chair and leaned across his desk. As he did, his robe fell open and exposed more of himself than either of us wanted to see. "Listen, I'm not mad, but you owe me for *Jolene*. Crank out a few dozen masterpieces and all is forgiven. We'll each make a few million, then you can get back to your normal schedule. Deal?"

"I'll see what I can do," Michael said.

"I need a stronger commitment than that." He held up the sheet of paper again. "These people aren't used to waiting."

And Michael wasn't used to being pressured. On any other day, he might have told Thatcher off for pushing so hard, but he felt bad for destroying a painting this man had paid a ton of money for. Then there were the lawyers who'd appeared just when he needed them. "Give me a few days and I'll come up with something."

"Sounds like my golden boy talking." Thatcher retied his robe and grabbed a cigar from a drawer in his desk. "Hey, want to jump in the hot tub with me and Tiff to celebrate?"

"No thanks."

As we walked together down the long driveway toward the street, Michael spoke to me. "Did you hear what Thatcher said? 'Crank out a few dozen masterpieces and all is forgiven'? Who does he think he is?"

I answered the only way I knew, using another ability I'd discovered by accident a long time ago. The words started in my mind and entered like a whisper in his: *He's a businessman, not an artist. What did you expect him to say?*

"He never even looks at them. It's only the signature he cares about."

Remember what he did for you in Chicago. At least he was there when you needed him.

Michael smirked. "I thought that was your job."

I was there, too. But you wouldn't listen.

"That's over now. Time to get to work." He turned away from the house and saw something that caused him to break into a run. "Hey, get away from my car!"

On the street a tow truck had hoisted the back end of Michael's Hyundai into the air. The driver stood at the lift controls. Tall and thick-bearded, wearing a denim ball cap and matching coveralls, the man didn't react when Michael sprinted toward him.

"What are you doing? This is my car!"

"My job," the man said.

"Are you a car thief?"

"Repo man, actually." The driver pulled a handkerchief from the front pocket of his coveralls and turned away from us.

Michael checked the towing mechanism under his bumper. He knew at first glance he could never unhook it by himself. "This is a mistake. You've got the wrong vehicle."

The driver kept his back to us, working his hands, fidgeting with something we couldn't see. "I hear that every day. But this is what happens when you don't make your payments."

"I paid cash for this car. Like I said, you've got the wrong—"

The driver spun around and covered Michael's nose and mouth with the handkerchief. He pressed it hard over his face, forced him backward, and drove him to the ground. Michael gasped, then everything went black.

That's how I lost him. It happened right in front of me, faster than a blink. And all I did was watch.

**Thanks for reading this sample of *The Keeper*
by T. F. Allen, available now at Amazon.**

ABOUT THE AUTHOR

T. F. Allen writes suspense thrillers injected with an element of the supernatural. His short stories have appeared in *Futures Mystery Anthology Magazine*, *Thought Magazine*, and *Chiron Review*. His debut thriller, *The Keeper*, was named a finalist for the Claymore Award. He lives in Spring, Texas, with his wife and three sons.

Made in the USA
Las Vegas, NV
16 November 2020